THE MAN IN GREY

During the Napoleonic era, a band of criminals who became known as the Chouans, terrorised the countryside. Disguised Royalist sympathisers, they ranged from aristocrats to humble peasants and spent their time in pillage, murder and arson.

Some were brought to justice by a mysterious secret agent called the Man in Grey. Known only as Fernand by the local police, he tracked down the miscreants one by one by his ingenious and methodical investigations.

In this exciting book the Man in Grey rivals the famous Scarlet Pimpernel.

The Man In Grey

Baroness Orczy

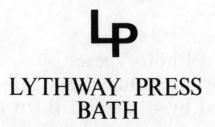

LP

LYTHWAY PRESS
BATH

First published 1918
by
Cassell & Co. Ltd.,
This Large Print edition published by
Lythway Press Ltd.,
Combe Park, Bath
by
arrangement with the copyright holder
1975

ISBN 0 85046 613 X

Phototypeset by
Woodspring Press Ltd.,
Printed by Redwood Burn Ltd.,
Trowbridge & Esher
Bound by Cedric Chivers Ltd., Bath

CONTENTS

THE MAN IN GREY

PROEM

IT has been a difficult task to piece together the fragmentary documents which alone throw a light—dim and flickering at the best—upon that mysterious personality known to the historians of the Napoleonic era as the Man in Grey. So very little is known about him. Age, appearance, domestic circumstances, everything pertaining to him has remained a matter of conjecture—even his name! In the reports sent by the all-powerful Minister to the Emperor he is invariably spoken of as "The Man in Grey." Once only does Fouché refer to him as "Fernand."

Strange and mysterious creature! Nevertheless, he played an important *part—the* most important, perhaps—in bringing to justice some of those reckless criminals who, under the cloak of Royalist convictions and religious and political aims, spent their time in pillage, murder, and arson.

Strange and mysterious creatures, too,

1

these men so aptly named Chouans—that is, "chats-huants"; screech-owls—since they were a terror by night and disappeared within their burrows by day. A world of romance lies buried within the ruins of the châteaux which gave them shelter—Tournebut, Bouvesse, Donnai, Plélan. A world of mystery encompasses the names of their leaders and, above all, those of the women—ladies of high degree and humble peasants alike—often heroic, more often misguided, who supplied the intrigue, the persistence, the fanatical hatred which kept the fire of rebellion smouldering and spluttering even while it could not burst into actual flame. D'Aché Cadoudal, Frotté Armond le Chevallier, Marquise de Combray, Mme. Aquet de Férolles—the romance attaching to these names pales beside that which clings to the weird anonymity of their henchmen—"Dare-Death," "Hare-Lip," "Fear-Nought," "Silver-Leg," and so on. Theirs were the hands that struck whilst their leaders planned—they were the screech-owls who for more than twenty years terrorised the western provinces of France and, in the name of God and their King, committed every crime that could besmirch the Cause which they professed to uphold.

Whether they really aimed at the restoration of the Bourbon kings and at bolstering up the fortunes of an effete and dispossessed monarchy with money wrung from peaceable citizens, or whether they were a mere pack of lawless brigands made up of deserters from the army and fugitives from conscription, of felons and bankrupt aristocrats, will for ever remain a bone of contention between the apologists of the old régime and those of the new.

With partisanship in those strangely obscure though comparatively recent episodes of history we have nothing to do. Facts alone—undeniable and undenied—must be left to speak for themselves. It was but meet that these men—amongst whom were to be found the bearers of some of the noblest names in France—should be tracked down and brought to justice by one whose personality has continued to be as complete an enigma as their own.

I

SILVER-LEG

"FORWARD now! And at foot-pace, mind, to the edge of the wood—or——"

The ominous click of a pistol completed the peremptory command.

Old Gontran, the driver, shook his wide shoulders beneath his heavy caped coat and gathered the reins once more in his quivering hands; the door of the coach was closed with a bang; the postilion scrambled into the saddle; only the passenger who had so peremptorily been ordered down from the box-seat beside the driver had not yet climbed back into his place. Well! old Gontran was not in a mood to fash about the passengers. His horses, worried by the noise, the shouting, the click of firearms and the rough handling meted out to them by strange hands in the darkness, were very restive. They would have liked to start off at once at a brisk pace so as to leave these disturbers of their peace as far behind them as possible, but Gontran was holding them in with a firm hand and they had to

4

walk—walk!—along this level bit of road, with the noisy enemy still present in their rear.

The rickety old coach gave a lurch and started on its way; the clanking of loose chains, the grinding of the wheels in the muddy roads, the snorting and travail of the horses as they finally settled again into their collars, drowned the coachman's muttered imprecations.

"A fine state of things, forsooth!" he growled to himself more dejectedly than savagely. "What the Emperor's police are up to no one knows. That such things can happen is past belief. Not yet six o'clock in the afternoon, and Alençon less than five kilometres in front of us."

But the passenger who, on the box-seat beside him, had so patiently and silently listened to old Gontran's florid loquacity during the early part of the journey, was no longer there to hear these well-justified lamentations. No doubt he had taken refuge with his fellow-sufferers down below.

There came no sound from the interior of the coach. In the darkness, the passengers—huddled up against one another, dumb with fright and wearied with excitement—had not yet found vent for their outraged feelings in whispered words or smothered oaths. The coach lumbered on at foot-pace. In the affray the head-light had been broken; the two lanterns that remained lit up fitfully the tall pine trees on either side of the road and gave momentary glimpses of a mysterious, fairy-like world beyond, through the curtain of dead branches and the veil of tiny bare twigs.

Through the fast gathering gloom the circle of light toyed with the haze of damp and steam which rose from the cruppers of the horses, and issued from their snorting nostrils. From far away came the cry of a screech-owl and the call of some night beasts on the prowl.

Instinctively, as the road widened out towards the edge of the wood, Gontran gave a click with his tongue and the horses broke into a leisurely trot. Immediately from behind, not forty paces to the rear, there came the sharp detonation of a pistol shot. The horses, still quivering from past terrors, were ready to plunge once more, the wheelers stumbled, the leaders reared, and the team would again have been thrown into confusion but for the presence of mind of the driver and the coolness of the postilion.

"Oh! those accursed brigands!" muttered Gontran through his set teeth as soon as order was restored. "That's just to remind us that they are on the watch. Keep the leaders well in hand, Hector," he shouted to the postilion; "don't let them trot till we are well out of the wood."

Though he had sworn copiously and plentifully at first, when one of those outlaws held a pistol to his head whilst the others ransacked the coach of its contents and terrorised the passengers, he seemed inclined to take the matter philosophically now. Afterall, he himself had lost nothing; he was too wise a man, was old Gontran, to carry his wages in his breeches pocket these days, when those accursed Chouans robbed, pillaged and plundered rich and poor alike. No! Gontran flattered himself that the rogues had got nothing out of him; he had lost nothing—not even prestige, for it had been a case of twenty to one at the least, and the brigands had been armed to the teeth. Who could blame him that in such circumstances the sixty-two hundred francs, all in small silver and paper

7

money—which the collector of taxes of the Falaise district was sending up to his chief at Alençon—had passed from the boot of the coach into the hands of that clever band of rascals?

Who could blame him? I say. Surely, not the Imperial Government up in Paris who did not know how to protect its citizens from the depredations of such villains, and had not even succeeded in making the high road between Caën and Alençon safe for peaceable travellers.

Inside the coach the passengers were at last giving tongue to their indignation. Highway robbery at six o'clock in the afternoon, and the evening not a very dark one at that! It were monstrous, outrageous, almost incredible, did not the empty pockets and ransacked valises testify to the scandalous fact. M. Fouché, Duc d'Otrante, was drawing a princely salary as Minister of Police, and yet allowed a mail-coach to be held up and pillaged—almost by daylight and within five kilometres of the county town!

The last half-hour of the eventful journey flew by like magic: there was so much to say that it became impossible to keep count of time. Alençon was reached before everyone had had a chance of saying just what he or she thought of the whole affair, or of consigning M. le Duc d'Otrante and all his myrmidons to that particular chamber in Hades which was most suitable for their crimes.

Outside the "Adam et Eve," where Gontran finally drew rein, there was a gigantic clatter and din as the passengers tumbled out of the coach, and by the dim light of the nearest street lantern tried to disentangle their own belongings from the pile of ransacked valises which the ostlers had unceremoniously tumbled out in a heap upon the cobble stones. Everyone was talking—no one in especial seemed inclined to listen—anecdotes of former outrages committed by the Chouans were bandied to and fro.

Gontran, leaning against the entrance of the inn, a large mug of steaming wine in his hand, watched with philosophic eye his former passengers struggling with their luggage. One or two of them were going to spend the night at the "Adam et Eve": they had already filed past him into the narrow passage beyond, where they were now deep in an altercation with Gilles Blaise, the proprietor, on the subject of the price and the situation of their rooms; others had homes or friends in the city, and with their broken valises and bundles in their hands could be seen making their way up the narrow main street, still gesticulating excitedly.

"It's a shocking business, friend Gontran," quoth Gilles Blaise as soon as he had settled with the last of his customers. His gruff voice held a distinct note of sarcasm, for he was a powerful fellow and feared neither footpads nor midnight robbers, nor any other species of those *satané* Chouans. "I wonder you did not make a better fight for it. You had three or four male passengers aboard——"

"What could I do?" retorted Gontran irritably. "I had my horses to attend to, and did it, let me tell you, with the muzzle of a pistol pressing against my temple."

"You didn't see anything of those miscreants?"

"Nothing. That is——"

"What?"

"Just when I was free once more to gather the reins in my hands and the order 'Forward' was given by those impudent rascals, he who had spoken the order

10

stood for a moment below one of my lanterns."

"And you saw him?"

"As plainly as I see you—except his face, for that was hidden by the wide brim of his hat and by a shaggy beard. But there is one thing I should know him by, if the police ever succeed in laying hands on the rogue."

"What is that?"

"He had only one leg, the other was a wooden one."

Gilles Blaise gave a loud guffaw. He had never heard of a highwayman with a wooden leg before. "The rascal cannot run far if the police ever do get after him," was his final comment on the situation.

Thereupon Gontran suddenly bethought himself of the passenger who had sat on the box-seat beside him until those abominable footpads had ordered the poor man to get out of their way.

"Have you seen anything of him, Hector?" he queried of the postilion.

"Well, now you mention him," replied the young man slowly, "I don't remember that I have."

"He was not among the lot that came out of the coach."

"He certainly was not."

"I thought when he did not get back to his seat beside me, he had lost his nerve and gone inside."

"So did I."

"Well, then?" concluded Gontran.

But the puzzle thus propounded was beyond Hector's powers of solution. He scratched the back of his head by way of trying to extract thence a key to the enigma.

"We must have left him behind," he suggested.

"He would have shouted after us if we had," commented Gontran. "Unless——" he added with graphic significance.

Hector shook himself like a dog who has come out of the water. The terror of those footpads and of those pistols clicking in the dark, unpleasantly close to his head, was still upon him.

"You don't think——" he murmured through chattering teeth.

Gontran shrugged his shoulders.

"It won't be the first time," he said sententiously, "that those miscreants have added murder to their other crimes."

"Lost one of your passengers, Gontran?" queried Gilles Blaise blandly.

12

"If those rogues have murdered him——" quoth Gontran with an oath.

"Then you'd have to make a special declaration before the chief commissary of police, and that within an hour. Who was your passenger, Gontran?"

"I don't know. A quiet, well-mannered fellow. Good company he was, too, during the first part of the way."

"What was his name?"

"I can't tell. I picked him up at Argentan. The box-seat was empty. No one wanted it, for it was raining then. He paid me his fare and scrambled up beside me. That's all I know about him."

"What was he like? Young or old?"

"I didn't see him very well. It was already getting dark," rejoined Gontran impatiently. "I couldn't look him under the nose, could I?"

"But *sacrebleu*! Monsieur le Commissaire de Police will want to know something more than that. Did you at least see how he was dressed?"

"Yes," replied Gontran, "as far as I can recollect he was dressed in grey."

"Well then, friend Gontran," concluded Gilles Blaise with a jovial laugh, "you can go at once to Monsieur le Commissaire de

13

Police, and you can tell him that an industrious Chouan, who has a wooden leg and a shaggy beard but whose face you did not see, has to the best of your belief murdered an unknown passenger whose name, age, and appearance you know nothing about, but who, as far as you can recollect, was dressed in grey—— And we'll see," he added with a touch of grim humour, "what Monsieur le Commissaire will make out of this valuable information."

The men were cowering together in a burrow constructed of dead branches and caked mud, with a covering of heath and dried twigs. Their heads were close to one another and the dim light of a dark lantern placed upon the floor threw weird, sharp shadows across their eager faces, making them appear grotesque and almost ghoulish—the only bright spots in the surrounding gloom.

One man on hands and knees was crouching by the narrow entrance, his keen eyes trying to pierce the density of the forest beyond.

The booty was all there, spread out upon the damp earth—small coins and bundles of notes all smeared with grease and mud; there were some trinkets, too, but of obviously little value: a pair of showy gold earrings, one or two signets, a heavy watch in a chased silver case. But these had been contemptuously swept aside—it was the money that mattered.

The man with the wooden leg had counted it all out and was now putting coins and notes back into a large leather wallet.

"Six thousand two hundred and forty-seven francs," he said quietly, as he drew the thongs of the wallet closely together and tied them securely into a knot.

"One of the best hauls we've ever had. 'Tis Madame who will be pleased."

"Our share will have to be paid out of that first," commented one of his companions.

"Yes, yes!" quoth the other lightly. "Madame will see to it. She always does. How many of you are there?" he added carelessly.

"Seven of us all told. They were a pack of cowards in that coach."

"Well!" concluded the man with the wooden leg, "we must leave Madame to settle accounts. I'd best place the money in

15

safety now."

He struggled up into a standing position—which was no easy matter for him with his stump and in the restricted space—and was about to hoist the heavy wallet on to his powerful shoulders, when one of his mates seized him by the wrist.

"Hold on, Silver-Leg!" he said roughly, "we'll pay ourselves for our trouble first. Eh, friends?" he added, turning to the others.

But before any of them could reply there came a peremptory command from the man whom they had called "Silver-Leg."

"Silence!" he whispered hoarsely. "There's someone moving out there among the trees."

At once the others obeyed, every other thought lulled to rest by the sense of sudden danger. For a minute or so every sound was hushed in the narrow confines of the lair save the stertorous breathing which came from panting throats. Then the look-out man at the entrance whispered under his breath:

"I heard nothing."

"Something moved, I tell you," rejoined Silver-Leg curtly. "It may only have been a beast on the war-path."

But the brief incident had given him the opportunity which he required; he had shaken off his companion's hold upon his wrist and had slung the wallet over his shoulder. Now he stumped out of the burrow.

"Friend Hare-Lip," he said before he went, in the same commanding tone wherewith he had imposed silence awhile ago on his turbulent mates, "tell Monseigneur that it will be 'Corinne' this time, and you, Mole-Skin, ask Madame to send Red-Poll over on Friday night for the key."

The others growled in assent and followed him out of their hiding-place. One of the men had extinguished the lantern, and another was hastily collecting the trinkets which had so contemptuously been swept aside.

"Hold on, Silver-Leg!" shouted the man who had been called Hare-Lip; "short reckonings make long friends. I'll have a couple of hundred francs now," he continued roughly. "It may be days and weeks ere I see Madame again, and by that time God knows where the money will be."

But Silver-Leg stumped on in the gloom, paying no heed to the peremptory calls of his mates. It was marvellous how fast he contrived to hobble along, winding his way in and out in the darkness, among the trees, on the slippery carpet of pine needles and carrying that heavy wallet—six thousand two hundred francs, most of it in small coin—upon his back. The others, however, were swift and determined, too. Within the next minute or two they had overtaken him, and he could no longer evade them; they held him tightly, surrounding him on every side and clamouring for their share of the spoils.

"We'll settle here and now, friend Silver-Leg," said Hare-Lip, who appeared to be the acknowledged spokesman of the malcontents. "Two hundred francs for me out of that wallet, if you please, ere you move another step, and two hundred for each one of us here, or——"

The man with the wooden leg had come to a halt, but somehow it seemed that he had not done so because the others held and compelled him, but because he himself had a desire to stand still. Now when Hare-Lip paused, a world of menace in every line of his gaunt, quivering body, Silver-Leg laughed with gentle irony, as a man would laugh at the impotent vapourings of a child.

"Or what, my good Hare-Lip?" he queried slowly.

Then as the other instinctively lowered his gaze and mumbled something between his teeth, Silver-Leg shrugged his shoulders and said with a kind indulgence, still as if he were speaking to a child:

"Madame will settle, my friend. Do not worry. It is bad to worry. You remember Fear-Nought: he took to worrying—just as you are doing now—wanted to be paid out of his turn, or more than his share, I forget which. But you remember him?"

"I do," muttered Hare-Lip with a savage oath. "Fear-Nought was tracked down by the police and dragged to Vincennes, or Force, or Bicêtre—we never knew."

"To the guillotine, my good Hare-Lip," rejoined Silver-Leg blandly, "along with some other very brave Chouans like yourselves, who also had given their leaders some considerable trouble."

"Betrayed by you," growled Hare-Lip menacingly.

"Punished—that's all," concluded Silver-Leg as he once more turned to go.

"Treachery is a game at which more than one can play."

19

"The stakes are high. And only one man can win," remarked Silver-Leg dryly.

"And one man must lose," shouted Hare-Lip, now beside himself with rage, "and that one shall be you this time, my fine Silver-Leg. *A moi*, my mates!" he called to his companions.

And in a moment the men fell on Silver-Leg with the vigour born of terror and greed, and for the first moment or two of their desperate tussle it seemed as if the man with the wooden leg must succumb to the fury of his assailants. Darkness encompassed them all round, and the deep silence which dwells in the heart of the woods. And in the darkness and the silence these men fought—and fought desperately—for the possession of a few hundred francs just filched at the muzzle of a pistol from a few peaceable travellers.

Pistols of course could not be used; the police patrols might not be far away, and so they fought on in silence, grim and determined, one man against half a dozen, and that one halt, and weighted with the spoils. But he had the strength of a giant, and with his back against a stately fir tree he used the heavy wallet as a flail, keeping his assailants at arm's length with the

20

menace of death-dealing blows.

Then, suddenly, from far away, even through the dull thuds of this weird and grim struggle, there came the sound of men approaching—the click of sabres, the tramp and snorting of horses, the sense of men moving rapidly even if cautiously through the gloom. Silver-Leg was the first to hear it.

"Hush!" he cried suddenly, and as loudly as he dared, "the police!"

Again, with that blind instinct born of terror and ever-present danger, the others obeyed. The common peril had as swiftly extinguished the quarrel as greed of gain had fanned it into flame.

The cavalcade was manifestly drawing nearer.

"Disperse!" commanded Silver-Leg under his breath. "Clear out of the wood, but avoid the tracks which lead out of it, lest it is surrounded. Remember 'Corinne' for Monseigneur, and that Red-Poll can have the key for Madame on Friday."

Once again he had made use of his opportunity. Before the others had recovered from their sudden fright he had quietly stumped away, and in less than five seconds was lost in the gloom among the trees. For a moment or two longer an ear, attuned by terror or the constant sense of danger, might have perceived the dull, uneven thud of his wooden leg against the soft carpet of pine needles, but even this soon died away in the distance, and over the kingdom of darkness which held sway within the forest there fell once more the pall of deathlike silence. The posse of police in search of human quarry had come and gone, the stealthy footsteps of tracked criminals had ceased to resound from tree to tree; all that could be heard was the occasional call of a night-bird, or the furtive movement of tiny creatures of the wild.

Silence hung over the forest for close upon an hour. Then from behind a noble fir a dark figure detached itself and, more stealthily, more furtively than any tiny beast, it stole along the track which leads to the main road. The figure, wrapped in a dark mantle, glided determinedly along despite the difficulties of the narrow track, complicated now by absolute darkness. Hours went by ere it reached the main road, on the very spot where some few hours ago the mail-coach had been held up and robbed by a pack of impudent thieves.

Here the figure halted for awhile, and just then the heavy rain clouds, which had hung over the sky the whole evening, slowly parted and revealed the pale waning moon. A soft light gradually suffused the sky and vanquished the impenetrable darkness.

Not a living soul was in sight save that solitary figure by the roadside—a man, to all appearances, wearing a broad-brimmed hat casting a deep shadow over his face; the waning moon threw a cold light upon the grey mantle which he wore. On ahead the exquisite tower of the church of Notre Dame appeared vague and fairylike against the deep sapphire of the horizon far away. Then the solitary figure started to walk briskly in the direction of the city.

M. le Procureur Impérial, sitting in his comfortable armchair in the well-furnished apartment which he occupied in the Rue St. Blaise at Alençon, was surveying his visitor with a quizzical and questioning gaze.

On the desk before him lay the letter which that same visitor had presented to him the previous evening—a letter penned

23

by no less a hand than that of M. le Duc d'Otrante himself, Minister of Police, and recommending the bearer of this august autograph to the goodwill of M. de Saint-Tropèze, Procureur Imperial at the tribunal of Alençon. Nay, more! M. le Ministre in that same autograph letter gave orders, in no grudging terms, that the bearer was to be trusted implicitly, and that every facility was to be given him in the execution of his duty: said duty consisting in the tracking down and helping to bring to justice of as many as possible of those saucy Chouans who, not content with terrorising the countryside, were up in arms against the Government of His Imperial Majesty.

A direct encroachment this on the rights and duties of M. le Procureur Impérial; no wonder he surveyed the quiet, insignificant-looking individual before him with a not altogether benevolent air.

M. le Préfet sitting on the opposite side of the high mantelpiece was discreetly silent until his chief chose to speak.

After a brief while the Procureur Impérial addressed his visitor.

"Monsieur le Duc d'Otrante," he said in that dry, supercilious tone which he was

wont to affect when addressing his subordinates, "speaks very highly of you,
Monsieur—Monsieur—— By the way,
the Minister, I perceive, does not mention
your name. What is your name,
Monsieur?"

"Fernand, Monsieur le Procureur,"
replied the man.

"Fernand? Fernand what?"

"Nothing, Monsieur le Procureur. Only
Fernand."

The little Man in Grey spoke very
quietly in a dull, colourless tone which
harmonised with the neutral tone of his
whole appearance. For a moment it
seemed as if a peremptory or sarcastic
retort hovered on M. le Procureur's lips.
The man's quietude appeared like an
impertinence.

M. de Saint-Tropèze belonged to the
old Noblesse. He had emigrated at the
time of the Révolution and spent a certain
number of years in England, during which
time a faithful and obscure steward
administered his property and saved it
from confiscation.

The blandishments of the newly-
crowned Emperor had lured M. de Saint-
Tropèze back to France. Common sense

and ambition had seemingly got the better of his antiquated ideals, whilst Napoléon was only too ready to surround himself with as many scions of the ancient nobility as were willing to swear allegiance to him. He welcomed Henri de Saint-Tropèze and showered dignities upon him with a lavish hand; but the latter never forgot that the Government he now served was an upstart one, and he never departed from that air of condescension and high breeding which kept him aloof from his more plebeian subordinates and which gave him an authority and an influence in the province which they themselves could never hope to attain.

M. le Préfet had coughed discreetly. The warning was well-timed. He knew every word of the Minister's letter by heart, and one phrase in it might, he feared, have escaped M. le Procureur's notice. It ordered that the bearer of the Ministerial credentials was to be taken entirely on trust—no questions were to be pressed on him save those to which he desired to make reply. To disregard even the vaguest hint given by the all-powerful Minister of Police was, to say the least, hazardous. Fortunately, M. de Saint-

Tropèze understood the warning. He pressed his thin lips tightly together and did not pursue the subject of his visitor's name any farther.

"You propose setting to work immediately, Monsieur—er—Fernand?" he asked with frigid hauteur.

"With your permission, Monsieur le Procureur," replied the Man in Grey.

"In the matter of the highway robbery the other night, for instance?"

"In that and other matters, Monsieur le Procureur."

"You were on the coach which was attacked by those damnable Chouans, I believe?"

"Yes, Monsieur le Procureur. I picked up the coach at Argentan and sat next to the driver until the vehicle was ordered to halt."

"Then what happened?"

"A man scrambled up on the box-seat beside me, and holding a pistol to my head commanded me to descend."

"And you descended?"

"Yes," replied the man quietly. He paused a moment and then added by way of explanation: "I hurt my knee coming down; the pain caused me to lose some

27

measure of consciousness. When I returned to my senses, I found myself on the roadside—all alone—there was no sign either of the coach or of the footpads."

"An unfortunate beginning," said M. de Saint-Tropèze with a distinct note of sarcasm in his voice, "for a secret agent of His Majesty's Police sent down to track some of the most astute rascals known in the history of crime."

"I hope to do better in the future, Monsieur le Procureur," rejoined the Man in Grey simply.

M. de Saint-Tropèze made no further remark, and for a moment or two there was silence in the room. The massive Louis XIV clock ticked monotonously; M. de Saint-Tropèze seemed to be dissociating his well-bred person from the sordid and tortuous affairs of the police. The Man in Grey appeared to be waiting until he was spoken to again, and M. le Préfet had a vague feeling that the silence was becoming oppressive, as if some unspoken enmity lurked between the plebeian and obscure police agent and the highly connected and influential Procurator of His Majesty the Emperor. He threw himself blandly into the breach.

"Of course, of course," he said genially. "You, Monsieur—er—Fernand, are lucky to have escaped with your life. Those rascals stick at nothing nowadays. The driver of the coach fully believed that you had been murdered. I suppose you saw nothing of the rogue?"

But this was evidently not one of the questions which the Man in Grey had any desire to answer, and M. Vimars did not insist. He turned obsequiously to M. le Procureur.

"The driver," he said, "spoke of one having a wooden leg. But the worthy Gontran was very vague in all his statements. I imagine that he and all the male passengers must have behaved like cowards or the rascals would never have got so clean away."

"The night was very dark, Monsieur le Préfet," observed the Man in Grey dryly, "and the Chouans were well armed."

"Quite so," here broke in M. le Procureur impatiently, "and no object can be served now in recriminations. See to it, my good Vimars," he continued in a tone that was still slightly sarcastic but entirely peremptory, "that the Minister's orders are obeyed to the last letter. Place yourself and all your personnel and the whole of the local police at Monsieur —er—Fernand's disposal, and do not let me hear any more complaints of inefficiency or want of goodwill on your part until those scoundrels have been laid by heel."

M. de Saint-Tropèze paused after his peroration. With an almost imperceptible nod of his handsome head he indicated both to his visitor and to his subordinate that the audience was at an end. But M. le Préfet, though he knew himself to be dismissed, appeared reluctant to go. There was something which M. le Procureur had forgotten, and the worthy préfet was trying to gather up courage to jog his memory. He had a mightily wholesome respect for his chief, had M. Vimars, for the Procureur was not only a man of vast erudition and of the bluest blood, but one who was held in high consideration by His Majesty's government in Paris, aye, and, so 'twas said, by His Majesty himself.

So M. Vimars hummed and hawed and gave one or two discreet little coughs, whilst M. le Procureur with obvious impatience was drumming his well-manicured nails against the arm of his chair. At last he said testily:

"You have something you wish to say to me, my good Monsieur Vimars?"

"Yes, Monsieur le Procureur," hazarded the préfet in reply, "that is—there is the matter of the burglary—and—and the murder last night—that is——"

M. le Procureur frowned: "Those are local matters," he said loftily, "which concern the commissary of police, my good Vimars, and are beneath the notice of Monsieur le Ministre's secret agent."

The préfet, conscious of a reprimand, blushed to the very roots of his scanty hair. He rose with some haste and the obvious desire to conceal his discomfiture in a precipitate retreat, when the Man in Grey interposed in his quiet, even monotone:

"Nothing is beneath the notice of a secret agent, Monsieur le Procureur," he said; "and everything which is within the province of the commissary of police concerns the representative of the Minister."

M. Vimars literally gasped at this presumption. How anyone dared thus to run counter to M. le Procureur's orders simply passed his comprehension. He looked with positive horror on the meagre, insignificant personage who even now was meeting M. le Procureur's haughty, supercilious glance without any sign of contrition or of shame.

M. de Saint-Tropèze had raised his aristocratic eyebrows, and tried to wither the audacious malapert of his scornful glance, but the little Man in Grey appeared quite unconscious of the enormity of his offence; he stood by—as was his wont—quietly and silently, his eyes fixed inquiringly on the préfet, who was indeed hoping that the floor would open conveniently and swallow him up ere he was called upon to decide whether he should obey the orders of his social chief, or pay heed to the commands of the accredited agent of M. the Minister of Police.

But M. le Procureur decided the question himself and in the only way possible. The Minister's letter with its peremptory commands lay there before him—the secret agent of His Majesty's Police was to be aided and obeyed implicitly in all matters relating to his work; there was nothing to be done save to comply with those orders as graciously as he could, and without further loss of dignity.

"You have heard the wishes of Monsieur le Ministre's agent, my good Vimars," he said coldly; "so I pray you speak to him of the matter which exercises your mind, for of a truth I am not well acquainted with all the details."

Whereupon he fell to contemplating the exquisite polish on his almond-shaped nails. Though the over-bearing little upstart in the grey coat could command the obsequiousness of such men as that fool Vimars, he must be shown at the outset that his insolence would find no weak spot in the armour of M. de Saint-Tropèze's lofty self-respect.

"Oh! it is very obvious," quoth the préfet, whose only desire was to conciliate both parties, "that the matter is not one which affects the graver question of those *satané* Chouans. At the same time both the affairs of last night are certainly mysterious and present some unusual features which have greatly puzzled our exceedingly able commissary of police. It seems that in the early hours of this morning the library of Monseigneur the

Constitutional Bishop of Alençon was broken into by thieves. Fortunately nothing of any value was stolen, and this part of the affair appeared simple enough, until an hour or two later a couple of peasants, who were walking from Lonrai towards the city, came across the body of a man lying face upwards by the roadside. The man was quite dead—had been dead some time apparently. The two louts hurried at once to the commissariat of police and made their depositions. Monsieur Lefèvre, our chief commissary, proceeded to the scene of the crime; he has now the affair in hand."

The prefet had perforce to pause in his narrative for lack of breath. He had been talking volubly and uninterruptedly, and indeed he had no cause to complain of lack of attention on the part of his hearer. M. le Ministre's secret agent sat absolutely still, his deep-set eyes fixed intently upon the narrator. Alone M. le Procureur Impérial maintained his attitude of calm disdain. He still appeared deeply absorbed in the contemplation of his finger-nails.

"At first," resumed the prefét after his dramatic pause, "these two crimes, the greater and the less, seemed in no way

34

connected, and personally I am not sure even now that they are. A certain air of similarity and mystery, however, clings to them both, for in both cases the crimes appear at the outset so very purposeless. In the case of the burglary in Monseigneur's palace the thieves were obviously scared before they could lay hands on any valuables, but even so there were some small pieces of silver lying about which they might have snatched up, even if they were in a vast hurry to get away; whilst in the case of the murder, though the victim's silver watch was stolen and his pockets ransacked, the man was obviously poor and not worth knocking down."

"And is the identity of the victim known to the police?" here asked the Man in Grey in his dull, colourless voice.

"Indeed it is," replied the préfet; "the man was well known throughout the neighbourhood. He was valet to Madame la Marquise de Plélan."

M. le Procureur looked up suddenly from his engrossing occupation.

"Ah!" he said, "I did not know that. Lefèvre did not tell me that he had established the identity of the victim."

He sighed and once more gazed meditatively upon his finger-nails.

"Poor Maxence! I have often seen him at Plélan. There never was a more inoffensive creature. What motive could the brute have for such a villainous murder?"

The prefet shrugged his shoulders.

"Some private quarrel, I imagine," he said.

"A love affair?" queried the Man in Grey.

"Oh, no, Monsieur. Maxence was the wrong side of fifty."

"A smart man?"

"Anything but smart—a curious, shock-headed, slouch-looking person with hair as red as a fox's."

Just for the space of one second the colourless eyes of the Man in Grey lit up with a quick and intense light; it seemed for the moment as if an exclamation difficult to suppress would escape his thin, bloodless lips, and his whole insignificant figure appeared to be quivering with a sudden, uncontrollable eagerness. But this departure from his usual quietude was so momentary that M. le Préfet failed to notice it, whilst M. le Procureur remained as usual uninterested and detached.

"Poor Maxence!" resumed M. Vimars after awhile. "He had, as far as is known, not a single enemy in the world. He was devoted to Madame la Marquise and enjoyed her complete confidence; he was not possessed of any savings, nor was he of a quarrelsome disposition. He can't have had more than a few francs about his person when he was so foully waylaid and murdered. Indeed, it is because the crime is ostensibly so wanton that the police at once dismissed the idea that those abominable Chouans had anything to do with it."

"Is the road where the body was found very lonely of nights?" asked the Man in Grey.

"It is a lonely road," replied the préfet, "and never considered very safe, as it is a favourite haunt of the Chouans—but it is the direct road between Alençon and Mayenne, through Lonrai and Plélan."

"Is it known what business took the confidential valet of Madame la Marquise de Plélan on that lonely road in the middle of the night?"

"It has not been definitely established," here broke in M. le Procureur curtly, "that the murder was committed in the middle of the night."

"I thought——"

"The body was found in the early morning," continued M. de Saint-Tropèze, with an air of cold condescension; "the man had been dead some hours—the leech has not pronounced how many. Maxence had no doubt many friends or relations in Alençon: it is presumed that he spent the afternoon in the city and was on his way back to Plélan in the evening when he was waylaid and murdered."

"That presumption is wrong," said the Man in Grey quietly.

"Wrong?" retorted M. le Procureur frigidly. "What do you mean?"

"I was walking home from Plélan towards Alençon in the small hours of the morning. There was no dead body lying in the road then."

"The body lay by the roadside, half in the ditch," said M. le Procureur dryly; "you may have missed seeing it."

"Possibly," rejoined the Man in Grey equally dryly, "but unlikely."

"Were you looking out for it then?" riposted the Procureur. But no sooner were the words out of his mouth than he realised his mistake. The Man in Grey made no reply; he literally appeared to withdraw himself into an invisible shell, to efface himself yet further within a colourless atmosphere, out of which it was obviously unwise to try to drag him. M. le Procureur pressed his thin lips together, impatient with himself at an unnecessary loss of dignity. As usual M. le Préfet was ready to throw himself into the breach.

"I am sure," he said with his usual volubility, "that we are wasting Monsieur le Procureur's valuable time now. I can assure you Monsieur—er—Fernand, that our chief commissary of police can give you all the details of the crime—if, indeed, they interest you. Shall we go now?—that is," he added, with that same feeling of hesitation which overcame him every time he encountered the secret agent's calm, inquiring look, "that is—er—unless there's anything else you wish to ask of Monsieur le Procureur."

"I wish to know with regard to the murder, what was the cause of death," said the Man in Grey quietly.

"A pistol shot, sir," replied M. de Saint-Tropèze coldly, "right between the shoulder blades, delivered at short range apparently, seeing that the man's coat was charred and blackened with powder. The leech avers that he must have fallen instantly."

"Shot between the shoulders, and yet found lying on his back," murmured the Man in Grey. "And was nothing at all found upon the body that would give a clue to the motive of the crime?"

"Nothing, my dear sir," broke in the préfet glibly, "nothing at all. In his breeches pocket there was a greasy and crumpled sheet of letter-paper, which on examination was found to be covered with a row of numerals all at random—like a child's exercise-book."

"Could I see the paper?"

"It is at the commissariat of police," explained the Procureur curtly.

"Where I can easily find it, of course," concluded the Man in Grey with calm decision. "In the meantime perhaps Monsieur le Préfet will be kind enough to tell me something more about the burglary at the Archbishop's palace."

"There's very little to tell, my good Monsieur Fernand," said M. Vimars, who, far more conscious than was the stranger of the Procureur's growing impatience, would have given a month's salary for the privilege of making himself scarce.

"With what booty did the burglars make off?"

"With nothing of any value; and what they did get they dropped in their flight. The police found a small silver candle-stick and a brass paper weight in the street close to the gate of Monseigneur's palace, also one or two books which no doubt the burglars had seized in the hope that they were valuable editions."

"Nothing, then, has actually been stolen?"

"Nothing. I believe that Monseigneur told the chief commissary that one or two of his books are still missing, but none of any value. So you see, my good Monsieur—er—Fernand," concluded M. Vimars blandly, "that the whole matter is quite beneath your consideration. It is a case of a vulgar murder with only a private grudge by way of motive—and an equally vulgar attempt at burglary, fortunately with no evil results. Our local police—though none too efficient, alas! in these strenuous days, when His Majesty's army claims the flower of our manhood—is well able to cope with these simple matters, which, of course, must occur in every district from time to time. You may take it from me—and I have plenty of experience, remember—that the matter has no concern whatever with the Chouans and with your mission here. You can quite conscientiously devote the whole of your time to the case of the highway robbery the other night, and the recovery of the sixty-two hundred francs which were stolen from the coach, as well as the tracking of that daring rascal with the wooden leg."

Satisfied with his peroration, M. Vimars at last felt justified in moving towards the door.

"I don't think," he concluded with suave obsequiousness, "that we need take up any more of Monsieur le Procureur's valuable time, and with his gracious permission——"

To his intense relief, M. Vimars perceived that the Man in Grey was at last prepared to take his leave.

M. de Saint-Tropèze, plainly at the end of his patience, delighted to be rid of his tiresome visitors, at once became pleasantly condescending. To the secret agent of His Majesty's Police he gave a quite gracious nod, and made the worthy prefet proud and happy by whispering in his ear:

"Do not allow that little busybody to interfere with you too much, my dear Monsieur Vimars. I am prepared to back your skill and experience in such matters against any young shrimp from Paris."

The nod of understanding which accompanied this affable speech sent M. Vimars into an empyrean of delight. After which M. le Procureur finally bowed his visitors out of the room.

The little Man in Grey walked in silence beside M. Vimars along the narrow network of streets which led to the Hôtel de Ville. The préfet had a suite of apartments assigned to him in the building, and once he was installed in his own well-furnished library, untrammelled by the presence of his chief, and with the accredited agent of His Majesty's Minister sitting opposite to him, he gave full rein to his own desire for perfect amity with so important a personage.

He began by a lengthy disquisition on the merits of M. le Procureur Impérial. Never had there been a man of such consideration and of such high culture in the city. M. de Saint-Tropèze was respected alike by the municipal officials, by the townspeople and by the landed aristocracy of the neighbourhood and he was a veritable terror to the light-fingered gentry, as well as to the gangs of Chouans that infested the district.

The Man in Grey listened to the fulsome panegyric with his accustomed deep attention. He asked a few questions as to M. de Saint-Tropèze's domestic circumstances. "Was he married?" "Was he wealthy?" "Did he keep up a luxurious mode of life?"

To all these questions M. Vimars was only too ready to give reply. No, Monsieur le Procureur was not married. He was presumably wealthy, for he kept up a very elegant bachelor establishment in the Rue St. Blaise with just a few old and confidential servants. The sources of his income were not known, as Monsieur de Saint-Tropèze was very proud and reserved, and would not condescend to speak of his affairs with anyone.

Next the worthy préfet harked back, with wonted volubility, to the double outrage of the previous night, and rehearsed

44

at copious length every circumstance connected with it. Strangely enough, the secret agent, who had been sent by the Minister all the way from Paris in order to track down that particular band of Chouans, appeared far more interested in the murder of Mme. de Plélan's valet and the theft of a few books out of Monseigneur the Bishop's library than he was in the daring robbery of the mail-coach.

"You knew the unfortunate Maxence, did you not, Monsieur le Préfet?" he asked.

"Why, yes," replied M. Vimars, "for I have often paid my respects to Madame la Marquise de Plélan."

"What was he like?"

"You can go over to the commissariat of police and see what's left of the poor man," rejoined the préfet, with a feeble attempt at grim humour. "The most remarkable feature about him was his red hair—an unusual colour among our Normandy peasantry."

Later M. Vimars put the finishing touch to his amiability by placing his services unreservedly at the disposal of M. le Ministre's agent.

"Is there anything that I can do for you,

my good Monsieur Fernand?" he asked urbanely.

"Not for the moment, I thank you," replied Fernand. "I will send to you if I require any assistance from the police. But in the meanwhile," he added, "I see that you are something of a scholar. I should be greatly obliged if you could lend me a book to while away some of my idle hours."

"A book? With pleasure!" quoth M. Vimars, not a little puzzled. "But how did you know?"

"That you were a scholar?" rejoined the other with a vague smile. "It was a fairly simple guess, seeing your well-stocked cases of books around me, and that a well-figured volume protrudes even now from your coat pocket."

"Ah! Ah!" retorted the préfet ingenuously, "I see that truly you are a great deal sharper, Monsieur Fernand, than you appear to be. But in any case," he added, "I shall be charmed to be of service to you in the matter of my small library. I flatter myself that it is both comprehensive and select—so if there is anything you especially desire to read——"

"I thank you, sir," said the Man in Grey;

46

"as a matter of fact I have never had the opportunity of reading Madame de Staël's latest work, *Corinne*, and if you happen to possess a copy——"

"With the greatest of pleasure, my dear sir," exclaimed the préfet. He went at once to one of his well-filled bookcases, and after a brief search found the volume and handed it with a smile to his visitor.

"It seems a grave pity," he added, "that no new edition of this remarkable work has ever been printed. But Madame de Staël is not in favour with His Majesty, which no doubt accounts for the publisher's lack of enterprise."

A few more words of polite farewell: after which M. Vimars took final leave of the Minister's agent. The little Man in Grey glided out of the stately apartment like a ghost, even his footsteps failing to resound along the polished floor.

Buried in a capacious armchair, beside a cheerfully blazing fire, M. le Procureur Impérial had allowed the copy of the *Moniteur* which he had been reading to drop from his shapely hands on to the floor. He had closed his eyes, and half an hour had gone by in peaceful somnolence, even while M. Lefèvre, chief commissary of police, was cooling his heels in the ante-chamber, preparatory to being received in audience on most urgent business.

M. le Procureur Impérial never did any-thing in a hurry, and, on principle, always kept a subordinate waiting until any officiousness or impertinence which might have been lurking in the latter's mind had been duly squelched by weariness and sore feet.

So it was only after he had indulged in a short and refreshing nap that M. de Saint-Tropèze rang for his servant, and ordered him to introduce M. Lefèvre, chief com-missary of police. The latter, a choleric, apoplectic, loud-voiced official, entered the audience chamber in a distinctly chastened spirit. He had been shown the original letter of credentials sent to M. le Procureur by the Minister, and yesterday he had caught sight of the small grey-clad figure as it flitted noiselessly along the narrow streets of the city. And inwardly the brave commissary of police had then and there perpetrated an act of high treason, for he had sworn at the in-eptitude of the grand Ministries in Paris, which sent a pack of incompetent agents to interfere with those who were capable of dealing with their own local affairs.

Monsieur le Procureur Impérial, who no doubt sympathised with the worthy man's grievances, was inclined to be gracious.

"Well? And what is it now, my good Monsieur Lefèvre?" he asked as soon as the commissary was seated.

"In one moment, Monsieur le Procureur," growled Lefèvre. "First of all, will you tell me what I am to do about that secret agent who has come here, I suppose, to poke his ugly nose into my affairs?"

"What you are to do about him?" rejoined M. de Saint-Tropèze with a smile. "I have shown you the Minister's letter: he says that we must leave all matters in the hands of his accredited agent."

"By your leave," quoth Lefèvre wrathfully, "that accredited agent might as well be polishing the flagstones of the Paris boulevards, for all the good that he will do down here."

"You think so?" queried M. le Procureur, and with a detached air, he fell into his customary contemplation of his nails.

"And with your permission," continued the commissary, "I will proceed with my own investigations of the outrages committed by those abominable Chouans, for that bundle of conceit will never get the hang of the affair."

"But the Minister says that we must not interfere. We must render all the assistance that we can."

"Bah! we'll render assistance when it is needed," retorted Lefèvre captiously. "But in the meantime I am not going to let that wooden-legged scoundrel slip through my fingers, to please any grey-coated marmoset, who thinks he can lord it over me in my own district."

M. de Saint-Tropèze appeared interested.

"You have a clue?" he asked.

"More than that. I know who killed Maxence."

"Ah! You have got the man? Well done, my brave Lefèvre," exclaimed M. le Procureur, without however, a very great show of enthusiasm.

"I haven't got him yet," parried Lefèvre. "But I have the description of the rascal. A little patience and I can lay my hands on him—provided that busybody does not interfere."

"Who is he, then?" queried M. de Saint-

Tropèze.

"One of those damned Chouans."

"You are sure?"

"Absolutely. All day yesterday I was busy interrogating witnesses, who I knew must have been along the road between Lonrai and the city in the small hours of the morning—workpeople and so on, who go to and from their work every morning of their lives. Well! after a good deal of trouble we have been able to establish that the murder was actually committed between the hours of five and half-past, because although no one appears actually to have heard the pistol shot, the people who were on the road before five saw nothing suspicious, whilst the two louts who subsequently discovered the body actually heard the tower clock of Notre Dame striking the half-hour at the very time."

"Well? And——"

"No fewer than three of the witnesses state that they saw a man with a queer-shaped lip, dressed in a ragged coat and breeches, and with stockingless feet thrust into sabots, hanging about the road shortly before five o'clock. They gave him a wide berth, for they took him to be a

Chouan."

"Why should a Chouan trouble to kill a wretched man who has not a five-franc piece to bless himself with?"

"That's what we've got to find out," rejoined the commissary of police, "and we will find it out, too, as soon as we've got the ruffian and the rest of the gang. I know the rogue, mind you—the man with the queer lip. I have had my eye on him for some time. Oh! he belongs to the gang, I'll stake mine oath on it: a youngish man who should be in the army and is obviously a deserter—a ne'er-do-well who never does a day's honest work and disappears o' nights. What his name is and where he comes from I do not know. But through him we'll get the others, including the chief of the gang—the man with the wooden leg."

"God grant you may succeed!" ejaculated M. le Procureur sententiously. "These perpetual outrages in one's district are a fearful strain on one's nerves. By the way," he added, as he passed his shapely hand over a number of miscellaneous papers which lay in a heap upon his desk, "I don't usually take heed of anonymous letters, but one came to me this morning which might be worth your consideration."

He selected a tattered, greasy paper from the heap, fingering it gingerly, and having carefully unfolded it, passed it across the table to the chief commissary of police. Lefèvre smoothed the paper out: the writing was almost illegible, and grease and dirt had helped further to confuse the characters, but the commissary had had some experience of such communications, and contrived slowly to decipher the scrawl.

"It is a denunciation, of course," he said. "The rogues appear to be quarrelling amongst themselves. 'If,' says the writer of the epistle, 'M. le Procureur will send his police to-night between the hours of ten and twelve to the Cache-Renard woods and they follow the directions given below, they will come across the money and valuables which were taken from the mail-coach last Wednesday, and also those who robbed the coach and murdered Mme. de Plélan's valet. Strike the first bridle-path on the right after entering the wood by the main road, until you come to a fallen fir tree lying across another narrow path; dismount here and follow

53

this track for a further three hundred metres, till you come to a group of five larches in the midst of a thicket of birch and oak. Stand with your back to the larch that is farthest from you, and face the thicket; there you will perceive another track which runs straight into the depths of the wood; follow it until you come to a tiny clearing, at the bottom of which the thicket will seem so dense that you would deem it impenetrable. Plunge into it boldly to where a nest of broken branches reveals the presence of human footsteps, and in front of you you will see a kind of hut composed of dead branches and caked mud and covered with a rough thatch of heather. In that hut you will find that for which you seek."

"Do you think it worth while to act upon this anonymous denunciation?" queried M. de Saint-Tropèze when Lefèvre had finished reading.

"I certainly do," replied the commissary. "In any case it can do no harm."

"You must take plenty of men with you."

"Leave that to me, Monsieur le Procureur," rejoined Lefèvre, "and I'll see that they are well armed, too."

"What about the secret agent?"

Lefèvre swore.

"That worm?" was his sole but very expressive comment.

"Will you see him about the matter?"

"What do you think?"

"I suppose you must."

"And if he gives me orders?"

"You must obey them, of course. Have you seen him this morning?"

"Yes. He had ordered me to come to his lodgings in the Rue de France."

"What did he want?"

"The scrap of paper which we had found in the breeches pocket of Maxence."

"You gave it to him?"

"Of course," growled Lefèvre savagely. "Haven't we all got to obey him?"

"You left him in his lodgings, then?"

"Yes."

"Doing what?"

"Reading a book."

"Reading a book?" exclaimed M. de Saint-Tropèze with a harsh laugh. "What book?"

"I just noticed the title," replied Lefèvre, "though I'm nothing of a scholar and books don't interest me."

"What was the title?"

55

"*Corinne*," said the commissary of police.

Apparently M. le Procureur Impérial had come to the end of the questions which he desired to put to the worthy M. Lefèvre, for he said nothing more, but remained leaning back in his chair and gazing straight out of the window beside him. His pale, aristocratic profile looked almost like chiselled marble against the purple damask of the cushions. He seemed absorbed in thought, or else supremely bored; M. Lefèvre—nothing of a psychologist, despite his calling—could not have said which.

The ticking of the massive Louis XIV clock upon the mantelpiece and the sizzling of damp wood on the hearth alone broke the silence which reigned in the stately apartment. Through the closed window the manifold sounds which emanate from a busy city came discreet and subdued.

Instinctively M. Lefèvre's glance followed that of his chief: he, too, fell to gazing out of the window where only a few passers-by were seen hurrying homewards on this late dreary October afternoon. Suddenly he perceived the narrow, shrinking figure of the little Man in Grey gliding swiftly down the narrow street. The commissary of police smothered the savage oath which had risen to his lips: he turned to his chief, and even his obtuse perceptions were aroused by what he saw. M. le Procureur Impérial was no longer leaning back listlessly against the damask cushions: he was leaning forward, his fine, white hands clutching the arms of his chair. He, too, had apparently caught sight of the grey-clad figure, for his eyes, wide open and resentful, followed it as it glided along, and on his whole face there was such an expression of hatred and savagery that the worthy commissary felt unaccountably awed and subdued. Next moment, however, he thought he must have been dreaming, for M. de Saint-Tropèze had once more turned to him with that frigid urbanity which became his aristocratic personality so well.

"Well, my good Lefèvre," he said, "I don't really think that I can help you further in any way. I quite appreciate your mistrust of the obtrusive stranger, and personally I cannot avoid a suspicion that he will hamper you by interfering at a critical moment to-night during your expedition against the Chouans. He may just be the cause of their slipping through your fingers, which would be such a terrible pity now that you have gathered the net so skilfully around them."

Lefèvre rose, and with firm, deliberate movements tightened the belt round his portly waist, re-adjusted the set of his tunic, and generally contrived to give himself an air of determination and energy.

"I'll say nothing to the shrimp about our expedition to-night," he said with sullen resolution. "That is, unless you, Monsieur le Procureur, give me orders to do so."

"Oh, I?" rejoined M. de Saint-Tropèze carelessly. "I won't say anything one way or the other. The whole matter is out of my hands and you must act as you think best. Whatever happens," he added slowly and emphatically, "you will get no blame from me."

Which was such an extraordinary thing for M. le Procureur to say—who was one of the most pedantic, most censorious and most autocratic of men—that Lefèvre spoke of it afterwards to M. le Préfet and to one or two of his friends. He could not understand this attitude of humility and obedience on the part of his chief: but everyone agreed that it was small wonder M. le Procureur Impérial was upset, seeing that the presence of that secret police agent in Alençon was a direct snub to all the municipal and departmental authorities throughout the district, and M. de Saint-Tropèze was sure to resent it more than anyone else, for he was very proud, and acknowledged to be one of the most capable of highly-placed officials in the whole of France.

The night that followed was unusually dark. Out in the Cache-Renard woods the patter of the rain on the tall crests of the pines and the soughing of the wind through the branches of the trees drowned every other sound. In the burrow built of dead branches, caked mud and dried heather, five men sat waiting, their ears strained to the cracking of every twig, to the fall of every drop of moisture from the overladen boughs. Among them the dark lantern threw a dim, flickering light on their sullen, glowering faces. Despite the cold and the damp outside, the atmosphere within was hot to suffocation; the men's breath came panting and laboured, and now and again they exchanged a few whispered words.

"In any case," declared one of them, "if we feel that he is playing us false we shall have to do for him to-night, eh, mates?"

A kind of muffled assent went round the circle, and one man murmured:

"Do you really mistrust him, Hare-Lip?"

"I should," replied Hare-Lip curtly, "if I thought he knew about Red-Poll."

"You don't think that he suspects?" queried another.

"I don't see how he can. He can't have shown his face, or rather his wooden leg, inside Alençon since the mail-coach episode. The police are keen after him. But if he did hear rumours of the death of Red-Poll he will also have heard that the murder was only an ordinary case of robbery—watch and money stolen—and that a sheet of letter-paper covered with random numerals was found in the breeches pocket of the murdered man."

One of the men swore lustily in the dark.

"The paper covered with numerals!" he muttered savagely under his breath. "You clumsy fool to have left that behind!"

"What was the use——" began another.

But Hare-Lip laughed, and broke in

quietly:

"Do ye take me for a fool, mates? I was not going to take away that original sheet of paper and proclaim to our chiefs, that it was one of us who killed Red-Poll. No! I took the sheet of letter-paper with me when I went to meet Red-Poll. After he fell—I shot him between the shoulders—I turned him over on his back and ransacked his pockets; that was a blind. Then I found the paper with the figures and copied them out carefully—that was another blind—in case Silver-Leg heard of the affair and suspected us."

One or two of the others gave a growl of dissent.

"You might have been caught while you were playing that silly game," said one of the men, "which would not deceive a child."

"Silver-Leg is no baby," murmured another.

"Well, he'll be here anon," concluded Hare-Lip lightly. "If you think he means to play a dirty trick, he can go and join Red-Poll, that's all."

"He may not come, after all."

"He must come. I had his message to meet him here to-night without fail. The chiefs have planned another attack: on the Orléans coach this time. Silver-Leg wants us to be of the party."

"We ought to have got hold of the last booty before now!"

"Impossible! Mole-Skin and I have not figured out all the directions from the book and the numerals yet. It is not an easy task, I tell you, but it shall be done soon, and we can take you straight to the spot as soon as we have the directions before us."

"Unless Silver-Leg and Madame remove the booty in the meanwhile," grunted one of the party caustically.

"I sometimes wonder——" said another. But he got no further. A peremptory "Hush!" from Hare-Lip suddenly silenced them all.

With a swift movement one of them extinguished the lantern, and now they cowered in absolute darkness within their burrow like so many wild beasts tracked to earth by the hunters. The heat was suffocating: the men vainly tried to subdue the sound of their breath as it came panting from their parched throats.

"The police!" Hare-Lip muttered hoarsely.

But they did not need to be told. Just like tracked beasts, they knew every sound which portended danger, and already from afar off, even from the very edge of the wood, more than a kilometre away, their ears, attuned to every sound, had perceived the measured tramp of horses upon the soft, muddy road. They cowered there, rigid and silent. The darkness encompassed them, and they felt safe enough in their shelter in the very heart of the woods, in this secret hiding-place which was known to no living soul save to them. The police on patrol duty had often passed them by: the nearest track practicable on horseback was four hundred metres away, the nearest footpath made a wide detour round the thicket, wherein these skulking miscreants had contrived to build their lair.

As a rule, it meant cowering, silent and motionless, inside the burrow whilst perhaps one posse of police, more venturesome than most, had dismounted at the end of the bridle-path and plunged afoot into the narrower track, scouring the thicket on either side for human quarry. It involved only an elementary amount of danger, distant and intangible, not worth an accelerated heart-beat, or even a gripping of knife or pistol wherewith to sell life and liberty at a price.

And so, for the first five minutes, while the tramp of horses' hoofs drew nearer, the men waited in placid silence.

"I hope Silver-Leg has found shelter," one of the men murmured under his breath.

"He should have been here by now," whispered another.

Then they perceived the usual sound of men dismounting, the rattle of chains, the champing of bits, peremptory words of command. Even then they felt that they had nothing to fear: these were all sounds they had heard before. The thicket and the darkness were their allies; they crouched in silence, but they felt that they were safe. Their ears and senses, however, were keenly on the alert: they heard the crackling of dried twigs under the heavy footsteps of the men, the muttered curses that accompanied the struggle against the density of the thicket, the clashing of metal tools against dead branches of intervening trees. Still they did not move. They were not afraid—not yet! But somehow in the obscurity which held them as in a pall their

64

attitude had become more tense, their breathing more laboured, and one or two strong quivering hands went out instinctively to clutch a neighbouring one.

Then suddenly Hare-Lip drew in his breath with a hissing sound like that of an angry snake. He suppressed an imprecation which had forced itself to his lips. Through the almost imperceptible aperture of the burrow he had perceived the flicker of lanterns: and sounds of broken twigs, of trampling feet, of moving, advancing humanity appeared suddenly to be strangely near.

"By Satan!" he said almost inaudibly; "they are in the clearing!"

"They are attacking the thicket," added Mole-Skin in a hoarse whisper.

Never before had the scouring posse of police come so near to the stronghold of these brigands. It was impossible to see how many of them there were, but that they were both numerous and determined could not for a moment be disputed. Voices now became more distinct.

"This way!" "No—that!" "Here, Marcel, where's your pick?" "Lend us your knife, Jules Marie; the bramble has got into my boots."

Some of the men were joking, others swearing lustily. But there were a great number of them, and they were now desperately near.

"They are on us!" came in a husky murmur from Hare-Lip. "They know their way."

"We are betrayed!" was the stifled response.

"By Silver-Leg!" ejaculated Hare-Lip hoarsely, and with such an intensity of vengeful hatred as would have made even the autocratic wooden-legged chief of this band of brigands quake. "The accursed informer! By all the demons in hell he shall pay for his treachery!"

Indeed, there was no longer any doubt that it was not mere chance which was guiding the posse of police to this secret spot. They were making their way unhesitatingly by the dim light of the dark lanterns which their leaders carried before them. One of the men suddenly hit upon the almost imperceptible track which led straight to the burrow. There was no mistaking the call which he gave to his comrades.

"I have it now, mates!" he shouted. "Follow me!"

The sharp report of a pistol came by way of a reply from the lurking-hole of the Chouans, and the man who had just uttered the call to his mates fell forward on his face.

"Attention, my men!" commanded the officer in charge. "Close the lanterns and put a charge of powder into the brigand's den."

Once more the report of a pistol rang out through the night. But the men of the police, though obviously scared by the mysterious foe who struck at them out of the darkness, were sufficiently disciplined not to give ground: they fought their way into line, and the next moment a terrific volley of gunfire rent the echoes of the wood from end to end. In front of the men now there was a wide clearing, where the undergrowth had been repeatedly broken and trampled upon. This they had seen, just before the lanterns were closed, and beyond it the burrow with its thatch of heather and its narrow aperture which revealed the muzzle of two or three muskets, and through the aperture several pairs of glowing eyes and shadowy forms vaguely discernible in the gloom.

"Up with the lights and charge!"

67

commanded the officer.

The lanterns were opened, and three sharp reports came in immediate answer from the lair.

One or two men of the police fell amidst the bed of brambles; but the others, maddened by this resistance and by the fall of their comrades, rushed forward in force.

Dividing their line in the centre, they circled round the clearing, attacking the stronghold from two sides. The commissary of police, leaving nothing to chance, had sent half a company to do the work. In a few seconds the men were all over the burrow, scrambling up the thatch, kicking aside the loose walls of dead branches, and within two minutes they had trampled every fragment of the construction under foot.

But of the gang of Chouans there remained only a few traces, and two or three muskets abandoned in their hasty flight: they had succeeded in making good their escape under cover of the darkness. The sergeant in command of the squad of police ordered the debris of the den to be carefully searched. Very little of importance was found beyond a few proofs that the robbery of the mail-coach the other night, the murder of Maxence, and the abortive burglary in Monseigneur's palace were the work of the same gang. One or two watches and pocket-books were subsequently identified by the passengers of the coach that had been held up; there was the silver watch which had belonged to the murdered valet, and a couple of books which bore Monseigneur the Bishop of Alençon's book-plate.

But of the man with the wooden leg and his rascally henchmen, or of the sixty-two hundred francs stolen from the coach, there was not a sign.

The chief commissary of police swore lustily when his men returned to the bridle-path where he had been waiting for them, and the sergeant reported to him that the rogues had made good their escape. But even his wrath—violent and wordy as it was—was as nothing to the white heat of anger wherewith M. le Procureur Impérial received the news of the dire failure of the midnight raid in the Cache-Renard woods.

Indeed, he appeared so extraordinarily upset at the time that his subsequent illness was directly attributable to this cause. The leech vowed that his august patient was suffering from a severe shock to his nerves. Be that as it may, M. de Saint-Tropèze, who was usually in such vigorous health, was confined to his room for some days after the raid. It was a fortnight and more ere he again took his walks abroad, as had been his wont in the past, and his friends, when they saw him, could not help but remark that something of M. le Procureur's elasticity and proud bearing had gone. He who used to be so upright now walked with a decided stoop; his face looked at times the colour of ashes; and now and again, when he was out in the streets, he would throw a look around him almost as if he were afraid.

On the other hand, the secret agent of His Imperial Majesty's Police had received the news of the escape of the Chouans with his habitual quietude and equanimity.

He did not make any comment on the commissary's report of the affair, nor did he offer the slightest remonstrance to M. le Procureur Impérial for having permitted the expedition without direct instructions from the official representative of the

Minister.

Nothing was seen of the little Man in Grey for the next two or three weeks: he appeared absorbed in the books which M. le Préfet so graciously lent him, and he did not trouble either the latter or M. le Procureur, or the commissary of police with many visits.

The matter of the highway robbery, as well as that of the murdered valet Maxence, appeared to be already relegated to the growing list of the mysterious crimes perpetrated by those atrocious Chouans, with which the police of His Imperial Majesty were unable to cope. The appearance of the enigmatic person in grey had had no deterrent effect on the rascals, nor was it likely to have any, if he proved as inept as the local officials had been in dealing with such flagrant and outrageous felony.

And once again the silence of the forest was broken in the night by the sound of human creatures on the prowl. Through the undergrowth which lies thickest at the Lonrai end of the woods, to the left of the intersecting main road, the measured tread of a footfall could be faintly

71

perceived—it was a strange and halting footfall, as of a man walking with a stump.

Behind the secular willow, which stands in the centre of the small clearing beside the stagnant pool in the very heart of this dense portion of the forest, a lonely watcher crouched, waiting. He had lain there and waited night after night, and for hours at a stretch the surrounding gloom held him in its close embrace: his ears and senses were strained to hear that uneven footfall, whenever its faint thud broke the absolute silence. To no other sound, no other sight, did he pay any attention, or no doubt he would have noticed that in the thicket behind him another watcher cowered. The stalker was stalked in his turn: the watcher was watched. Someone else was waiting in this dense corner for the man with the wooden leg—a small figure wrapped in a dark mantle, a silent, furtive creature, more motionless, more noiseless than any beast in its lair.

At last, to-night, that faint, uneven thud of a wooden stump against the soft carpet of the woods reached the straining ears of the two watchers. Anon the feeble flicker of a dark lantern was vaguely discernible in the undergrowth.

The man who was crouching behind the willow drew in his breath with a faint, hissing sound; his hand grasped more convulsively the pistol which it held. He was lying flat upon his stomach, like a creeping reptile watching for its prey; his eyes were fixed upon the tiny flickering light as it slowly drew near towards the stagnant pool.

In the thicket behind him the other watcher also lay in wait: his hand, too, closed upon a pistol with a firm and determined grip; the dark mantle slid noiselessly down from his shoulders. But he did not move, and not a twig that helped to give him cover quivered at his touch.

The next moment a man dressed in a rough blouse and coarse breeches and with a woollen cap pulled over his shaggy hair came out into the clearing. He walked deliberately up to the willow tree. In addition to the small dark lantern which he held in one hand, he carried a spade upon his shoulder. Presently he threw down the spade and then proceeded so to arrange the lantern that its light fell full upon one particular spot, where the dry moss appeared to have been recently disturbed. The man crouching behind the willow watched his every movement; the other behind the thicket hardly dared to breathe.

Then the new-comer did a very curious thing. Sitting down upon the soft, sodden earth, he stretched his wooden stump out before him: it was fastened with straps to the leg which was bent at the knee, the shin and foot beyond appearing like a thick and shapeless mass, swathed with bandages. The supposed maimed man, however, now set to work to undo the straps which bound the wooden stump to his leg, then he removed the stump, straightened out his knee, unwound a few metres of bandages which concealed the shape of his shin and foot, and finally stood up on both legs, as straight and hale as nature had originally made him. The watcher behind the willow had viewed all his movements with tense attention. Now he could scarcely repress a gasp of mingled astonishment and rage, or the vengeful curse which had risen to his lips.

The new-comer took up his spade and, selecting the spot where the moss and the earth bore traces of having been disturbed, he bent to his task and started to dig. The man behind the tree raised his pistol and fired: the other staggered backwards with a groan—partly of terror and partly of pain, and his left hand went up to his right shoulder with a quick, convulsive gesture. But already the assassin, casting his still smoking pistol aside, had fallen upon his victim; there was a struggle, brief and grim, a smothered call for help, a savage exclamation of rage and satisfied vengeance, and the wounded man fell at last with a final cry of horror, as his enemy's grip fastened around his throat.

For a second or two the murderer stood quite still contemplating his work. With a couple of vigorous kicks with his boot he turned the body callously over. Then he picked up the lantern and allowed the light to play on the dead man's face; he gave one cursory glance at the straight, marble-like features and at the full, shaggy beard and hair which disfigured the face, and another contemptuous one at the wooden stump which still lay on the ground close by.

"So dies an informer!" he ejaculated with a harsh laugh.

He searched for his pistol, and, having found it, he tucked it into his belt; then putting his fingers to his lips he gave a cry like that of a screech-owl. The cry was answered by a similar one some little distance away: a minute or two later another man appeared through the undergrowth.

"Have you done for him?" queried this stranger in a husky whisper.

"He is dead," replied the other curtly. "Come nearer, Mole-Skin," he added; "you will see something that will amaze you."

Mole-Skin did as his mate ordered; he, too, stood aghast when Hare-Lip pointed to the wooden stump and to the dead man's legs.

"It was not a bad idea!" said Hare-Lip after a while. "It put the police on a wrong scent all the time; while they searched for a man with one leg he just walked about on two. Silver-Leg was no fool. But," he added savagely, "he was a traitor, and now he'll neither bully nor betray us again."

"What about the money?"

"We'd best get that now. Didn't I tell you that Silver-Leg would come here sooner or later? We lost nothing by lying in wait for him."

Without another word Mole-Skin

picked up the spade, and in his turn began to dig at the spot where Silver-Leg had toiled when the bullet of his betrayed comrade laid him low. There was only the one spade, and Hare-Lip kept watch while his comrade dug. The light from the dark lantern revealed the two miscreants at their work.

While Hare-Lip had thus taken the law into his own hands against the informer, the watcher in the thicket had not stirred. But now he, also, began to crawl slowly and cautiously out of his hiding-place. No snake, or lizard, or crawling, furtive beast could have been more noiseless than he was; the moss beneath him dulled the sound of every movement, till he too had reached the willow tree.

The two Chouans were less than thirty paces away from him. Intent upon their work, they had been oblivious of every other sound. Now, when the tracker of his human quarry raised his arm, to fire, Hare-Lip suddenly turned and at once gave a warning call to his mate. But the call broke upon his lips; there came a sharp report, immediately followed by another—the two brigands, illumined by the lantern, had been an easy target, and

77

the hand which wielded the pistol was steady and unerring.

And now stillness more absolute than before reigned in the heart of the forest. Summary justice had been meted out to a base informer by the vengeful arm of the comrades whom he had betrayed, and to the two determined criminals by an equally relentless and retributive hand.

The man who had so inexorably accomplished this last act of unfaltering justice waited for a moment or two until the last lingering echo of the double pistol shot had ceased to resound through the woods. Then he put two fingers to his lips and gave a shrill, prolonged whistle, after which he came out from behind the willow. He was small and insignificant-looking, with a pale face and colourless eyes. He was dressed in grey and a grey cap was pulled low down over his forehead. He went up to where the two miscreants whom he had shot were lying, and with a practised eye and hand assured himself that they were indeed dead. He turned the light of the dark lantern first on the man with the queer-shaped lip and then on the latter's companion. The two Chouans had at any rate paid for some of their crimes with their lives; it remained for the Almighty Judge to pardon or to punish as they deserved. The third man lay, stark and rigid, where a kick from the other man had roughly cast him aside. His eyes, wide open and inscrutable, had still around them a strange look of authority and pride; the features appeared calm and marble-like; the mouth under the obviously false beard was tightly closed, as if it strove even in death to suppress every sound which might betray the secret that had been so jealously guarded throughout his life. Near by lay the wooden stump which had thrown such a cloud of dust into the eyes of good M. Lefèvre and his local police.

With slow deliberation the Man in Grey picked up the wooden stump, and so replaced it against the dead man's leg that in the feeble light and dense black shadows it looked as real as it had done in life—a support for an amputated limb. A moment or two later the flickering light of a lantern showed through the thicket, and soon the lusty voice of the commissary of police broke in on the watcher's loneliness.

"We heard three distinct shots," explained M. Lefèvre, as soon as he reached the clearing and caught sight of the secret agent.

"Three acts of justice," replied the Man in Grey quietly, as he pointed to the bodies of the three Chouans.

"The man with the wooden leg! exclaimed the commissary in tones wherein astonishment and unmistakable elation struggled with a momentary feeling of horror. "You have got him?"

"Yes," answered the Man in Grey simply. "Where are your men?"

"I left them at the junction of the bridle-path as you ordered me to do," growled the commissary sullenly, for he still felt sore and aggrieved at the peremptory commands which had been given to him by the secret agent earlier on that day.

"Then go back and send half a dozen of them here with improvised stretchers to remove the bodies."

"Then it was you who——" murmured Lefèvre, not knowing, indeed, what to say or do in the face of this puzzling and grim emergency.

"What else would you have had me do?" rejoined the Man in Grey as, with a steady hand, he removed the false hair and beard which disguised the pale, aristocratic face

80

of M. de Saint-Tropèze.

"Monsieur le Procureur Impérial!" ejaculated Lefèvre hoarsely. "I—I—don't understand—you—you—have killed him —he—oh, my God!"

"The Chouans whom he betrayed killed him, my good Lefèvre," replied the Man in Grey quietly. "He was their chief, and kept the secret of his anonymity even from them. When he was amongst them and led them to their many nefarious deeds he was not content to hide his face behind a tangle of false and shaggy hair, or to appear in rough clothes and with grimy hands. No! His artistry in crime went a step farther than that: he strapped a wooden leg to his own whole one, and while you scoured the countryside in search of a Chouan with a wooden leg, the latter had resumed his personality as the haughty and well-connected Monsieur de Saint-Tropèze, Procureur at the tribunal of Alençon to His Majesty the Emperor. Here is the stump," added the Man in Grey, as with the point of his boot he kicked the wooden stump aside, "and there," he concluded, pointing to the two dead Chouans, "are the men who wreaked their vengeance upon their chief."

"But how——" interjected Lefèvre, who was too bewildered to speak or even to think coherently, "how did you find out—how——"

"Later I may tell you," broke in the Man in Grey shortly, "now we must see to the removal of the bodies. But remember," he added peremptorily and with solemn earnestness, "that everything you have seen and heard to-night must remain for ever a secret within your breast. For the honour of our administration, for the honour of our newly-founded Empire, the dual personality and countless crimes of such a highly placed official as Monsieur de Saint-Tropèze must never be known to the public. I saved the hangman's work when I killed these two men—there is no one living now, save you and I, who can tell the tale of Monsieur de Saint-Tropèze's double entity. Remember that to the public who knew him, to his servants, to your men who will carry his body in all respect and reverence, he has died here by my side in the execution of his duty—disguised in rough clothes in order to help me track these infernal Chouans to their lair. I shall never speak of what I know, and as for you——"

82

The Man in Grey paused, and, even through the gloom, the commissary felt the strength and menace of those colourless eyes fixed steadfastly upon him.

"Your oath, Monsieur le Commissaire de Police," concluded the secret agent in firm, commanding tones.

Awed and subdued—not to say terrified—the chief commissary gave the required oath of absolute secrecy.

"Now go and fetch your men, my good Lefèvre," enjoined the Man in Grey quietly.

Mechanically the commissary turned to go. He felt as if he were in a dream from which he would presently awake. The man whom he had respected and feared, the Procurator of His Majesty the Emperor, whose authority the whole countryside acknowledged, was identical with that nefarious Chouan with the wooden leg whom the entire province loathed and feared.

Indeed, the curious enigma of that dual personality was enough to addle even a clearer intellect than that of the worthy commissary of police. Guided by the light of the lantern he carried, he made his way back through the thicket whence he had come.

Alone in the forest, the Man in Grey watched over the dead. He looked down meditatively on the pale, aristocratic face of the man who had lied and schemed and planned, robbed and murdered, who had risked so much and committed such villainies, for a purpose which would henceforth and for ever remain an unfathomable mystery.

Was passionate loyalty for the decadent Royalist Cause at the root of all the crimes perpetrated by this man of culture and position—or was it merely vulgar greed, vulgar and insatiable worship of money, that drove him to mean and sordid crimes? To what uses did he put the money wrung from peaceable citizens? Did it go to swell the coffers of a hopeless Cause, or to contribute to M. de Saint-Tropèze's own love of luxury?

The Man in Grey pondered these things in the loneliness and silence of the night. All such questions must henceforth be left unanswered. For the sake of officialdom, of the government of the new Empire, the memory of such a man as M. de Saint-Tropèze must remain for ever untarnished.

Anon the posse of police under the command of a sergeant arrived upon the scene. They had improvised three stretchers; one of these was reverently covered with a mantle, upon which they laid the body of M. le Procureur Impérial, killed in the discharge of his duty whilst aiding to track a gang of desperate Chouans.

In the forenoon of the following day the chief commissary of police, having seen M. le Préfet on the subject of the arrangements for the public funeral of M. de Saint-Tropèze, called at the lodgings of the secret agent of His Imperial Majesty's Police.

After the usual polite formalities Lefèvre plunged boldly into the subject of his visit.

"How did you find out?" he asked, trying to carry off the situation with his accustomed bluff. "You owe me an explanation, you know, Monsieur—er—Fernand. I am chief commissary of this district, and by your own statement you stand convicted of having killed two men. Abominable rogues though they were, the laws of France do not allow——"

"I owe you no explanation, my good Lefèvre," interrupted the Man in Grey in his quiet monotone, "as you know. If you would care to take the responsibility on yourself of indicting me for the wilful murder of those two men, you are of course at liberty to do so. But——"

The commissary hastened to assure the secret emissary of His Majesty that what he had said had only been meant as a joke.

"Only as a spur," he added affably, "to induce you to tell me how you found out the secret of Monsieur de Saint-Tropèze."

"Quite simply," replied the Man in Grey, "by following step by step the series of crimes which culminated in your abortive expedition against the Chouans. On the evening of the attack on the coach on the 10th of October last, I lay hidden and forgotten by the roadside. The coach had driven away; the footpads were making off with their booty. I followed them. I crawled behind them on my hands and knees till they came to their burrow—the place where you made that foolish and ill-considered attack on them the other night. I heard them quarrelling over their loot; I heard enough to guess that sooner or later a revolt would break out amongst them and that the man whom they called Hare-Lip meant to possess himself of a large share of the spoils. I also heard the man with the wooden leg say something about a book named *Corinne* which was to be mentioned to 'Monseigneur,' and a key which would be sent to 'Madame' by the intermediary of Red-Poll.

"Within two days of this I learned that a man who had red hair and was valet to Madame la Marquise de Plélan had been murdered, and that a sheet of notepaper covered with random numerals was found upon his person; at the same time a burglary had been committed in the house of Monseigneur the Bishop of Alençon and all that had been stolen was some books. At once I recognised the hand of Hare-Lip and his gang. They had obviously stolen the book from Monseigneur's library and then murdered Red-Poll, in order to possess themselves of the cipher, which I felt sure would prove to be the indication of the secret hiding-place of the stolen booty. It was easy enough to work out the problem of the book and the key. The numerals on the sheet of notepaper referred to pages, lines and words in the book—a clumsy enough cipher at best. It gave me—just as I expected—clear indications of the very place, beside the willow tree and the pool. Also—just as I anticipated—Silver-Leg, the autocratic chief, had in the meanwhile put his threat into execution and punished his rebellious followers by betraying them to the police."

"Great God!" exclaimed Lefèvre, recollecting the anonymous letter which M. le Procureur had handed to him.

"I dare say you recollect this phase of the episode," continued the Man in Grey. "Your expedition against the Chouans nearly upset all my plans. It had the effect of allowing three of them to escape. However, let that pass for the moment. I could not help but guess, when I heard of the attack, that Hare-Lip and his mates would wish to be revenged on the informer. Their burrow was now known to the police, but there was still the hiding-place of the booty, to which sooner or later I knew that Silver-Leg must return.

"You remember the orders I gave you a full month ago; to be prepared to go on any day and at an instant's notice with a dozen of your men to a certain point on the main road at the Lonrai end of the wood which I had indicated to you, whenever I sent you a peremptory message to do so, and there to wait in silence and on the alert until a shrill whistle from me brought you to my side. Well! in this matter you did your duty well, and the Minister shall hear of it.

"As for me, I was content to bide my time. With the faithful henchman whom you placed at my disposal I lay in wait for Monsieur de Saint-Tropèze in the Rue St. Blaise during all those weary days and nights when he was supposed to be too ill to venture out of his house. At last he could refrain no longer; greed or perhaps sheer curiosity, or that wild adventurous spirit which made him what he was, drove him to lend a deaf ear to the dictates of prudence and to don once again the shaggy beard, the rough clothes and wooden stump of his lawless and shady life.

"I had so placed your man that from where he was he could not see Monsieur le Procureur, whenever the latter came out of his house, nor did he know whom or what it was that I was watching; but as soon as I saw Monsieur de Saint-Tropèze emerging stealthily from his side gate, I dispatched your man to you with the peremptory message to go at once to the appointed place, and then I started in the wake of my quarry.

"You, my good Lefèvre, have no conceptions what it means to track—unseen and unheard—one of those reckless Chouans who are more alert than any wild beast. But I tracked my man; he came out of his house when the night was at its darkest and first made his way to that small derelict den which no doubt you know and which stands just off the main road on the fringe of the Cache-Renard wood. This he entered and came out about a quarter of an hour later, dressed in his Chouan rig-out. I must own that for a few seconds he almost deceived me, so marvellous was his disguise; the way he contrived that wooden leg was positively amazing.

"After that he plunged into the woods. But I no longer followed him; I knew whither he was going and was afraid lest, in the depths and silence of the forest, he would hear my footfall and manage to give me the slip. Whilst he worked his way laboriously with his wooden stump through the thicket and the undergrowth, I struck boldly along the main road, and plunged into the wood at the point which had been revealed to me by the cipher. I had explored the place many a time during the past month, and had no difficulty in finding the stagnant pool and the willow tree. Hare-Lip and his mate were as usual on the watch. No sooner had Silver-Leg appeared on the scene than the others meted out to him the full measure of their vengeful justice. But I could not allow them to be taken alive. I did not know how much they knew or guessed of their leader's secret, or how much they might reveal at their first interrogation. The gallows had already claimed them for its own; for me they were a facile prey. I shot them both deliberately and will answer to His Majesty's Minister of Police alone for my actions."

The Man in Grey paused. As he completed his narrative Lefèvre stared at him, dumbfounded at the courage and determination, the dogged perseverance which alone could have brought this amazing undertaking to its grim and gruesome issue.

"After this, my good Lefèvre,"

remarked the secret agent more lightly, "we shall have to find out something about 'Madame' and quite a good deal about 'Monseigneur.' "

II

THE SPANIARD

THE man with the wooden leg was still at large, and M. le Procureur Impérial had died a hero's death whilst helping to capture a gang of desperate Chouans in the Cache-Renard woods. This was the public version of the tragic epilogue to those three mysteries,, which had puzzled and terrified the countryside during the early days of October, 1810—the robbery of the mail-coach, the burglary in the Palace of Monseigneur the Constitutional Bishop of Alençon, and the murder of Mme. la Marquise de Plélan's valet, Maxence.

The intelligent section of the public was loud in its condemnation of the ineptitude displayed by the police in the matter of those abominable crimes, and chief commissary Lefèvre, bound by oath—not to say terror—to hold his tongue as to the real facts of the case, grumbled in his beard and muttered curses on the accredited representative of the Minister of Police—aye, and on M. le Duc d'Otrante himself.

On top of all the public unrest and dissatisfaction came the outrage at the house of M. de Kerblay, a noted advocate of the Paris bar and member of the Senate, who owned a small property in the neighbourhood of Alençon, where he spent a couple of months every year with his wife and family, entertaining a few friends during the shooting season.

In the morning of November the 6th, the neighbourhood was horrified to hear that on the previous night, shortly after ten o'clock, a party of those ruffianly Chouans had made a descent on M. de Kerblay's house, Les Ormeaux. They had demanded admittance in the name of the law. All the servants had gone to bed with the exception of Hector, M. de Kerblay's valet, and he was so scared that he allowed the *scélérats* to push their way into the house before he had realised who they were. Ere he could call for help he was set upon, gagged, and locked up in his pantry. The Chouans then proceeded noiselessly upstairs. Mme. de Kerblay was already in bed. The Senator was in his dressing-room, half undressed. They took him completely by surprise, held a pistol to his head, and demanded the immediate payment of twenty-five thousand francs. Should the Senator summon his servants, the rogues would shoot him and his wife and even his children summarily, if they were stopped in their purpose or hindered in their escape.

M. de Kerblay was considerably over sixty. Not too robust in health, terrorised and subdued, he yielded, and with the muzzle of a pistol held to his head and half a dozen swords gleaming around him, he produced the keys of his secretaire and handed over to the Chouans not only all the money he had in the house—something over twenty thousand francs—but a diamond ring, valued at another twenty thousand, which had been given to him by the Emperor in recognition of signal services rendered in the matter of the affairs of the ex-Empress. Whereupon the wretches departed as silently as they had come, and by the time the hue and cry was raised they had disappeared, leaving no clue or trace.

The general consensus of opinion attributed the outrage to the man with the wooden leg. M. Lefèvre, chief commissary of police, who knew that that particular scoundrel was reposing in the honoured vault of the Saint-Tropèze family, was severely nonplussed. Since the sinister episode of the dual personality of M. Saint-Tropèze he realised more than ever how difficult it was to deal with these Chouans. Here to-day, gone to-morrow, they were veritable masters in the art of concealing their identity, and in this quiet corner of Normandy it was impossible to shake a man by the hand without wondering whether he did not perchance belong to that secret gang of malefactors.

M. de Kerblay, more distressed at the loss of his ring than of his money, offered a reward of five thousand francs for its recovery; but while M. Lefèvre's zeal was greatly stimulated thereby, the Man in Grey appeared disinclined to move in the matter, and his quiet, impassive attitude grated unpleasantly on the chief commissary's feelings.

About a week after the outrage, on a cold, wet morning in November, M. Lefèvre made a tempestuous irruption into the apartments in the Rue de France occupied by the secret agent of the Minister of Police.

"We hold the ruffians!" he cried, waving his arms excitedly. "That's the best of those scoundrels! They are always quarrelling among themselves! They lie and they cheat and betray one another into our hands!"

The Man in Grey, as was his wont, waited patiently until the flood of M. Lefèvre's impassioned eloquence had somewhat subsided, then he said quietly:

"You have had the visit of an informer?"

"Yes," replied the commissary, as he sank, panting, into a chair.

"A man you know?"

"By sight. Oh, one knows those rogues vaguely. One sees them about one day—they disappear the next—they have their lairs in the most inaccessible corners of this cursed country. Yes! I know the man by sight. He passed through my hands into the army a year ago. A deserter, of course. Though his appearance does not tally with any of the descriptions we have received from the Ministry of War, we know that these fellows have a way of altering even their features on occasions, and this man has 'deserter' written all over his ugly countenance."

"Well! And what has he told you?"

"That he will deliver to us the leader of the gang who broke into Monsieur de Kerblay's house the other night."

"On conditions, of course."

"Of course."

"Immunity for himself?"

"Yes."

"And a reward?"

"Yes."

"You did not agree to that, I hope," said the Man in Grey sternly.

M. Lefèvre hummed and hawed.

"There must be no question of bribing these men to betray one another," resumed the secret agent firmly, "or you'll be falling into one baited trap after another."

"But there's Monsieur de Kerblay's offer of a reward for the recovery of the ring, and in this case——" protested Lefèvre sullenly.

"In no case," broke in the Man in Grey.

"Then what shall I do with the man?"

"Promise him a free pardon for himself and permission to rejoin his regiment if his information proves to be correct. Keep him in the police-cells, and come and report to me directly you have extracted from him all he knows, or is willing to tell."

The chief commissary of police was well aware that when the Minister's secret agent assumed that quiet air of authority, neither argument nor resistance was advisable. He muttered something between his teeth, but receiving no further response from the Man in Grey he turned abruptly on his heels and stalked out of the room, murmuring inaudible things about "officiousness" and "incompetence."

The man who had presented himself that morning at the commissariat of police offering valuable information as to the whereabouts of the leaders of his own gang, appeared as the regular type of the unkempt, out-at-elbows, down-at-heels, unwashed Chouans who had of a truth become the pest and terror of the countryside. He wore a long shaggy beard, his hair was matted and tousled, his blouse and breeches were in rags, and his bare feet were thrust into a pair of heavy leather shoes. During his brief sojourn in the army, or in the course of his subsequent lawless life, he had lost one eye, and the terrible gash across that part of his face gave his countenance a peculiarly sinister expression.

He stood before the commissary of police, twirling a woollen cap between his grimy fingers, taciturn, sullen and defiant.

"I'll say nothing," he repeated for the third time, "unless I am paid to speak."

"You are amenable to the law, my man," said the chief commissary dryly. "You'll be shot, unless you choose to earn a free pardon for yourself by making a frank confession of your misdeeds."

"And what's a free pardon to me," retorted the Chouan roughly, "if I am to starve on it?"

"You will be allowed to at once rejoin your regiment."

"Bah!"

The man spat on the ground by way of expressing his contempt at the prospect.

"I'd as lief be shot at once," he declared emphatically.

M. Lefèvre could have torn his scanty hair with rage. He was furious with the Chouan and his obstinacy, and furious with that tiresome man in the grey coat who lorded it over every official in the district and assumed an authority which he ought never to have been allowed to wield.

The one-eyed Chouan was taken back to the police-cells, and M. Lefèvre gave himself over to his gloomy meditations. Success and a goodly amount of credit—not to mention the five thousand francs reward for the recovery of the ring—appeared just within his reach. A couple of thousand francs out of the municipal funds to that wretched informer, and the chiefs of one of the most desperate gangs of Chouans would fall into M. Lefèvre's hands, together with no small measure of glory for the brilliant capture. It was positively maddening!

It was not till late in the afternoon that the worthy commissary had an inspiration—such a grand one that he smacked his high forehead, marvelling it had not come to him before. What were two thousand francs out of his own pocket beside the meed of praise which would fall to his share if he succeeded in laying one or two of those Chouan leaders by the heels? He need not touch the municipal funds. He had a couple of thousand francs put by and more; and surely that sum would be a sound investment for future advancement and the recognition of his services on the part of the Minister himself, in addition to which there would be his share in M. de Kerblay's reward.

So M. Lefèvre sent for the one-eyed Chouan and once more interrogated him, cajoling and threatening alternately, with a view to obtaining gratis the information which the man was only prepared to sell.

"I'll say nothing," reiterated the Chouan obstinately, "unless I am paid to speak."

"Well, what will you take?" said the commissary at last.

"Five thousand francs," replied the man glibly.

"I'll give you one," rejoined M. Lefèvre. "But mind," he added with uncompromising severity, "you remain here in the cells as hostage for your own good faith. If you lie to me you will be shot—summarily and without trial."

"Give me three thousand and I'll speak," said the Chouan.

"Two thousand," rejoined the commissary, "and that is my last word."

For a moment or two the man appeared to hesitate; with his one eye he tried to fathom the strength of M. le Commissaire's determination. Then he said abruptly:

"Very well, I'll take two thousand francs. Give me the money now and I'll speak."

Without another superfluous word M. Lefèvre counted out twenty one-hundred franc notes and gave them into the Chouan's grimy hand. He thought it best to appear open-handed and to pay cash down; the man would be taken straight back to the cells presently, and if he played a double game he would anyhow forfeit the money together with his life.

"Now," said Lefèvre as soon as the man had thrust the notes into the pocket of his breeches, "tell me who is your chief and where a posse of my police can lay hands upon him."

"The chief of my gang," rejoined the Chouan, "is called 'The Spaniard' amongst us; his real name is Carrerra, and he comes from Madrid. We don't often see him, but it was he who led the expedition to the house of Monsieur de Kerblay."

"What is he like?"

"A short man with dark, swarthy skin, small features, keen jet-black eyes, no lashes, and very little eyebrow, a shock of coal-black hair and a square black beard and moustache; he speaks French with a Spanish accent."

"Very good! Now tell me where we can find him."

"At Chéron's farm on the Chartres road between la Mesle and Montagne. You know it?"

"I know the farm. I don't know Chéron. Well?"

"The Spaniard has arranged to meet a man there—a German Jew—while Chéron himself is away from home. The idea is to dispose of the ring."

"I understand. When is the meeting to take place?"

"To-night! It is market day at Chartres and Chéron will be absent two days. It was all arranged yesterday. The Spaniard and his gang will sleep at the farm; the following morning they will leave for Paris, en route some of them, so 'tis said, for Spain."

"And the farmer—Chéron? What has he to do with it all?"

"Nothing," replied the Chouan curtly. "He is just a fool. His house stands isolated in a lonely part of the country, and his two farm hands are stupid louts.

So, whenever the Spaniard wants to meet any of his accomplices privately, he selects a day when Chéron is from home, and makes use of the farm for his own schemes."

"You owe him a grudge, I suppose," sneered Lefèvre, who had taken rapid notes of all the man had told him:

"No," replied the Chouan slowly, "but those of us who helped to work the *coup* at Monsieur de Kerblay's the other night were each to receive twenty francs as our share of the spoils. It was not enough!"

The commissary of police nodded complacently. He was vastly satisfied with the morning's work. He had before now heard vague hints about this Spaniard, one of those mysterious and redoubtable Chouan leaders who had given the police of the entire province no end of trouble and grave cause for uneasiness. Now by his—Lefèvre's—own astuteness he stood not only to lay the villain by the heels and earn commendation for his zeal from the Minister himself, but, if this one-eyed scoundrel spoke the truth, also to capture some of his more prominent accomplices, not to mention the ring and M. de Kerblay's generous reward.

Incidentally he also stood to put a spoke in the wheel of that over-masterful and interfering man in the grey coat, which would be a triumph not by any means to be depreciated.

So the Chouan was taken back to the cells and the chief commissary of police was left free to make his arrangements for the night's expedition, without referring the matter to the accredited agent of His Majesty's Police.

Lefèvre knew that he was taking a grave risk when, shortly after eight o'clock on that same evening, he ordered a squadron of his police to follow him to Chéron's farm on the Chartres road. At the last moment he even had a few misgivings as to the wisdom of his action. If the expedition did not meet with the measure of success which he anticipated, and the accredited agent of the Minister came to hear of it, something exceedingly unpleasant to the over-zealous commissary might be the result. However, after a few very brief moments of this unworthy hesitation, M. Lefèvre chid himself for his cowardice and started on his way.

Since his interview with the one-eyed

Chouan he had been over to the farm in order to get a thorough knowledge of the topography of the buildings and of their surroundings. Disguised as a labourer he had hung about the neighbourhood in the wet and cold until he felt quite sure that he could find his way anywhere around the place in the dark.

The farm stood a couple of kilometres or so from the road, on the bank of a tiny tributary of the Mayenne, surrounded by weeping willows, and stripped of their leaves, and flanked by a couple of tumble-down heather-thatched sheds. It was a square building, devoid of any out-standing architectural features, and look-ing inexpressibly lonely and forlorn. There was not another human habitation in sight, and the wooded heights which dominated the valley appeared to shut the inhabitants of the little farm away from the rest of mankind. As he looked at the vast and mournful solitude around, Lefèvre easily recognised how an astute leader, such as the Spaniard appeared to be, would choose it as headquarters for his schemes. Whenever the house itself became unsafe the thicket of willow and chestnut close by, and the dense undergrowth on the heights above, would afford perfect shelter for fugitive marauders.

It was close on ten o'clock of an exceptionally dark night when the posse of police, under the command of the chief commissary, dismounted at the "Grand Duc," a small wayside inn on the Chartres road, and, having stabled their horses, started on foot across country at the heels of their chief. The earth was sodden with recent rains, and the little troop moved along in silence, their feet encased in shoes of soft leather, making no sound as they stealthily advanced.

The little rivulet wound its sluggish course between flat banks bordered by waste land on either side. Far ahead a tiny light gleamed intermittently like a will-o'-the-wisp, as intervening groups of trees alternately screened it and displayed it to view.

After half an hour of heavy walking the commissary called a halt. The massive block of the farmhouse stood out like a dense and dark mass in the midst of the surrounding gloom. M. Lefèvre called softly to his sergeant.

"Steal along, Hippolyte," he whispered,

"under cover of those willow trees, and when you hear me give the first command to open, surround the house so that the rascals cannot escape either by the door or the windows."

Silently and noiselessly these orders were executed, whilst the commissary himself stole up to the house. He came to a halt before the front door and paused a moment, peering anxiously round about him and listening for any sound which might come from within. The house appeared dark and deserted; only from one of the windows on the ground floor a feeble light filtered through the chinks of an ill-fitting shutter, and a mingled murmur of voices seemed to travel thence intermittently. But of this the eager watcher could not be sure. The north-westerly wind, soughing through the bare branches of the trees behind him, also caused the shutters to creak on their hinges and effectually confused every other sound.

The chief commissary then rapped vigorously against the door with the hilt of his sword.

"Open!" he called peremptorily, "in the name of the law!"

Already he could hear the sergeant and his men stealing out from under the trees; but from the stronghold of the Chouans there came no answer to his summons; absolute silence reigned inside the farm-house; the dismal creaking of a half-broken shutter and the murmur of the wind in the leafless willows alone roused the dormant echoes of the old walls.

Lefèvre rapped once more against the massive panels.

"Open!" he called again, "in the name of the law!"

The men following their sergeant had now reached the open. In an instant, from somewhere in the gloom behind them, there came the report of two musket shots in rapid succession. Someone was hit, for there was the sound of a groan and a curse; but in the darkness it was impossible to see who it was.

The men halted irresolute.

"Run to the back of the house, some of you!" commanded the commissary, "and in Heaven's name do not allow a single ruffian to escape."

The men obeyed as quickly as the dark-ness would allow, and again two musket shots rang out from among the trees; this time the sergeant fell forward on his face.

"Corporal Crosnier, are you there?" called Commissary Lefèvre.

"Present, my commandant!" was the quick reply.

"Take Jean Marie and Dominique and two or three others with you, and put up the game that is lurking under those willows."

Crosnier obeyed; he called half a dozen men to him and marched them up towards the thicket. The cowering enemy lay low; only from time to time shots rang out simultaneously out of the darkness. Sometimes they made a hit, but not often; one or two of the men received a stray bullet in shoulder or leg—a random shot which came from out of the gloom and to which they could not reply, for it was impossible to see whence it had come. Presently even that intermittent fire ceased. It seemed as if the thicket had finally swallowed up the lurking quarry.

In the meantime Lefèvre had ordered two or three of his picked men to use the butt-end of their muskets against the door.

"Batter it in, my men," he commanded, "and arrest everyone you find inside the house."

Strangely enough, considering the usually desperate tactics of these Chouan gangs when brought to bay, no resistance was offered from the interior of their stronghold. Whether the rascals were short of ammunition and were saving it for a hand-to-hand fight later, or whether they were preparing some bold *coup*, it was impossible to say. Certain it was that the vigorous atracks against the front door were met by absolute silence—so absolute, indeed, as vaguely to disconcert the commissary of police.

Still the men continued to pound away with their muskets against the panels of the door; but the latter was extraordinarily massive in comparison with the want of solidity of the rest of the house. It resisted every onslaught for some time, until at last it fell in with a terrific crash, and Lefèvre, leaving half a dozen men on guard outside, took another half-dozen with him and entered.

He had picked his men from among those whom he knew to be most intrepid, for he had expected a desperate resistance on the part of the Chouans; he was prepared to be greeted with a volley of musket-fire as he and his men crossed the threshold; he had anticipated a hand-to-hand fight across that battered door. In fact, M. Lefèvre, chief commissary of police, had made ready for everything excepting the death-like stillness which he encountered by way of welcome.

Darkness and silence held undisputed sway everywhere. The men, with dark lanterns fixed to their belts and holding loaded muskets in their hands, paused for one moment irresolute. Then they started to make a thorough search of the place; first the ground floor, then the entrance hall and staircase, then the cellars. They explored every nook and cranny where human quarry might find shelter, but there was not a sign, hardly a trace of any Chouans, save in one small room on the ground floor which certainly appeared as if it had been recently occupied; the chairs had been hastily pushed aside, on the centre table were half a dozen mugs and two or three jugs, one of which was still half filled with wine, a handful of ashes smouldered on the hearth, and the lamp which hung from the ceiling above was alight. But for this, Lefèvre might have thought that he must have been dreaming when he stood by the front door and saw

112

the narrow stream of light through the chink of a shutter.

Indeed, there was something unspeakably dreary and desolate in this dark and empty house, in which undoubtedly a gang of malefactors had lately held revel; and when the men went upstairs in order to explore the floor above, they were, every one of them, conscious of the quick sense of unreasoning terror when a weird and intermittent sound suddenly reached their ears.

The sound came from over their heads—it was like a wail, and was piteous and disconcerting in the extreme.

"Like someone groaning," said one of the men in a hoarse whisper.

Soon their momentary feeling of dread passed away, and two or three of the men had already scaled the narrow, ladder-like stairs which led to a loft that ran the whole length and breadth of the house under the sloping roof.

But here an extraordinary sight met their gaze. Huddled up against a large supporting beam were an old man, a woman and two young girls. They had been tied together by ropes to the beam. Each of the unfortunates was in acute distress or bodily pain. The atmosphere of the place was both stuffy and bitterly cold. Incessant moaning came from the woman, sobbing from the girls; the man appeared stunned and dazed. When the light from one of the dark lanterns fell upon him, he blinked his eyes and gazed vacantly on the men who were already busy with the ropes, freeing him and the women from their bonds.

They all appeared in the last stage of exhaustion and clung to one another for support and warmth, when Lefèvre with kindly authority ordered them to move. Fortunately one of the men recollected the jug of wine which had been left in the room on the ground floor. He ran to fetch it, and returned very soon, jug and glasses in hand. In the meanwhile Lefèvre had remained staring at the wretched people and trying to extract a few words of explanation from them.

So far he had only been able to elicit the information that four members of the farmer Chéron's family, his father, his wife and his two daughters, stood before him in this pitiable plight. It was only after they had drunk a little wine that they were able to speak coherently. In short, jerky sentences and with teeth still chattering with cold and terror, the old man tried to reply to the commissary's questions.

"How in the world came you to be up here," M. Lefèvre asked, "tied like cattle to a beam in your son's house?"

"My son is away at Chartres, Monsieur le Commissaire," replied the old man; "he won't return till to-morrow. We should have perished of hunger and cold if you had not come to our rescue."

"But where are those blackguardly Chouans? And who in the devil's name fired on us from under your trees?"

"Those execrable Chouans took possession of my son's house this morning, Monsieur le Commissaire, soon after his departure," answered the old man dolefully. "They seized me and my daughter-in-law and my two grand-children, forced us to give up the little bit of money which my son had left for our use, stole food from the larder and wine from the cellar; and when we protested they dragged us up here—as you say—like cattle, tied us to a beam and left us to perish unless my son should chance to come home."

Lefèvre would have liked to say that

twenty-four hours spent in a draughty loft does not necessarily mean starvation, but on the whole he refrained from badgering the poor people, who had suffered quite enough, with further expostulation.

"But what has happened to the Chouans?" he reiterated with a hearty curse.

"Gone, Monsieur le Commissaire," here interposed the woman woefully. "Gone! They caroused all day, and left about a couple of hours ago; since then the house has been as silent as the grave."

Lefèvre said nothing very coherent for the moment; he was mentally embracing the Chouans, the lying informer and his own folly in one comprehensive curse.

"But my men were fired on from behind the trees," he urged feebly after a while.

"I heard the firing, too, Monsieur le Commissaire," rejoined the old man. "It terrified us, for the Chouans had threatened to shoot us all if they were attacked by the police; and these two young girls—think of it, Monsieur le Commissaire—at the mercy of those brutes. I suppose," he added with a shudder, "that while the leaders of the gang made good their escape, they left a couple of men behind to cover their retreat."

Nothing more could be got out of these poor people. They had been set upon quite early in the day by the Chouans, and knew little or nothing of what had gone on in the house while they were prisoners in the loft. They did not know how many of the ruffians there were—six or eight, they thought. The chief was a man with swarthy skin and a long black beard, who spoke French with a strange foreign accent.

The commissary of police went nearly mad with rage. He set his best men to search the farm-house through and through, in the hope that some of the rascals might still be lurking about the place. But the men ransacked the house in vain. They found neither trap-door nor secret panel, nor slinking quarry, and after a couple of hours' hunt were forced to own themselves defeated.

M. Lefèvre returned to Alençon with his posse of police in the small hours of the morning. He dismissed the men at the commissariat, and sought his own lodgings in the Rue Notre Dame, his mind a prey to the bitterest feeling of disappointment—not unmixed with misgivings at thought of M. le Ministre's agent, should he get wind of the miscarriage.

To his terror and amazement, no sooner had he entered the house than the concierge came out of his lodge to tell him that a gentleman was upstairs in his rooms, waiting for him.

"Who is it?" he asked sharply. "You have no right to admit anyone to my rooms at this hour of the night."

"I could not help myself," retorted the concierge sullenly. "He exhibited some sort of order from the Ministry of Police, and was so high-handed and peremptory that I dared not refuse."

Filled with vague apprehension M. Lefèvre ran quickly up to his rooms. He was greeted in the antechamber by the Man in Grey.

"I was unfortunately too late to catch you before you started," said the latter as soon as Lefèvre had closed the door. He spoke in his even monotone—his face was calm and expressionless, but there was something about his attitude which jarred unpleasantly on the commissary's nerves.

"I—that is——" he stammered, despite his stern effort to appear confident and at his ease.

"You have disobeyed the Minister's orders," interposed the secret agent quietly. "But there is no time now to discuss your conduct. The blunder which you have just committed is mayhap beyond repair; in which case——"

He broke off abruptly and M. Lefèvre felt a cold shiver running down his spine.

"There was no time to consult you——" he began.

"I said that I would not discuss that," interposed the Man in Grey quietly. "Tell me where you have been."

"To Chéron's farm on the Chartres road," replied the commissary.

"The informer gave you directions?"

"Yes."

"That you would find his leader there?"

"Yes, the man whom they call 'The Spaniard,' and some of his accomplices. The informer——"

"The informer escaped from the cells during your absence this evening," said the Man in Grey curtly.

"Malédiction!"

"Do not curse, my good man," advised

the other dryly. "The rascal's escape may be the means of retrieving your blunder, since it gave me the knowledge of the whole affair."

"But how did it happen?"

"Surveillance slackened while you went off on your wild-goose chase. Your prisoner used some of the money wherewith you had bribed him—against my express command, remember—to bribe his warder in his turn. Your sergeant-in-charge came to me in his distress when he found that his bird had flown."

Lefèvre had no longer the strength to argue or even to curse. He hung his head in silent dejection.

"I sent for you," continued the Man in Grey mercilessly. "When I found that you had gone no one knew whither, and that you had taken a posse of your men with you, I guessed the whole extent of your damnable blunder. I have waited here for you ever since."

"What can I do now?" murmured Lefèvre gloomily.

"Collect ten or twelve of the men whom you can most confidently trust, and then pick me up at my lodgings in the Rue de France. We'll go back to Chéron's farm—together."

"But there is no one there," said Lefèvre with a dejected sigh, "only Chéron's father, his wife and two daughters."

"I know that well enough, you fool!" exclaimed the Man in Grey, departing for the first time from his habitual calm, and starting to pace up and down the narrow room like a caged and fretting animal; "and that every proof against the villains who robbed Monsieur de Kerblay has no doubt vanished whilst you were getting the wrong sow by the ear. To bring the crime home to them now will be very difficult. 'Tis red-handed we ought to have caught them, with the Jew there, and the ring, and the Spaniard bargaining, whereas now——"

Suddenly he paused and stood quite still; the anger and impatience died out of his face, leaving it pale and expressionless as was its wont; only to Lefevre who was watching him with keen anxiety it seemed as if for one fraction of a second a curious glitter had lit up his colourless eyes.

"In Heaven's name!" he resumed impatiently after a while, "let us get to horse, or I may be tempted to tell you what I think of your folly."

The commissary, trounced like a recalcitrant schoolboy and not a little terrified at the consequences of his blunder, was only too ready to obey. Within half an hour he was in the saddle. He had Corporal Crosnier with him and half a dozen picked men, and together they went to the Rue de France, where the Minister's agent was waiting for them.

It was close upon five o'clock of a raw, damp morning when the little party drew rein once more at the wayside inn on the Chartres road. The men appeared tired out and were grateful for the hot coffee which a sleepy ostler hastily prepared for then; but the Man in Grey seemed indefatigable. Wrapped to the chin in a long, dark mantle, he had ridden the whole way by the side of the commissary, plying him with questions the while. Bit by bit he had extracted from him the full history of the futile expedition, the description of the house, its situation and structure, and of the members of the Chéron family. Now, whilst sipping his coffee, he made Lefèvre give him final and minute directions how to reach the farmhouse.

Ten minutes later he started on his way—alone and on foot.

"Follow me in about five minutes," were his last commands to the commissary. "Then lie low under the trees. When you hear a pistol shot from inside the house rush in and seize every man, woman, or child whom you find; if you meet with any resistance order your men to use their muskets. Leave the corporal with a strong guard outside the house, both back and front, and bid him shoot on sight anyone who attempts to escape."

After he had walked on through the darkness for a couple of metres or so, he threw off his mantle and hat and kicked off his shoes. The commissary of police, had he been near him now, would of a truth have been staggered at his appearance. He wore a pair of ragged breeches, and a stained and tattered blouse; his hair was unkempt, and his feet and legs were bare to the knees.

"Now for a little bit of luck," he murmured as he started to run. His bare feet squelched through the wet earth and spattered him with mud from head to foot, and as he ran the perspiration streamed down his face and mingled with the grime.

Indeed, it seemed as if he took a special delight in tiring himself out, in getting breathless and hot, and by his active exercise making himself look even dirtier and more disreputable than he had been before.

When he reached the riverside and the row of willow trees, he halted; the house, he knew, must be quite close now on the right, and as he peered into the darkness he perceived a tiny streak of light glimmering feebly through the gloom some way off. Throwing himself flat upon his stomach, he bent his ear to the ground; it was attuned to the slightest sound, like that of the Indian trackers, and he heard at a distance of four hundred metres behind him the measured tramp of Lefèvre's men. Then he rose to his feet and, stealthily as a cat, crept up to the house.

The slender streak of light guided him and, as he drew nearer, he heard a confused murmur of voices raised in merriment. The occupants of the house were apparently astir; the light came through a half-open shutter on the ground floor as did the sound of the voices, through which presently there rang a loud and prolonged peal of laughter. The secret agent drew a deep sigh of satisfaction; the birds—thank goodness—had not yet flown. Noiselessly he approached the front door, the battered and broken appearance of which bore testimony to Lefèvre's zeal.

A bright patch of light striking through an open door on the right illumined a portion of the narrow hall beyond, leaving the rest in complete darkness. The Man in Grey stepped furtively over the threshold. Immediately he was challenged: "Who goes there?" and he felt rather than saw a gun levelled at his head.

"A friend," he murmured timidly.

At the instant the challenge had resounded through the house the light in the inner room on the right was suddenly extinguished; deathly silence had succeeded the debauch.

"What's your business?" queried a muffled voice peremptorily.

Before the Man in Grey could reply there was a commotion in the inner room as of chairs hastily thrust aside, and presently another voice—one both gruff and commanding—called out: "What is it, Pierre?"

A dark lantern was flashed about; its light fell full on the miserable apparition of the Man in Grey.

"What do you want?" queried the commanding voice out of the partial gloom. "Speak, or I fire!"

"A friend!" reiterated the Man in Grey timidly.

"Your name?"

"Nicaise, sir, from Mauger's farm on the Mayenne road. I was asleep under a haystack, when a stranger comes to me and shakes me roughly by the shoulder. 'Run,' he says to me, 'to Chéron's up by the Chartres road. Run as fast as your legs will take you. Walk in boldly; the door is open. You will find company inside the farm. Tell them the police are coming back in force. Someone will give you a silver franc for your pains if you get there in time.' So I took to my heels and ran."

While he spoke another man and a woman had entered. Their vague forms were faintly discernible through the darkness; the light from the lanterns still struck full on the Man in Grey, who looked the picture of woebegone imbecility.

From the group in the doorway there came a murmur: "The police!"

"A stranger, you say?" queried the man with the commanding voice. "What was he like?"

"I could not say," replied the secret agent humbly. "It was very dark. But he said I should get a silver franc for my pains, and I am a poor man. I thought at first it was a hoax, but when I crossed the meadow just now I saw a lot of men in hiding under the willow trees."

"Malédiction!" muttered the man, as he turned undecided towards his companions. "Oh, that I had that one-eyed traitor in my power!" he added with a savage oath.

"Did you speak to the men of the police?" asked a woman's voice out of the darkness.

"No, madame," replied the secret agent. "They did not see me. I was crawling on my hands and knees. But they are all round the house, and I heard one man calling to the sergeant and giving him orders to watch the doors and windows lest anyone tried to escape."

The group in the doorway was silent; the man who had been on guard appeared to have joined them, and they all went back into the room and held a hurried consultation.

"There is nothing for it," said one man,

"but to resume our former roles as members of the Chéron family, and to do it as naturally as before."

"They suspect us now," said another, "or they would not be here again so soon."

"Even so; but if we play our parts well they can only take us back to the commissariat and question us; they must release us in the end; they have no proof."

In the meantime someone had relighted the lamp. There appeared to be a good deal of scurrying and scrambling inside the room; the Man in Grey tip-toed up to the doorway to see what was going on. Evidently, disguises which had hastily been put aside had been resumed; the group stood before him now just as Lefèvre had originally described them: the old man, the woman, the two young girls; the latter were striding about the room and holding their skirts up clumsily with both hands, as men are wont to do when they don women's clothes; the old man, on whom grey locks and well-stencilled wrinkles were the only signs of age, was hastily putting these to rights before a mirror on the wall.

But it was the woman's doings which compelled the attention of the Man in

Grey. She was standing on a chair with her back to him, intent on manipulating something up the huge open chimney.

"It will be quite safe there," she said.

She appeared to be closing some heavy iron door which fell in its place with a snap. Then she turned to her companions and slowly descended from the chair. "When the present storm has blown over," she said, "we'll come and fetch it. Chéron will never guess; at any rate, we are sure the police cannot discover this most excellent hiding-place."

She was a short, square-built woman, with a dark, almost swarthy skin, keen jet-black eyes which appeared peculiarly hard and glittering owing to the absence of lashes, a firm, thin-lipped mouth, square chin, and low forehead crowned by a shock of thick, black hair cut short like a boy's. The secret agent kept his eyes fixed upon her while she spoke to her friends. He noted the head so full of character, and the strength and determination expressed in every line of the face; he marvelled why the features—especially those glittering jet-black eyes—appeared familiar, as something he had known and heard of before. And suddenly it came to him in a flash; he remembered the informer's description of the leader named "The Spaniard": a dark, swarthy skin, jet-black hair, keen dark eyes with no lashes to soften their glitter, the beard, the man's attire, the foreign accent. Soh! these marauding Chouans slipped in and out of their disguises and changed even their sex outwardly as easily as men change their coats; whilst the very identity of their leader was more often unknown to them than known!

As the secret agent's practised glance took in during these few seconds the whole personality of the woman before him, he knew that his surmises—based on intuition and on reasoning—were correct. It was the Spaniard who stood before him now, but the Spaniard was a woman. And as he gazed on her, half in pity because of her sex, and half in admiration for her intrepidity, she turned, and their glances met. She looked at him across the narrow room, and each knew that the other had guessed.

The woman never flinched; she held the agent's glance and did not utter either word or cry whilst with a slow, deliberate movement, she drew a pistol from beneath her kerchief. But he, as quick and resourceful, had instantly stepped back into the hall. He seized the door, and, with a loud bang, closed it to between himself and the Chouans. Then, with lightning rapidity, he pushed the heavy bolt home.

The report of a pistol rang out. It came from inside the room. The Man in Grey was leaning his full weight against the door, wondering whether Lefèvre and his men would come to his assistance before the trapped Chouans had time to burst the panels.

He heard Lefèvre's call outside and the heavy tramp of the men. A few seconds of agonising suspense, whilst he literally felt the massive door heaving behind him under the furious onslaught of the imprisoned Chouans, and the commissary with the men of the police burst into the hall. The door fell in with a terrific crash.

The Chouans, caught like foxes run to earth, offered a desperate resistance. But the odds were too great; after a grim struggle across the threshold, which lasted close on ten minutes and left several men of the police bleeding or dead upon the floor, the gang were captured, securely bound and locked in one of the cellars

131

underneath the house, where they were left in charge of half a dozen men until such time as they could be conveyed to Alençon and thence to Bicêtre to await their trial.

It has been impossible, owing to the maze of records, to disentangle the subsequent history of three of these Chouans. The Spaniard, however, was, we know, kept in prison for over five years until, after the Restoration, her friends succeeded in laying her petition for release before the King and she was granted a free pardon and a small pension from the privy purse, "in consideration of the services she had rendered to His Majesty and the martyrdom she had suffered in his cause." On the official list of pensioners in the year 1816 her name appears as "Caroline Mercier, commonly called the Spaniard."

But at Chéron's farm, when all was still, the men of the police gone and the prisoners safely under lock and key, the Man in Grey and the commissary returned to the little room which had been the scene of the Chouan's final stand. A broken chair was lying by the side of the tall, open chimney wherein the woman with the swarthy skin and jet-black eyes had concealed the stolen treasure. The accredited agent had no difficulty in finding the secret hiding-place; about a foot up the chimney an iron door was let into the solid wall. A little manipulation of his deft fingers soon released the secret spring, and the metal panel glided gently in its grooves.

M. de Kerblay's precious ring and some twenty thousand francs in money gladdened the sight of the worthy com-missary of police.

"But how did you guess?" he asked of the Man in Grey, when, half an hour later, the pair were ambling along the road back towards Alençon.

"While you were getting ready for our second expedition, my dear Monsieur Lefèvre," replied the Man in Grey, "I took the simple precaution of ascertaining whether the farmer Chéron had a wife, a father, and two daughters. Your own records at the commissariat furnished me with this information. From them I learned that though he had a wife, he had no father living, and that he had three grown-up sons, long ago started out into the world. After that, everything became very simple."

"I suppose," quoth the commissary ruefully, "that I ought to have found out about the man Chéron and his family before I went off on that fool's errand."

"You ought, above all, to have consulted me," was the Man in Grey's calm reproof.

III

THE MYSTERY OF MARIE VAILLANT

AFTER the capture of the Spaniard at Cheron's farm on that dark night, M. Lefèvre realised that when M. le Duc d'Otrante sent down that insignificant-looking little man in the grey coat to help in the hunt after the astute but infamous Chouans, he had acted—as he always did—with foresight and unerring knowledge of human nature and human capacity.

Henceforward M. Lefèvre became the faithful panegyrist and henchman of the Minister's anonymous agent. He haunted the latter's apartments in the Rue de France, he was significantly silent when the Man in Grey was sneered and jeered at in the higher official circles, and, what is more, when M. Leblanc, sous-préfet of Bourg-le-Roi, had such grave misgivings about his children's governess, it was the commissary who advised him to go for counsel and assistance to the mysterious personage who enjoyed the special confidence and favour of M. le Duc d'Otrante himself.

M. Leblanc, who had an inordinate belief in his own perspicacity, fought for some time against the suggestion; but, after a while, the mystery which surrounded Mademoiselle Vaillant reached such a bewildering stage, whilst remaining outside the scope of police interference, that he finally decided to take his friend's advice, and one morning, about the end of November, he presented himself at the lodgings in Alençon occupied by the accredited agent of His Majesty's Minister of Police.

Of a truth, M. Leblanc was singularly agitated. His usually correct, official attitude had given place to a kind of febrile excitement which he was at great pains to conceal. He had just left Madame Leblanc in a state of grave anxiety, and he himself, though he would not have owned to it for the world, did not know what to make of the whole affair. But he did not intend that his own agitation should betray him into a loss of dignity in the presence of the little upstart from Paris; so, after the formal greetings, he sat down and plunged into a maze of conversational subjects—books, the theatres, the war, the victories of the Emperor and the rumoured alliance with the Austrian Archduchess—until the Man in Grey's quiet monotone broke in on the flow of his eloquence with a perfectly polite query:

"Has Monsieur le Sous-Préfet, then, honoured me with a visit at this early hour for the purpose of discussing the politics of the day?"

"Partly, my good Monsieur Fernand, partly," replied the sous-préfet airily. "I desired that we should become more closely acquainted—and," he added, as if with an after-thought, "I desired to put before you a small domestic matter which has greatly perturbed Madame Leblanc, and which, I confess, does appear even to me as something of a mystery."

"I am entirely at Monsieur le Sous-Préfet's service," rejoined the Man in Grey without the ghost of a smile.

"Oh! I dare say," continued M. Leblanc

in that off-hand manner which had become the rule among the officials of the district when dealing with the secret agent, "I dare say that when I think the matter over I shall be quite able to deal with it myself. At the same time, the facts are certainly mysterious, and I doubt not but that they will interest you, even if they do not come absolutely within the sphere of your province."

This time the Man in Grey offered no remark. He waited for M. le Sous-Préfet to proceed.

"As no doubt you know, Monsieur Fernand," resumed M. Leblanc after a slight pause, "I own a small house and property near Bourg-le-Roi, some eight kilometres from this city, where my wife and children live all the year round and where I spend as much of my leisure as I can spare from my onerous duties here. The house is called Les Colombiers. It is an old manor, which belonged to the Comtes de Mamers, a Royalist family who emigrated at the outset of the Revolution and whose properties were sold for the benefit of the State. The Mamers have remained—as perhaps you know—among the irreconcilables. His Majesty the

Emperor's clemency did not succeed in luring them away from England, where they have settled; and I, on the other hand, have continued in undisputed possession of a charming domain. The old moated house is of great archaeological and historical interest. It stands in the midst of a well-timbered park, is well secluded from the road by several acres of dense coppice, and it is said that, during the religious persecutions instituted by Charles IX at the instigation of his abominable mother, Les Colombiers was often the refuge of Huguenots, and the rallying-point for the followers of the proscribed faith. As I myself," continued M. Leblanc with conscious pride, "belong to an old Huguenot family, you will readily understand, my good Monsieur Fernand, that I feel an additional interest in Les Colombiers."

Pausing for a moment, the sous-préfet readjusted the set of his neckcloth, crossed one shapely leg over the other and added with an affable air of condescension:

"I trust that I am not trespassing upon your valuable time, my dear friend, by recounting these seemingly irrelevant but quite necessary details."

"On the contrary, Monsieur le Sous-Préfet," rejoined the Man in Grey quietly, "I am vastly and, I may say, respectfully interested."

Thus encouraged, M. Leblanc boldly continued his narrative.

"My household," he said, "consists, I must tell you, of my wife and myself and my two children—a boy and a girl—Adèle, aged fourteen, and Ernest, just over twelve. I keep a couple of men and two maids indoors, and three or four men in the garden. Finally, there is my children's governess, Marie Vaillant. She came to us last summer warmly recommended by Monseigneur the Constitutional Bishop of Alençon, and it is her conduct which of late has so gravely disquieted Madame Leblanc and myself.

"But you shall judge.

"At first my wife and I had every reason to congratulate ourselves on having secured such a competent, refined and charming woman to preside over the education of our children. Marie Vaillant was gay, pretty and full of spirits. The children loved her, especially Ernest, who set his entire childish affections upon his young and attractive governess. During the summer lessons were done out of doors, and long expeditions were undertaken in the woods, whence Ernest and Adèle would return, hot, tired and happy. They had played at being explorers in virgin forests, so they told their mother.

"It was only when the evenings waxed longer," continued the sous-préfet, in a tone of growing embarrassment, now that he was nearing the climax of his story, "that Mademoiselle Vaillant suddenly changed. She developed a curious proclivity for promiscuous coquetry."

"Coquetry?" broke in the secret agent with a smile.

"Yes! Marie began to flirt—shamelessly, openly, with every man she came across, visitors, shopkeepers, friends and gardeners. She exercised an almost weird fascination over them; one and all would anticipate her slightest wish; in fact, the men about the house and grounds of Les Colombiers appeared to be more her servants than ours. Moreover, she made an absolute fool of our butler, Lavernay—a middle-aged man who ought to have known better. He has not only pursued Mademoiselle Vaillant with his attentions but also with his jealousy, until

140

Madame Leblanc felt that her whole household was becoming the laughing-stock of the neighbourhood."

"And have you or Madame Leblanc done anything in the matter?" asked the Man in Grey, while M. le Sous-Préfet paused to draw breath.

"Oh, yes! Madame spoke to the girl and I trounced Lavernay. Marie was humble and apologetic and Lavernay very contrite. Both promised to be discreet and sensible in future. At the same time I confess that I was not at all reassured. Within a fortnight we heard through the gossip of a busybody that Marie Vaillant was in the habit of stealing out of the house in the evenings, at an hour when respectable people should be in bed, and after five minutes' start she was usually followed on these peregrinations by the butler. There was no doubt about the whole thing: even our sergeant of police had witnessed these clandestine meetings and had reported the matter to the local commissary.

"There was nothing for it now but to dismiss the flirtatious governess as quickly as possible. I may say that Madame Leblanc, who had been genuinely fond of the girl, acquitted herself of the task with remarkable tact and gentleness. Marie Vaillant, indeed, belied her name when she received the news of her dismissal. She begged and implored my wife's forgiveness, swore by all she could think of that she had only erred from ignorance; she had no thought of doing wrong; she was innocent of anything but the merest flirtation. Fond of breathing the midnight air which was so balmy and sweet in the woods, she had lately got into the habit of strolling out when she could not sleep and sitting for an hour or so dreaming among the trees. She admitted that once or twice she had been followed by Lavernay, had been very angry with him, and had seriously rebuked him; but it should never, never happen again—she vowed and swore it should not—if only Madame would forgive her and not send her away from Les Colombiers, which was like a home to her, and from Ernest and Adèle, whom she loved as if they were her brother and sister.

"But Madame Leblanc was inexorable. Perhaps she felt that quite so much ignorance of the ways of the world and the decorum prescribed to every well-educated woman was not altogether credible; perhaps she thought that the lady did protest too much. Certain it is that though she went back on her original pronouncement that the girl must leave the house within twenty-four hours, she refused to consider the question of allowing her to remain permanently.

"It was finally agreed that Marie Vaillant should leave Les Colombiers at the end of the month; but that at the slightest transgression or repetition of the old offence she would be dismissed with contumely and turned out of the house at an hour's notice.

"This happened exactly a fortnight ago," went on M. Leblanc, who was at last drawing to the end of what had proved a lengthy soliloquy; "and I may tell you that since then Mademoiselle Vaillant has grown the model of all the proprieties. Sober, demure, well-conducted, she has fulfilled her duties with a conscientiousness which is beyond praise. When those heavy rains set in a week ago, outdoor life at once became impossible. Adèle and Ernest took seriously to their books and Mademoiselle devoted herself to them in a manner which has been absolutely exemplary. She has literally given up her whole time to their welfare, not only—so Madame Leblanc tells me—by helping with their clothes, but she has even taken certain menial tasks upon herself which are altogether outside her province as a governess. She has relieved the servants by attending to the children's bedroom; she has been making their beds and even washing their stockings and pocket-handkerchiefs. She asked to be allowed to do these things in order to distract her mind from the sorrow caused by Madame's displeasure.

"Of course, I gave Lavernay a stern scolding; but he swore to me that though he had followed Mademoiselle during her evening walks, he had done it mostly without her knowledge and always without her consent; a fit of his former jealousy had seized him, but she had reprimanded him very severely and forbidden him ever to dog her footsteps again. After that he, too, appeared to turn over a new leaf. It seemed as if his passion for Marie was beginning to burn itself out, and that we could look forward once again to the happy and peaceful days of the summer."

M. le Sous-Préfet had talked uninterruptedly for a quarter of an hour; his pompous, somewhat laboured diction and his loud voice had put a severe strain upon him. The Man in Grey had been an ideal listener. With his eyes fixed on M. Leblanc, he had sat almost motionless, not losing a single word of the prolix recital, and even now when the sous-préfet paused—obviously somewhat exhausted—he did not show the slightest sign of flagging interest.

"Now, my good Monsieur Fernand," resumed M. Leblanc, with something of his habitual, condescending manner, "will you tell me if there is anything in what I have just told you—I fear me at great length—that is not perfectly simple and even stereotyped? A young and pretty girl coming into a somewhat old-fashioned and dull household and finding a not altogether commendable pleasure in turning the heads of every susceptible man she meets! Indiscretions follow and the gossips of the neighbourhood are set talking. Admonished by her mistress, the girl is almost broken-hearted; she begs for forgiveness and at once sets to work to re-establish herself in the good graces of her employers. I dare say you are surprised that I should have been at such pains to re-count to you a series of commonplace occurrences. But what to an ordinary person would appear in the natural order of things, strikes me as not altogether normal. I mistrust the girl. I do not believe in her contrition, still less in her re-formation. Moreover, what worries me, and worries Madame Leblanc still more, is the amazing ascendency which Marie Vaillant exercises over our boy Ernest. She seems to be putting forth her fullest powers of fascination—I own that they are great—to cementing the child's affection for her. For the last few weeks the boy has become strangely nervy, irritable and jealous. He follows Marie wherever she goes, and hangs upon her lips when she speaks—so much so that my wife and I look forward now with dread to the day of parting. When Marie goes I do verily believe that Ernest, who is a very highly-strung child, will fall seriously ill with grief."

Again M. Leblanc paused. A look of genuine alarm had overspread his other-wise vapid face. Clearly he was a man deeply attached to his children and, despite his fatuous officiousness, was not prepared to take any risks where their welfare was concerned. He mopped his face with his handkerchief, and for the first time since the beginning of the interview he threw a look of almost pathetic appeal at the agent of the Minister of Police.

"Otherwise, Monsieur le Sous-Préfet," said the latter, meeting that look of appeal with a quiet smile, "has nothing occurred to justify your mistrust of Mademoiselle Vaillant's good intentions?"

"Nothing at all," replied M. Leblanc with a nervous hesitation which belied his emphatic words, "except a vague sense of uneasiness—the unnatural quiet which came so quickly in the wake of the storm of a fortnight ago; and, as I say, the extraordinary pains which the girl has taken to captivate the boy: to such an extent that, thinking perhaps Marie still entertained hopes of our complete forgiveness and thought of using the child as an intermediary with us to allow her to remain, Madame Leblanc at my suggestion spoke yesterday very firmly to the girl, and told her that whatever happened our determination was irrevocable. We felt that we could trust her no longer and go she must."

"And how did Mademoiselle Vaillant take this final decision?" asked the police agent.

"With extraordinary self-possession. Beyond a humble 'Very well, Madame,' she never spoke a word during the brief interview. But in the evening, long after the children should have been in bed, Anne—my wife's confidential maid—happened to be in the passage outside Mademoiselle's room, the door of which was ajar. She distinctly heard Marie's voice raised in almost passionate supplication: 'Ernest, my darling little Ernest!' she was saying, 'will you always love me as you do now?' And the child answered fervently: 'I will always love you, my darling Marie. I would do anything for you—I would gladly die for you——' and so on—just the sort of *exalté* nonsense which a highly-strung, irresponsible child would talk. Anne did not hear any more then, but remained on the watch in a dark corner of the passage. Quite half an hour later, if not more, she saw Ernest slipping out of the governess's room clad only in his little nightgown and slippers and going back to his own room. This incident, which Anne reported faithfully to her mistress and to me, has caused my wife such anxiety that I determined to consult someone whom I could trust, and see whether the whole affair struck an impartial mind with the like ominous significance which it bears for me. My choice fell upon you, my dear Monsieur Fernand," concluded the sous-préfet with a return to his former lofty condescension. "I don't like to introduce gossiping neighbours into my private affairs, and I know enough about you to be convinced of your absolute discretion as well as of your undoubted merits."

The Man in Grey accepted M. Leblanc's careless affability with the same unconcern that he had displayed under the latter's somewhat contemptuous patronage. He said nothing for a moment or two, remaining apparently absorbed in his own thoughts. Then he turned to his visitor and in a quiet, professional manner, which nevertheless carried with it an unmistakable air of authority, intimated to him, by rising from his chair, that the interview was now at an end.

"I thank you, Monsieur le Sous-Préfet," he said, "both for the confidence which you have reposed in me, and for your clear *exposé* of the present situation in your household. For the moment I should advise you to leave all your work in the city which is not of national importance and go straight back to Les Colombiers. Madame Leblanc should not be left to face alone any difficulties which may arise. At the same time, should any fresh development occur, I beg that you will either send for me or come to me at once. I place myself entirely at your disposal."

He did not hold out his hand, only stood quietly beside his desk; but there was no mistaking the attitude, or the almost imperceptible inclination of the head. M. Leblanc was dismissed, and he was not accustomed to seeing himself and his affairs set aside so summarily. A sharp retort almost escaped him; but a glance from those enigmatic eyes checked the haughty words upon his lips. He became suddenly and unaccountably embarrassed, seeking for a phrase which would disguise the confusion he felt.

"My good Monsieur Fernand——" he began haltingly.

"My time is valuable, Monsieur le Sous-Préfet," interposed the man in Grey; "and at Les Colombiers your son's welfare is perhaps even now at stake."

M. Leblanc—awed and subdued despite himself—had no choice but to make as dignified an exit as was possible in the circumstances.

It was barely eight o'clock the next morning when M. Leblanc made an excited and noisy irruption into the apartments of the secret agent of the Minister of Police. The Man in Grey had risen betimes; had brewed himself a cup of coffee and partaken of breakfast. The tray stood on a table beside him, and he was at the moment engaged in the perusal of the newest copy of the *Moniteur*.

At sight of his visitor he quietly folded and put down his paper. M. Leblanc had literally staggered into the room. He wore riding breeches and boots and his clothes were covered with mud; he had ridden hard and fast, and though his face was deathly pale it was covered with perspiration. His lips were quivering and his eyes had a look of horror and fear which almost resembled madness.

The Man in Grey led him, firmly and gently, to a seat. Without a word he went to a cupboard, took out a flask and a mug and forced a few drops of brandy down the sous-préfet's throat. The latter's teeth were chattering, and through his trembling lips there came a few hoarsely whispered words:

"My son—my child—he has gone! Oh, my God!"

After he had drunk the brandy, he became a little more composed. He lay back in his chair, with eyes closed, and for a moment it seemed as if he had lost consciousness, for his lips were bloodless and his face was the colour of dead ashes. Presently he opened his eyes and rested them on the small grey figure which stood, quietly expectant, before him.

"My son," he murmured more distinctly. "Ernest—he has gone!"

"Try to tell me coherently what has happened," said the Man in Grey in a quiet tone, which had the effect of further soothing M. Leblanc's overstrung nerves.

After a great effort of will the unfortunate man was able to pull himself together. He was half demented with grief, and it was blind, unreasoning instinct that had led him to seek out the man who might help him in his trouble. With exemplary patience, the police agent dragged from the unfortunate man, bit by bit, a more or less intelligible account of the extraordinary sequence of events which had culminated a few hours ago in such a mysterious and appalling tragedy.

Matters, it seemed, had been brought to a climax through the agency of feminine gossip, and it was Ma'ame Margot, the wife of one of the labourers, who did the washing for the household at Les Colombiers, who precipitated the catastrophe.

Ma'ame Margot had brought the washing home on the previous afternoon and stopped to have a cup of coffee and a chat in the kitchen of the house. In the course of conversation she drew the attention of Anne, Madame Leblanc's maid, to the condition of Monsieur Ernest's underclothes.

"I have done my best with it," she said, "but I told Mademoiselle Vaillant that I was afraid the stains would never come out. She had tried to wash the things herself before she thought of sending them to me. Whoever heard," added the worthy soul indignantly, "of letting a child of Monsieur Ernest's age go running about like that in the wet and the mud? Why, he must have been soaked through to his waist to get his things in that state."

Later Anne spoke to Madame Leblanc of what the laundrywoman had said. Madame frowned, greatly puzzled. She had positively forbidden the children to go out while the heavy rains lasted. She sent for Ma'ame Margot, who was bold enough to laugh outright when Madame told her that she did not understand about Monsieur Ernest's things being so stained with wet and mud, as the children had not been out since the heavy rains had started.

"Not been out!" ejaculated Ma'ame Margot, quite as puzzled as her lady. "Why! my man, when he was looking after the sick cow the other night, saw Monsieur Ernest out with the governess. It was past midnight then and the rain coming down in torrents, and my man, he says to me——"

"Thank you, Ma'ame Margot," broke in Madame Leblanc, "that will do."

She waited quietly until the laundrywoman was out of the house, then she sent for Mademoiselle Vaillant. This time no prayers, no protestations would avail. The girl must leave the house not later than the following morning. What her object could have been in dragging her young pupil with her on her nocturnal expeditions Madame Leblanc could not of course conjecture; did she take the child with her as a chaperon on her meetings with Lavernay, or what? Well, whatever her motive, the girl was not a fit person to be in charge of young children, and go she must, decided Madame definitely.

This occurred late yesterday afternoon. Strangely enough, Marie Vaillant took her dismissal perfectly calmly. She offered neither explanation nor protest. Except a modest "Very well, Madame!" she never said a word during this final interview with her employer, who, outraged and offended at the girl's obstinacy and ingratitude, ordered her to pack up her things and leave the house early next morning, when a carriage would be ready to take her and her effects to Alençon.

Early this morning, not two hours ago in fact, Anne had come running into Madame Leblanc's room with a scared white face, saying that Monsieur Ernest was not in his room and was nowhere to be found. He appeared to have slipped on the clothes which he had worn the previous

155

night, as they were missing from their usual place.

Terribly alarmed, M. Leblanc had sent Anne to bring Mademoiselle Vaillant to him immediately; but Anne returned within a couple of minutes with the news that Mademoiselle had also disappeared. The house was scoured from attic to cellar, the gardens were searched, and the out-door labourers started to drag the moat. Madame Leblanc, beside herself with dread, had collapsed, half fainting in the hall, where Anne was administering restoratives to her. Monsieur Leblanc had ordered his horse, determined at once to inform the police. He was standing at his dressing-room window, putting on his riding clothes, when he saw Marie Vaillant running as fast as ever she could across the garden towards the house. Her dress clung wet and muddy round her legs, her hair was streaming down her back, and she held out her arms in front of her as she ran. Indeed, she looked more mad than sane, and there was such a look of fear and horror in her face and about her whole appearance, that the servants—stupid and scared—stood by gaping like gabies, not attempting to run after her. In a moment

M. Leblanc—his mind full of horrible foreboding—had flung out of his dressing-room, determined to intercept the woman and to wring from her an admission of what she had done with the boy.

He ran down the main staircase, as he had seen Marie make straight for the chief entrance hall, but, presumably checked in her wild career, the girl had suddenly turned off after she had crossed the bridge over the moat, and must have dashed into the house by one of the side doors, for at the moment that M. Leblanc reached the hall he could hear her tearing helter-skelter up the uncarpeted service stairs. No one so far had attempted to stop her. M. Leblanc now called loudly to the servants to arrest this mad woman in her flight; there was a general scrimmage, but before anyone could reach the top landing, Marie had darted straight into her employers' bedroom and had locked and bolted the heavy door.

"You may imagine," concluded the unfortunate sous-préfet, who had been at great pains to give this narrative some semblance of coherence, "that I was the first to bang against the bedroom door and to demand admittance of the

157

wretched creature. At first there was no reply, but through the solid panelling we could hear a distinct and steady hammering which seemed to come from the farther end of the room. All the doors in the old house are extraordinarily heavy, but the one that gives on my wife's and my bedroom is of unusually massive oak with enormous locks and bars of iron and huge iron hinges. I felt that it would be futile to try to break it open, and, frankly, I was not a little doubtful as to what the wretched woman might do if brought to bay. The windows of the bedroom as well as those of the dressing-room adjoining give directly on the moat, which at this point is over three metres deep. Placing two of the men-servants on guard outside the door, with strict orders not to allow the woman to escape, I made my way into the garden and took my stand opposite the bedroom windows. I had the width of the moat between me and the house. The waters lapped the solid grey walls and for the first time since I have lived at Les Colombiers the thought of the old Manor, with its lurking holes for unfortunate Huguenots, struck my heart with a sense of coldness and gloom. Up above Marie Vaillant had already taken the precaution of fastening the shutters; it was impossible to imagine what she could be doing, locked up in that room, or why she should refuse to come out, unless——"

The stricken father closed his eyes as he hinted at this awful possibility; a shiver went through him.

"A ladder——" suggested the Man in Grey.

"Impossible!" replied M. Leblanc. "The moat on that side is over eight metres wide. I had thought of that. I thought of everything; I racked my brains. Think of it, sir! My boy Ernest gone, and his whereabouts probably only known to that mad woman up there!"

"Your butler Lavernay?" queried the Man in Grey.

"It was when I realised my helplessness that I suddenly thought of him," replied the sous-préfet; "but no one had seen him. He too had disappeared."

Then suddenly the full force of his misery rushed upon him. He jumped to his feet and seized the police agent by the coat sleeve.

"I entreat you, Monsieur Fernand," he exclaimed in tones of pitiable entreaty, "do not let us waste any more time. We'll call at the commissariat of police first and get Lefèvre to follow on our heels with a posse of police. I beg of you to come at once!"

Gently the Man in Grey disengaged his arm from the convulsive grasp of the other. By your leave," he said, "we will not call in a posse of police just yet. Remember your own fears! Brought to bay, Marie Vaillant, if indeed she has some desperate deed to conceal, might jump into the moat and take the secret of your boy's whereabouts with her to her grave."

"My God, you are right!" moaned the unfortunate man. "What can I do? In Heaven's name tell me what to do."

"For the moment we'll just go quietly to Les Colombiers together. I always keep a horse ready saddled for emergencies at the 'Trois Rois' inn close by. Do you get to horse and accompany me thither."

"But——"

"I pray you, sir, do not argue," broke in the police agent curtly. "Every minute has become precious."

And silently M. Leblanc obeyed. He had all at once grown as tractable as a child. The dominating personality of that little Man in Grey had entire possession of him now, of his will and understanding.

The first part of the cross-country ride was accomplished in silence. M. Leblanc was in a desperate hurry to get on; he pushed his horse along with the eagerness of intense anxiety. For a while the police agent kept up with him in silence, then suddenly he called a peremptory "Halt!"

"Your horse will give out, Monsieur le Sous-Préfet," he said. "Allow him to walk for awhile. There are two or three questions I must put to you before we arrive at Les Colombiers."

M. Leblanc obeyed and set his horse to a walk. Of a truth he was more worn-out than his steed.

"Firstly, tell me what kind of fireplace you have in your bedroom," said the other abruptly, and with such strange irrelevance that the sous-préfet stared at him.

"Why," he replied submissively, "there is a fine old chimney, as there is in every room in the house."

"You have had a fire in it lately?"

"Oh, every day. The weather has been very cold."

161

"And what sort of bed do you sleep in?"

"An old-fashioned fourpost bedstead," replied M. Leblanc, more and more puzzled at these extraordinary questions, "which I believe has been in the house for two or three hundred years. It is the only piece of the original furniture left; everything else was sold by Monsieur de Mamers' agent before the State confiscated the house. I don't know why the bedstead was allowed to remain; probably because it is so uncommonly heavy and is also screwed to the floor."

"Thank you. That is interesting," rejoined the police agent dryly. "And now, tell me, what is the nearest house to yours that is of similar historical interest?"

"An old sixteenth-century house, you mean?"

"Yes."

"There is none at Bourg-le-Roi. If you remember, the town itself is comparatively modern, and every traveller will tell you that Les Colombiers is the only interesting piece of mediaeval architecture in the neighbourhood. Of course, there are the ruins at Saut-de-Biche."

"The ruins at Saut-de-Biche?"

"Yes; in the woods, about half a kilometre from Les Colombiers. They are supposed to be the remains of the old farmhouse belonging to the Manor; but only two or three walls are left standing. A devastating fire razed the place to the ground some ten years ago; since then the roof has fallen in, and the town council of Bourg-le-Roi has been using some of the stone for building the new town hall. The whole thing is just a mass of debris and charred wood."

While the two men were talking the time had gone by swiftly enough. Alençon was soon left far behind; ahead, close by, lay the coppice which sheltered Les Colombiers. Some twenty minutes later the two men drew rein in the fine old courtyard of the ancient manor. At a call from M. Leblanc one of his men rushed out of the house to hold the horses and to aid his master to dismount. The Man in Grey was already on his feet.

"What news?" he asked of the man.

The latter shrugged his shoulders. There was no change at Les Colombiers. The two labourers were still on sentry guard outside the bedroom door, whilst the indoor servants, with the head gardener, had remained down below by the side of the moat, staring up at the shuttered windows, and revelling in all the horrors which the aspect of the dark waters and of the windows above, behind which no doubt the mad woman was crouching, helped to conjure up before their sluggish minds.

Madame Leblanc was still lying on a couch in the hall, prostrate with grief. No one had caught sight of Marie Vaillant within her stronghold, and there was no sign either of M. Ernest or of the butler Lavernay.

Without protest or opposition on the part of the master of the house, the Man in Grey had taken command of the small army of scared domestics.

"Monsieur le Sous-Préfet," he said, "before I can help you in this matter, I must make a hurried inspection of your domain. I shall require three of your men to come with me. They must come armed with a stout joist, with pickaxes and a few heavy tools. You yourself and your women servants must remain on guard outside the bedroom door. Should Marie Vaillant attempt a sortie, seize her and, above all, see she does not do herself an injury. Your head gardener and indoor man must remain by the moat. I presume they can swim."

"Swim?" queried M. Leblanc vaguely.

"Why, yes! There is still the possibility of the girl trying to drown herself and her secret in the moat."

M. Leblanc promised most earnestly that he would obey the police agent's commands to the letter, and the Man in Grey, followed by the three labourers who carried their picks, a bag of tools and a stout joist, started on his way. Swiftly crossing the bridge over the moat, he strode rapidly across the park and plunged into the coppice. Then only did he ask the men to precede him.

"Take me straight to the ruins at Saut-de-Biche," he said.

The men obeyed, not pausing to reflect what could be the object of this little man in the grey coat in going to look at a pile of broken walls, while M. le Sous-Préfet was half demented with anxiety, and a mad woman might either set fire to the whole house or do herself some terrible injury. They walked on in silence, closely followed by the accredited representative of His Imperial Majesty's Minister of Police.

Within ten minutes the ruined farmhouse came in sight. It stood in the midst of a wide clearing; the woods which stretched all round it were so dense that even in mid-winter they screened it from the road. There was but little of the original structure left; a piece of wall like a tall arm stretching upwards to the skies, another forming an angle, some loose pieces of stone lying about in the midst of a medley of broken and charred wood, cracked tiles and twisted pieces of desolation. All round the ruined walls a forest of brambles, dead gorse and broom had sprung up rendering access to the house very difficult. For a moment or two the Man in Grey paused, surveying the surroundings with a keen, experienced eye. At a slight distance from him on the right, the gorse and bramble had apparently been hacked away in order to make a passage practicable to human feet. Without hesitation Fernand, ordering the three men to follow him, struck into this narrow track, which, as he surmised, led straight to the ruins. He skirted the up-standing wall, until an opening in the midst of the big masses of stone enabled him to reach what was once the interior of the house. Here progress became very

166

difficult; the debris from the fallen roof littered the ground, and there was grave danger of a hidden chasm below, where the cellars may have been.

The Man in Grey peered round him anxiously. Presently an exclamation of satisfaction rose to his lips. He called to the men. A few feet away from where he was standing the whole debris seemed to have been lately considerably augmented. Right in the midst of a pile of burned wood, tiles and metal, a large stone was embedded. It had evidently been very recently detached from the high upstanding wall, and had fallen down amidst a shower of the decayed mortar, wet earth, and torn lichen and moss, which littered the place.

In obedience to the commands of the Man in Grey, the labourers took up their picks, and set to work to clear the debris around the fallen stone, the police agent standing close by, watching them. They had not done more than bury their tools once in the litter of earth and mortar, when their picks encountered something soft.

"Drop your tools," commanded the Man in Grey. "Your hands will suffice to

167

unearth what lies below."

It was the body of a man crushed almost past recognition by the weight of the fallen masonry. The labourers extricated it from the fragments of wood and metal and dragged it into the open.

"By his clothes," said one of the men, in answer to a peremptory query from the Man in Grey, "I guess he must be the butler, François Lavernay."

The secret agent made no comment. Not a line of his pale, colourless face betrayed the emotion he felt—the emotion of the sleuth-hound which knows that it is on the track of its quarry. He ordered the body to be decorously put on one side and took off his own loose mantle to throw over it. Then he bade the men resume their work. They picked up their tools again and tried to clear the rubbish all round the fallen stone.

"We must move that stone from its place," the man in the grey coat had said, and the labourers, impelled by that air of assurance and authority which emanated from the insignificant little figure, set to with a will. Having cleared the debris, they put their shoulders to the stone, helped by the secret agent, whose strength appeared out of all proportion to his slender frame. By and by the stone became dislodged and, with another effort, rolled over on its flat side. After that it was easy to move it some three or four feet farther on.

"That will do!" commanded the Man in Grey.

Underneath the stone there now appeared a square flat slab of granite embedded in the soil with cement. One piece of this slab had seemingly been cut or chiselled away and then removed, displaying a cavity about a foot and a half square. In the centre of the slab was an iron ring to which a rope was attached, the other end being lost within the cavity.

The labourers were staring at their find open-mouthed; but the secret agent was already busy hauling up the rope. The end of it was formed into a loop not large enough to pass over a man's shoulders.

"Just as I thought," he muttered between his teeth.

Then he lay down on his stomach and with his head just over the small cavity he shouted a loud "Hallo!" From down below there came no answer save a dull, resounding echo. Again and again the

Man in Grey shouted his loud "Hallo!" into the depths, but, eliciting no reply, at last he struggled to his feet.

"Now then, my men," he said, "I am going to leave you here to work away at this slab. It has got to be removed within an hour."

The men examined the cement which held the heavy stone in its place.

"It will take time," one of them said. "This cement is terribly hard; we shall have to chip every bit of it away."

"You must do your best," said the Man in Grey earnestly. "A human life may depend on your toil. You will have no cause to grumble at the reward when your work is done. For reasons which I cannot explain, I may not bring any strangers to help you. So work away as hard as you can. I will return in about an hour with Monsieur le Sous-Préfet."

He waited to see the men swing their picks, then turned on his heel and started to walk back the way he came.

It was nearly two hours before the slab of granite was finally removed from its place. M. le Sous-Préfet was standing by with the Man in Grey when the stone was hoisted up and turned over. It disclosed a large cavity with, at one end of it, a flight of stone steps leading downwards.

"Now then, Monsieur le Sous-Préfet," said the police agent quietly, "will you follow me?"

M. Leblanc's face was ghastly in its pallor. The sudden hope held out to him by the Man in Grey had completely unnerved him. "Are you sure——" he murmured.

"That we shall find Monsieur Ernest down there?" broke in the other, as he pointed to the hollow. "Well, Monsieur le Sous-Préfet, I wish I were equally sure of a fortune!"

He had a lighted lantern in his hand and began to descend the stone stairs, closely followed by the sous-préfet. The labourers above were resting after their heavy toil. They could not understand all they had seen, and their slow wits would probably never grasp the full significance of their strange adventure. While in the depths below the Man in Grey, holding M. le Sous-Préfet by the arm and swinging the lantern in front, was exploring the mediaeval lurking-holes of the Huguenots, the three labourers were calmly munching their bread and cheese.

The searchers found the boy lying unconscious not very far from the stairs. A dark lantern had fallen from his hand and been extinguished. A large heavy box with metal handles stood close behind him; a long trail behind the box showed that the plucky child had dragged it along by its handle for a considerable distance. How he had managed to do so remained a marvel. Love and enthusiasm had lent the puny youngster remarkable strength. The broken-hearted father lifted his unconscious child in his arms. Obviously he had only fainted—probably from fright—and together the little procession now worked its way back into the open.

"Can you carry your boy home, Monsieur le Sous-Préfet," asked the Man in Grey, "while we attend to your unfortunate butler?"

But he had no need to ask. Already M. Leblanc, closely hugging his precious burden, was striding bravely and manfully through the coppice beyond.

The Man in Grey arrived at Les Colombiers a quarter of an hour after the sous-préfet had seen his boy snugly laid in his mother's arms. The child was far too weak and too highly strung to give a clear account of the events which had landed him alone and unconscious inside the disused hiding-place, with his only means of exit cut off. But the first words he spoke after he had returned to consciousness were, "Tell my darling Marie that I did my best."

Afterwards the Man in Grey graphically recounted to the sous-préfet how he came to seek for Ernest beneath the ruins of Saut-de-Biche.

"I followed Marie Vaillant's machinations in my mind," he said, "from the moment that she entered your service. Not a word of your narrative escaped me, remember! Recommended by the Bishop of Alençon, I guessed her to be a Royalist who had been placed in your house for some purpose connected with the Cause. What that purpose was it became my business to learn. It was a case of putting the proverbial two and two together. There was, on the one hand, an old moated Manor, once the refuge of persecuted Huguenots and therefore full of secret corners and hiding-places, and, on the other, an *émigré* Royalist family who had fled the country, no doubt leaving hidden treasures which they could not take away in their flight. Add to these facts a young girl recommended by the Bishop of Alençon, one of the most inveterate Royalist intriguers in the land, and you have as fine a solution of all that has puzzled you, Monsieur, as you could wish. Marie Vaillant had been sent to your house by the Royalist faction to secure the treasure hidden by the Comte de Mamers in one of the lurking-holes of Les Colombiers.

"With this certainty firmly fixed in my mind, I was soon able to explain her every action. The open-air life in the summer meant that she could not gain access to the hiding-place inside the house and she must seek an entrance outside. This manoeuvre suggested to me that the secret place was perhaps a subterranean passage which led from some distant portion of the domain to the house itself. There are a number of such passages in France, of mediaeval structure. Often they run under a moat.

"Then came the second phase: Marie Vaillant's coquetry. She either could not find or could not open the hiding-place; she needed a man's help. Lavernay, your butler, appeared susceptible—her choice fell on him. Night after night they stole out together in order to work away at the obstacle which blocked the entrance to the secret passage. Then they were discovered. Marie was threatened with dismissal, even before she had found the hidden treasure. She changed her tactics and inveigled your boy into her service. Why? Because she and Lavernay were too weak and clumsy. They had only succeeded in disclosing one small portion of the entrance to the secret lair; a portion not large enough to allow of the passage of an adult. So your boy was cajoled, endeared, fascinated. Highly strung and nervous, he was ready to dare all for the sake of the girl whom he loved with the ardour of unawakened manhood. He is dragged through the woods and shown the place; he is gradually familiarised with the task which lies before him. Then once more discovery falls on Marie Vaillant like a thunderbolt.

"There is only one more night wherein she can effect her purpose. Can you see them—she and Lavernay and your boy—stealing out at dead of night to the ruins; the boy primed in what he has to do, lowered by a cord into the secret passage, dark lantern in hand? Truly the heroism of so young a child passes belief! Lavernay and Marie Vaillant wait above, straining their ears to hear what is going on below. The underground passage, remember, is over half a kilometre in length. I explored it as far as I could. It goes under the moat and I imagine has its other entrance in your bedroom at Les Colombiers. Ernest had to go some way along it ere he discovered the box which contained the treasure. With truly super-human strength he seizes the metal handle and drags his burden wearily along. At last he has reached the spot where the cord still dangles from above. He gives the preconcerted signal but receives no reply. Distracted and terror-stricken, he calls again and again until the horror of his position causes him to lose consciousness.

"Above the tragedy is being consummated. Loosened by recent heavy rains, a large piece of masonry comes crashing down, burying in its fall the unfortunate Lavernay and hopelessly blocking the entrance to the secret passage. Picture to yourself Marie Vaillant pitting her feeble strength against the relentless stone, half-crazed with the thought of the child buried alive beneath her feet. An oath to her party binds her to secrecy! She dares not call for help. Almost demented, blind instinct drives her to the one spot whence she might yet be able to render assistance to the child—your bedroom, where I'll wager that either inside the chimney or behind the head of the old-fashioned bedstead you will find the panel which masks the other entrance to the secret passage."

The Man in Grey suspended his story and, guided by his host, made his way upstairs to the landing outside the bedroom door.

"Call to the poor woman, Monsieur le Sous-Préfet," he commanded. "Tell her that the child is safe and well. Perhaps she will come out of her own accord. It were a pity to break this magnificent door."

Presently Marie Vaillant, summoned by her employer, who assured her repeatedly that Ernest was safe and well, was heard to unlock the door and to draw the bolts. Next moment she stood under the heavy oak lintel, her face as white as a shroud, her eyes staring wildly before her, her gown stained, her hands bleeding. She had bruised herself sorely in a vain endeavour to move the massive bedstead which concealed the secret entrance to the underground passage.

One glance at M. Leblanc's face assured her that all was well with her valiant little helpmeet and that the two men before her were moved more by pity than by wrath. She broke down completely, but the violent fit of weeping eased her overburdened heart. Soon she became comforted with the kindly assurance that she would be allowed to depart in peace. Even the sous-préfet felt that the wretched girl had suffered enough through the tortuous intrigues of her fanatic loyalty to the cause of her party, whilst the Man in Grey saw to it that in the matter of the death of Lavernay His Majesty's Police were fully satisfied.

IV

THE EMERALDS OF MADEMOISELLE PHILIPPA

AT first there was a good deal of talk in the neighbourhood when the de Romaines returned from England and made their home in the tumbledown Lodge just outside St. Lô. The Lodge, surrounded by a small garden, marked the boundary of the beautiful domain of Torteron, which had been the property of the de Romaines and their ancestors for many generations. M. le Comte de Romaine had left France with his family at the very outset of the Revolution and, in accordance with the decree of February, 1792, directed against the Emigrants, his estates were confiscated and sold for the benefit of the State. The chateau of Torteron, being so conveniently situated near the town of St. Lô, was converted into a general hospital, and the farms and agricultural lands were bought up by various local cultivators. Only the little Lodge at the park gates had remained unsold, and when the Emigrés were granted a general amnesty, the de Romaines obtained permission to settle in it. Although it was greatly neglected and dilapidated, it was weather-proof, and by the clemency of the Emperor it was declared to be, indisputably their own.

M. le Comte de Romaine, worn out by sorrow and the miseries of exile, had died in England. It was Mme. la Comtesse, now a widow, who came back to Torteron along with M. le Comte Jacques, her son who had never set foot on his native soil since, as a tiny lad, he had been taken by his parents into exile, and Mademoiselle Mariette, her daughter, who, born in England, had never been in France at all.

People who had known Madame la Comtesse in the past thought her greatly aged, more so in fact than her years warranted. She had gone away in '91 a young and handsome woman well on the right side of thirty, fond of society and show; now, nineteen years later, she reappeared the wreck of her former self. Crippled with rheumatism, for ever wrapped up in shawls, with weak sight and impaired hearing, she at once settled down to a very secluded life at the Lodge, waited on only by her daughter, a silent, stately girl, who filled the duties of maid of all work, companion and nurse to her mother, and her brother.

On the other hand, young M. le Comte de Romaine was a regular "gadabout." Something of a rogue and a ne'er-do-well, he seemed to have no defined occupation, and soon not a café or dancing hall in St. Lô but had some story to tell of his escapades and merry living.

M. Moulin, the préfet, had received an order from the accredited agent of the

Minister of Police to keep an eye on the doings of these returned Emigrants, but until now their conduct had been above suspicion. Mme. la Comtesse and Mlle. Mariette went nowhere except now and again to the church of Notre Dame; they saw no one; and for the nonce the young Comte de Romaine devoted his entire attention to Mademoiselle Philippa, the charming dancer who was delighting the audiences of St. Lô with her inimitable art, and dazzling their eyes with her showy dresses, her magnificent equipage and her diamonds.

The préfet, in his latest report to the secret agent, had jocularly added that the lovely dancer did not appear at all averse from the idea of being styled Mme. la Comtesse one of these days, or of re-gilding the faded escutcheon of the de Romaines with her plebeian gold.

There certainly was no hint of Chouan-nerie about the doings of any member of the family, no communication with any of the well-known Chouan leaders, no visits from questionable personages.

Great therefore was the astonishment of M. Moulin when, three days later, he received a summons to present himself at

No.15 Rue Notre Dame, where the agent of His Majesty's Minister of Police had arrived less than an hour ago.

"I am here in strict incognito, my dear Monsieur Moulin," said the Man in Grey as soon as he had greeted the préfet, "and I have brought three of my men with me whom I know I can trust, as I am not satisfied that you are carrying out my orders."

"Your orders, Monsieur—er—Fernand?" queried the préfet blandly.

"Yes! I said my orders," retorted the other quietly. "Did I not bid you keep a strict eye on the doings of the Romaine family?"

"But, Monsieur Fernand——"

"From now onwards my men and I will watch Jacques de Romaine," broke in the secret agent in that even tone of his which admitted of no argument. "But we cannot have our eyes everywhere. I must leave the women to you."

"The old Comtesse only goes to church, and Mademoiselle Mariette goes sometimes to market."

"So much the better for you. Your men will have an easy time."

"But——"

"I pray you do not argue, my good Monsieur Moulin. Mademoiselle Mariette may be out shopping at this very moment."

And when the accredited agent said "I pray you," non-compliance was out of the question.

Later in the day the préfet talked the matter over with M. Cognard, chief commissary of police, who had had similar orders in the matter of the Romaines. The two cronies had had their tempers sorely ruffled by the dictatorial ways of the secret agent, whom they hated with all the venom that indolent natures direct against an energetic one.

"The little busybody," vowed M. Moulin, "sees conspirators in every harmless citizen and interferes in matters which of a truth have nothing whatever to do with him."

Then in the very midst of the complacency of these two worthies came the memorable day which, in their opinion, was the most turbulent one they had ever known during their long and otiose careers.

It was the day following the arrival of

183

the secret agent at St. Lô, and he had come to the commissariat that morning for the sole purpose—so M. Cognard averred—of making matters uncomfortable for everybody, when Mademoiselle de Romaine was announced. Mademoiselle had sent in word that she desired to speak with M. le Commissaire immediately, and a minute or two later she entered, looking like a pale ghost in a worn grey gown, and with a cape round her shoulders which was far too thin to keep out the cold on this winter's morning.

M. Cognard, fussy and chivalrous, offered her a chair. She seemed to be in a terrible state of mental agitation and on the verge of tears, which, however, with characteristic pride she held resolutely in check.

"I have come, Monsieur le Commissaire," she began in a voice hoarse with emotion, "because my mother—Madame la Comtesse de Romaine—and I are desperately anxious—we don't know—we—"

She was trembling so that she appeared almost unable to speak. M. Cognard, with great kindness and courtesy, poured out a glass of water for her. She drank a little of it, and threw him a grateful look, after which she seemed more tranquil.

"I beg you to compose yourself, Mademoiselle," said the commissaire. "I am entirely at your service."

"It is about my brother, Monsieur le Commissaire," rejoined Mademoiselle more calmly, "Monsieur le Comte Jacques de Romaine. He has disappeared. For three days we have seen and heard nothing of him—and my mother fears—fears——"

Her eyes became dilated with that fear which she dared not put into words. M. Cognard interposed at once, both decisively and sympathetically.

"There is no occasion to fear the worst, Mademoiselle," he said kindly. "Young men often leave home for days without letting their mother and sisters know where they are."

"Ah, but, Monsieur le Commissaire," resumed Mademoiselle with a pathetic break in her voice, "the circumstances in this case are exceptional. My mother is a great invalid, and though my brother leads rather a gay life he is devoted to her and he always would come home at nights. Sometimes," she continued, as a slight flush rose to her pale cheeks, "Mademoiselle Philippa would drive him home in her barouche from the theatre. This she did on Tuesday night, for I heard the carriage draw up at our door. I saw the lights of the lanterns; I also heard my brother's voice bidding Mademoiselle good night and the barouche driving off again. I was in bed, for it was long past midnight, and I remember just before I fell asleep again thinking how very quietly my dear brother must have come in, for I had not heard the opening and shutting of the front door, nor his step upon the stairs or in his room. Next morning I saw that his bed had not been slept in, and that he had not come into the house at all—as I had imagined—but had driven off again, no doubt, with Mademoiselle Philippa. But we have not seen him since, and——"

"And—h'm—er—have you communicated with Mademoiselle Philippa?" asked the commissary with some hesitation.

"No, Monsieur," replied Mariette de Romaine gravely. "You are the first stranger whom I have consulted. I thought you would advise me what to do."

"Exactly, exactly!" rejoined M.

Cognard, highly gratified at this tribute to his sagacity. "You may rely on me, Mademoiselle, to carry on investigations with the utmost discretion. Perhaps you will furnish me with a few details regarding this—er—regrettable occurrence."

There ensued a lengthy period of questioning and cross-questioning. M. Cognard was impressively official. Mademoiselle de Romaine, obviously wearied, told and retold her simple story with exemplary patience. The Man in Grey, ensconced in a dark corner of the room, took no part in the proceedings; only once did he interpose with an abrupt question:

"Are you quite sure, Mademoiselle," he asked, "that Monsieur le Comte did not come into the house at all before you heard the barouche drive off again?"

Mariette de Romaine gave a visible start. Clearly she had had no idea until then that anyone else was in the room besides herself and the commissary of police, and as the quaint, grey-clad figure emerged suddenly from out the dark corner, her pale cheeks assumed an even more ashen hue. Nevertheless, she replied quite steadily:

"I cannot be sure of that, Monsieur,"

she said; "for I was in bed and half asleep, but I am sure my brother did not sleep at home that night."

The Man in Grey asked no further questions; he had retired into the dark corner of the room, but—after this little episode—whenever Mariette de Romaine looked in that direction, she encountered those deep-set, colourless eyes of his fixed intently upon her.

After Mademoiselle de Romaine's departure, M. Cognard turned somewhat sheepishly to the Man in Grey.

"It does seem," he said, "that there is something queer about those Romaines, after all."

"Fortunately," retorted the secret agent, "you have complied with my orders, and your men have never once lost sight of Mademoiselle or of Madame her mother."

M. Cognard made no reply. His round face had flushed to the very roots of his hair.

"Had you not better send at once for this dancer—Philippa?" added the Man in Grey.

"Of course—of course——" stammered the commissary, much relieved.

Mademoiselle Philippa duly arrived, in the early afternoon, in her barouche drawn by two magnificent English horses. She appeared dressed in the latest Paris fashion and was greeted by M. Cognard with the gallantry due to her beauty and talent.

"You have sent for me, Monsieur le Commissaire?" she asked somewhat tartly, as soon as she had settled herself down in as becoming an attitude as the office chair would allow.

"Oh, Mademoiselle," said the commissary deprecatingly, "I did so with deep regret at having to trouble you."

"Well? And what is it?"

"I only desired to ask you, Mademoiselle, if you have seen the Comte de Romaine recently."

She laughed and shrugged her pretty shoulders.

"The young scamp!" she said lightly. "No, I haven't seen him for two days. Why do you ask?"

"Because the young scamp, as you so pertinently call him, has disappeared, and neither his mother nor his sister knows what has become of him."

"Disappeared?" exclaimed Mademoiselle Philippa. "With my emeralds!"

Her nonchalance and habitual gaiety suddenly left her. She sat bolt upright, her small hands clutching the arms of her chair, her face pale and almost haggard beneath the delicate layer of rouge.

"Your emeralds, Mademoiselle?" queried M. Cognard in dismay.

"My emeralds!" she reiterated with a catch in her voice. "A necklace, tiara and earrings—a gift to me from the Emperor of Russia when I danced before him at St. Petersburg. They are worth the best part of a million francs, Monsieur le Commissaire. Oh! Monsieur de Romaine cannot have disappeared—not like that—and not with my emeralds!"

She burst into tears, and M. Cognard had much ado to reassure her. Everything would be done, he declared, to trace the young scapegrace. He could not dispose of the emeralds, avowed the commissary, without being apprehended and his booty being taken from him.

"He can dispose of them abroad," declared Mademoiselle Philippa, who would not be consoled. "He may be on the high seas by now—the detestable young rogue."

"But how came Mademoiselle Philippa's priceless emeralds in the hands of that detestable young rogue?" here interjected a quiet, even voice.

Mademoiselle turned upon the Man in Grey like a young tiger-cat that has been teased.

"What's that to you?" she queried.

He smiled.

"Are we not all trying to throw light on a mysterious occurrence?" he asked.

"Monsieur de Romaine wanted to show my emeralds to his mother," rejoined Mademoiselle, somewhat mollified and not a little shamefaced. "I had promised to be his wife—Madame la Comtesse had approved—she looked upon me as a daughter—I had been up to her house to see her—she expressed a wish to see my emeralds—and so on Tuesday I entrusted them to Monsieur de Romaine—and—and——"

Once more her voice broke and she burst into tears. It was a pitiably silly story, of course—that of the clumsy trap set by a fascinating rogue—the trap into which hundreds of thousands of women have fallen since the world began, and into which as many will fall again so long as human nature does not undergo a radical change.

"And when you drove Monsieur de Romaine home on that Tuesday night," continued the Man in Grey, "he had your emeralds in his possession?"

"Yes," replied Mademoiselle through her tears. "He had them in the inside pocket of his coat. I took leave of him at the Lodge. He waved his hand to me and I drove off. That is the last I have seen of him—the scamp!"

Mademoiselle Philippa was evidently taking it for granted that Jacques de Romaine had stolen her emeralds, and she laughed derisively when M. Cognard suggested that mayhap the unfortunate young man had been waylaid and robbed and afterwards murdered by some malefactor who knew that he had the jewels in his possession.

"Well!" commented the dancer with a shrug of the shoulders, "'tis for you, my good Commissaire, to find either my emeralds for me or the murdered body of Monsieur le Comte de Romaine."

After which parting shot Mademoiselle took her departure, leaving an atmosphere of cosmetics and the lingering echo of the *frou-frou* of silken skirts.

The commissary accompanied Mademoiselle Philippa to the door. He was not looking forward with unadulterated pleasure to the next half-hour, when of a surety that fussy functionary from Paris would set the municipal authorities by the ears for the sake of an affair which, after all, was not so very uncommon in these days—a handsome rogue, a foolish, trusting woman, valuable jewellery. The whole thing was very simple and the capture of the miscreant a certainty. "How was he going to dispose of the emeralds," argued M. Cognard to himself, "without getting caught?" As for connecting such a mild affair with any of those darling Chouans, the idea was preposterous.

But when M. Cognard returned to his office, these specious arguments froze upon his lips. The Man in Grey was very unusually stern and uncompromising.

"Let me have your last reports about Mademoiselle de Romaine," he said peremptorily. "What did she do all day yesterday?"

The commissary, grumbling in his beard, found the necessary papers.

"She only went to church in the morning," he said in an injured tone of voice, "with Madame la Comtesse. It was the feast of St. Andrew——"

"Did either of the women speak to anyone?"

"Not on the way. But the church was very crowded—both ladies went to confession——"

The Man in Grey uttered an impatient exclamation.

"I fear we have lost the emeralds," he said, "but in Heaven's name do not let us lose the rogue. When brought to bay he may give up the booty yet."

"But, Monsieur Fernand——" protested the commissary.

The other waved aside these protestations with a quick gesture of his slender hand.

"I know, I know," he said. "You are not at fault. The rascal has been too clever for us, that is all. But we have not done with him yet. Send over to the Lodge at once," added the secret agent firmly, "men whom you can trust, and order them to apprehend Monsieur le Comte Jacques de Romaine and convey him hither."

"To the Lodge?"

"Yes! Mariette de Romaine lied when she said that her brother had not been in the house since Tuesday. He is in the house now. I had only been in St. Lô a few hours, but I had taken up my stand outside the Lodge that night, when Mademoiselle Philippa's barouche drew up there and Jacques de Romaine stepped out of it. I saw him wave his hand and then turn to go into the house. The next moment the door of the Lodge was opened and he disappeared within it. Since then he has not been outside the house. I was there the whole of that night with one of my men; two others have been on the watch ever since—one in front, the other at the back. The sister or the mother may have passed the emeralds on to a confederate in church yesterday—we don't know. But this I do know," he concluded emphatically, "that Jacques de Romaine is in the Lodge at this moment unless the devil has spirited him away up the chimney."

"There's no devil that will get the better of my men," retorted the commissary, carried away despite himself by the other's energy and sense of power. "We'll have the rogue here within the hour, Monsieur Fernand, I pledge you the honour of the municipality of St. Lô! And the emeralds, too," he added complacently, "if the robbers have not yet disposed of them."

"That's brave!" rejoined the Man in Grey in a tone of kindly encouragement. "My own men are still on the spot and will lend you a hand. They have at their fingers' ends all that there is to know on the subject of secret burrows and hiding-places. All that you have to remember is that Jacques de Romaine is inside the Lodge and that you must bring him here. Now go and make your arrangements; I will be at the Lodge myself within the hour."

It was quite dark when the Minister's agent arrived at the Lodge. M. Cognard met him outside the small garden gate. As soon as he caught sight of the slender, grey-clad figure he ran to meet it as fast as his portliness would allow.

"Nothing!" he said breathlessly.

"How do you mean—nothing?" retorted the secret agent.

"Just what I say," replied the commissaire. "We have searched this tumble-down barrack through and through. The women are there—in charge of my men.

They did not protest; they did not hinder us in any way. But I tell you," added M. Cognard, as he mopped his streaming forehead, "there's not a cat or a mouse concealed in that place. We have searched every hole and corner."

"Bah!" said the Man in Grey with a frown. "Some secret hiding-place has escaped you!"

"Ask your own trusted men," retorted the commissaire. "They have worked with ours."

"Have you questioned the women?"

"Yes! They adhere to Mademoiselle's story in every point."

"Do they know that I—a member of His Majesty's secret police force—saw Jacques de Romaine enter this house on Tuesday night, and that I swear he did not leave it the whole of that night; whilst my own men are equally ready to swear that he has not left it since?"

"They know that."

"And what is their answer?"

"That we must demand an explanation from the man who was lurking round here in the dark when Jacques de Romaine had priceless jewels in his possession," replied the chief commissary.

The stern features of the Man in Grey relaxed into a smile.

"The rogues are cleverer than I thought," he said simply.

"Rogues?" growled M. Cognard. "I for one do not believe that they are rogues. If Jacques de Romaine entered this house on Tuesday night and has not left it since, where is he now? Answer me that, Monsieur Fernand!"

"Do you think I have murdered him?" retorted the secret agent calmly.

Then he went into the house.

He found Mme. la Comtesse de Romaine entrenched within that barrier of lofty incredulity which she had set up the moment that she heard of the grave suspicion which rested upon her son.

"A Comte de Romaine, Monsieur," she said in her thin, cracked voice in answer to every query put to her by the Man in Grey, "who is also Seigneur de Mazaire and a peer of France, does not steal the jewels of a dancer. If, as that wench asserts, my son had her trinkets that night about his person, then obviously it is for you who were lurking round my house like a thief in the night to give an account of what became of him."

198

"Your son entered this house last Tuesday night, Madame," answered Fernand firmly, "and has not been out of it since."

"Then I pray you find him, sir," was Madame de Romaine's rejoinder.

Mademoiselle Mariette's attitude was equally uncompromising. She bore every question and cross-question unflinchingly. But when the secret agent finally left her in peace to initiate a thorough search inside that house which so bafflingly refused to give up its secret, she turned to the commissary of police.

"Who is that anonymous creature," she queried with passionate indignation, "who heaps insults and tortures upon my dear mother and me? Why is he not being questioned? Whose is the hidden hand that shields him when retribution should be marking him for its own?"

Whose indeed? The commissary of police was at his wits' end. Even the Man in Grey—resolute, systematic and untiring—failed to discover anything suspicious in the Lodge. It had often been said of him that no secret hiding-place, no hidden panel or lurking-hole could escape his eagle eye, and yet, to-day, after three hours' persistent search, he was forced to confess he had been baffled.

Either his men had relaxed their vigilance at some time since that fateful Tuesday night, and had allowed the rogue to escape, or the devil had indeed spirited the young Comte de Romaine up the chimney.

Public opinion at once went dead against the authorities. Mademoiselle de Romaine had taken good care that the story of the man lurking round the Lodge on the night her brother disappeared should be known far and wide. That that man happened to be a mysterious and anonymous member of His Majesty's secret police did not in any way allay the popular feeling. The worthy citizens of St. Lô loudly demanded to know why he was not brought to justice. The préfet, the commissary, the procureur, were all bombarded with correspondence. Indignation meetings were held in every parish of the neighbourhood. Indeed, so tense had the situation become that the chief departmental and municipal officials were tendering their resignations wholesale, for their position, which already was well-nigh intolerable, threatened to become literally dangerous. Sooner or later the public would have to be told that the Man in Grey, on whom so grave a suspicion now rested, had mysteriously vanished, no one knew whither, and that no one dared to interfere with his movements, on pain of having to deal with M. le Duc d'Otrante, His Majesty's Minister of Police, himself.

Towards the end of December Mme. la Comtesse de Romaine announced her intention of going abroad.

"There is no justice in this country," she had declared energetically, "or no power on earth would shield my son's murderer from the gallows."

Of Jacques de Romaine there had been no news, nor yet of the Man in Grey. The Procureur Imperial, feeling the sting of Madame's indignation, had been over-courteous in the matter of passports, and everything was got ready in view of the de Romaines departure. Madame had decided to go with Mademoiselle Mariette to Rome, where she had many friends, and the first stage of the long journey had been fixed for the 28th, when the two ladies proposed to travel by private coach as far as Caën, to sleep there, and thus be ready in the early morning for the mail-coach which would take them to Paris.

A start was to be made at midday. In the morning Mademoiselle de Romaine went to High Mass at Notre Dame, it being the feast of the Holy Innocents. The church was very crowded, but Mariette had arrived early, and she had placed her *prie-Dieu* behind the shelter of one of the pillars, where she sat quite quietly, fingering her rosary, while the large congregation filed in. But all the while her thoughts were plainly not on her devotions. Her dark eyes roamed restlessly over every face and form that gathered near her, and there was in her drawn face something of the look of a frightened hare, when it lies low within its form, fearful lest it should be seen.

It was a bitterly cold morning, and Mariette wore a long, full cape, which she kept closely wrapped round her shoulders. Anon a verger came round with foot-warmers which he distributed, in exchange for a few coppers, to those who asked for them. One of these he brought to Mariette and placed it under her feet. As he did so an imperceptible look of understanding passed from her to him. Then the

202

priests followed in, the choir intoned the Introit, the smoke of incense rose to the exquisitely carved roof, and everyone became absorbed in prayer.

Mariette de Romaine, ensconced behind the pillar, sat still, until during the Confiteor, when all heads were buried between clasped hands, she stooped and apparently rearranged the position of her foot-warmer. Anyone who had been closely watching her would have thought that she had lifted it from the ground and was hugging it tightly under her cloak. No doubt her hands were cold.

Just before the Elevation a man dressed in a rough workman's blouse, his bare feet thrust into shabby shoes of soft leather, came and knelt beside her. She tried to edge away from him, but the pillar was in the way and she could not retreat any farther. Then suddenly she caught the man's glance, and he—very slowly—put his grimy hand up to the collar of his blouse and, just for an instant, turned it back; on the reverse side of the collar was sewn a piece of white ribbon with a fleur-de-lis roughly embroidered upon it—the device of the exiled Bourbon princes. A look of understanding, immediately followed by one of anxious inquiry, spread over Mariette de Romaine's face, but the man put a finger to his lips and gave her a scarcely noticeable reassuring nod.

After the conclusion of the service and during the usual noise and bustle of the departing congregation the man drew a little nearer to Mariette and whispered hurriedly:

"Do not go yet—there are police spies outside."

Mariette de Romaine was brave, at times even reckless, but at this warning her pale cheeks became nearly livid. She hugged the bulky thing which she held under her cloak convulsively to her breast.

"What am I to do?" she whispered in response.

"Wait here quietly," rejoined the man, "till the people have left. I can take you through the belfry and out by a postern gate I know of."

"But," she gasped hoarsely, for her throat felt dry and parched, "afterwards?"

"You can come to my lodgings," he replied. "We'll let Madame know—and then we shall have to think what best to do."

"Can you find White-beak?" she asked.

"What for?"

"I could give him the——"

"Hush!" he broke in quickly.

"I should like Monsieur le Chanoine to keep them again; we shall have to make fresh arrangements——"

''Hush!'' he reiterated more peremptorily. "We can do nothing for the moment except arrange for your safety."

The man spoke with such calm and authority that instinctively Mariette felt reassured. The bustle round them, people coming and going, chairs creaking against the flagstones, had effectually drowned the whispered colloquy. Now the crowd was thinning: the man caught hold of Mariette's cloak, and she, obediently, allowed him to lead her. He seemed to know his way about the sacred edifice perfectly, and presently, after they had crossed the belfry and gone along a flagged corridor, he opened a low door, and she found herself in the open in the narrow passage behind the east end of the church. Her guide was supporting her by the elbow, and she, still hugging her precious burden, walked beside him without further question. He led her to a house in a street close by, where he appeared to be at home. After climbing three flights of steps, he knocked vigorously at a door, which was immediately opened by a man also dressed in a rough blouse, and ushered Mariette de Romaine into an apartment of the type usually inhabited by well-to-do artisans. After crossing a narrow hall she entered a sitting-room wherein the first sight that greeted her tired eyes was a bunch of crudely fashioned artificial white lilies in the centre of a large round table. Fully reassured, though thoroughly worn out with the excitement of the past few minutes, the girl sank into a chair and threw open the fastening of her cloak. The bulky parcel, cleverly contrived to look like a foot-warmer, lay upon her lap.

"Now we must let Madame la Comtesse know," said the man who had been her guide, in a quiet, matter-of-fact tone. "Oh, it will be quite safe," he added, seeing a look of terror had spread over Mariette de Romaine's face. "I have a comrade here, Hare's-Foot—you know him, Mademoiselle?"

She shook her head.

"He is well known in St. Lô," continued the man simply. "Supposed to be harmless. His real name is Pierre Legrand. The police spies have never suspected him—the fools. But he is one of us—and as intrepid as he is cunning. So if you will write a few words, Mademoiselle, Hare's-Foot will take them at once to Madame la Comtesse."

"What shall I say?" asked Mariette, as she took up pen and paper which her unknown friend was placing before her.

"Only that you became faint in church," he suggested, "and are at a friend's house. Then request that Madame la Comtesse should come to you at once. The bearer of your note will guide her."

Obediently the girl wrote as he advised, the man watching her the while. Had Mariette de Romaine looked up she might have seen a strange look in his face—a look that was almost of pity.

The letter was duly signed and sealed and handed over to Hare's-Foot—the man who had opened the door of the apartment—and he at once went away with it.

After that perfect quietude reigned in the small room. Mariette leaned her head against the back of her chair. She felt very tired.

"Let me relieve you of this," said her companion quietly, and without waiting for her acquiescence he took the bulky parcel from her and put it on the table. Then Mariette de Romaine fell into a light sleep.

She was aroused by the sound of her mother's voice. Madame la Comtesse de Romaine was in her turn being ushered into the apartment, and was already being put in possession of the facts connected with her daughter's letter which had summoned her hither.

"I guessed at once that something of the sort had happened," was Madame's dry and unperturbed comment. "Mariette was not likely to faint while she had those emeralds in her charge. You, my men," she added, turning to her two interlocutors. "have done well by us. I don't yet know how you came to render us and our King's cause this signal service, but you may be sure that it will not go unrewarded. His Majesty himself shall hear of it—on the faith of a de Romaine."

"And now, Madame la Comtesse," rejoined the man in the rough blouse quietly,

208

"I would suggest that Mademoiselle and yourself don a suitable disguise, while Hare's-Foot and I arrange for a safe conveyance to take you out of St. Lô at once. We have most effectually given the police spies the slip, and while they are still searching the city for you, you will be halfway on the road to Caën, and there is no reason why the original plans of your journey to Rome should be in any way modified."

"Perfect! Perfect!" exclaimed Madame enthusiastically. "You are a jewel, my friend."

There was nothing of the senile invalid about her now. She had cast off her shawl and her bonnet, and with them the lank, white wig which concealed her own dark hair. The man in the rough blouse smiled as he looked on her.

"My mate and I have a number of excellent disguises in this wardrobe here, Madame la Comtesse," he said, as he pointed to a large piece of furniture which stood in a corner of the room, "and all are at your service. I would suggest a peasant's dress for Mademoiselle, and," he added significantly, "a man's attire for Madame, since she is so very much at home in it."

"You are right, my man," rejoined Madame lightly. "I was perfectly at home in my son's breeches, and I shall never cease to regret that Jacques de Romaine must remain now as he is—vanished or dead—for as long as I live."

The two men then took their leave, and the ladies proceeded to select suitable disguises. Silently and methodically they proceeded in their task, Mariette de Romaine making herself look as like a labourer's wench as she could, whilst Mme. la Comtesse slipped into a rough garb of coat and breeches with the ease born of constant habit. Her short dark hair she tied into a knot at the nape of her neck and placed a shabby three-cornered hat jauntily upon it. Her broad, unfeminine figure, her somewhat hard-marked features and firm mouth and chin made her look a handsome and dashing cavalier.

When a few moments later the sound of voices in the hall proclaimed the return of the men, Mme. la Comtesse was standing expectant and triumphant facing the door, ready for adventure as she had always been, a light of daring and of recklessness in her eyes, love of intrigue and of tortuous paths, of dark conspiracies and even of unavowable crimes glowing in her heart—all for the sake of a King whom France with one voice had ejected from her shores, and a régime which the whole of France abhorred.

The door was opened: a woman's cry of joy and astonishment rang out.

"Why, Jacques, you young scamp!" exclaimed Mademoiselle Philippa, who, dressed in a brilliant dark green silk, with feathered hat and well-rouged cheeks, was standing under the lintel of the narrow door like a being from another world. "Where have you been hiding all this while?"

But her cry of mingled pleasure and petulance had already been followed by a double cry of terror. Mme. la Comtesse, white now to the lips, had fallen back against the table, to which she clung, whilst Mariette de Romaine, wide-eyed like a tracked beast at bay, was gazing in horror straight before her, where, behind Philippa's flaring skirts, appeared the stern, colourless face of a small man in a grey coat.

"It was for the mean spies of that Corsican Upstart," she exclaimed with passionate indignation, "to have devised such an abominable trick."

Already the Man in Grey had entered the room. Behind him, in the dark, narrow hall, could be seen vaguely the silhouettes of three or four men in plain clothes.

"Trick for trick, Mademoiselle, and disguise for disguise," said the secret agent quietly. "I prefer mine to the one which deceived and defrauded Mademoiselle Philippa here of close on a million francs' worth of jewels."

"A trick?" exclaimed the dancer, who was looking the picture of utter confusion and bewilderment. "My jewels?—I don't understand——"

"Madame la Comtesse de Romaine, otherwise Jacques, your fiancé and admirer, Mademoiselle, has time to explain. The private coach which will convey her to Rennes will not be here for half an hour. In the meanwhile," he added, as he took up the parcel of jewels which still lay upon the table, "you will find these at the commissariat of police whenever you care to call for them. Monsieur Cognard will have the privilege of returning them to you."

But Mademoiselle Philippa was far too much upset to wait for explanations. At the invitation of the Minister's accredited agent, she had followed him hither, for he had told her that she would see Jacques de Romaine once more. The disappointment and mingled horror and excitement when she realised what an amazing trick had been played upon her literally swept her off her nimble feet. It was a month or more before she was well enough to fulfil her outstanding engagements.

The de Romaines—mother and daughter—offered no resistance. Indeed, resistance would have been futile, and theirs was not the temperament to allow of hysterics or undignified protestations. Every courtesy was shown to them on their way to Rennes, where they were tried and condemned to five years' imprisonment. But twelve months later the Imperial clemency was exercised in their favour, and they were released; after the Restoration they were handsomely rewarded for their zeal in the service of the King.

The Comte Jacques de Romaine, who, as a little lad, had been taken over to England, never came to France till after Waterloo had been fought and won. At the time that his mother impersonated him so daringly and with such sinister results, he was serving in the Prussian Army. Mariette de Romaine subsequently married the Vicomte de Saint-Vaast. She and her husband emigrated with Charles X. in 1830, and their son married an Englishwoman, and died in a house at Hampstead in the early 'seventies.

<h2 style="text-align:center">V</h2>

THE BOURBON PRINCE

"I DON'T see how I can be of any assistance to you, my good Monsieur Moulin. I quite agree with you that it would be a real calamity if a member of the ex-Royal family were to effect a landing in our province, but——" And Monseigneur the Constitutional Bishop of Alençon shrugged his shoulders in token of his inability to deal with the matter.

He was sitting in a small room of his splendid private château, which was situated near Granville. Through the tall window on his left, the magnificent panorama of the rugged coast of Normandy and of the turbulent English Channel beyond was displayed in its limitless glory.

The point of Carolles still gleamed beneath the last rays of the cold, wintry sun, but the jagged Dog's Tooth rocks were already wrapped in twilight gloom.

"And it is for our people themselves to realise," continued Monseigneur, with his slow, somewhat pompous delivery, "how much happier they would be if they discarded for ever their misguided allegiance to those degenerate Bourbons, and became law-abiding citizens like the rest of France."

"They'll have no chance to do that," growled the préfet moodily, "once we get one of those Bourbons sowing rebellion and discontent all over the place. The landing of the Comte d'Artois must be prevented at all costs or we shall have the devil to pay. Those Chouans have been difficult enough to deal with, God knows, but hitherto their want of organisation, their lack of responsible leadership and of co-ordination have been our salvation. With the Comte d'Artois at their head, and a deal of fictitious enthusiasm aroused by him for the exiled Royal family over the water, we shall have bloodshed, misery, and civil war rife again in this corner of France."

"Monsieur le Ministre," rejoined Monseigneur blandly, "has plenty of spies here. Surely, even if the Comte d'Artois effect a landing, he cannot escape capture at the hands of your well-organised police. His death within your circuit, my dear préfet, would be a fine feather in your cap."

"Oh, we don't want another martyred Bourbon just yet!" retorted the préfet gruffly. "He'd better die in England, or on the high seas rather than in this part of Normandy. We should be accused of murdering him."

M. le Préfet was distinctly perturbed and irritable. A denunciation from some anonymous quarter had reached him that morning; a number of rough fellows—marauding Chouans—had, it appeared, halted at a wayside inn somewhere on the Caën road, and openly boasted that M. le Comte d'Artois, own brother to His Majesty the King, was about to land on the shores of France, and that a numerous and enthusisatic army was already prepared to rally round his flag, and to sweep the upstart Emperor from his throne and all the myrmidons of the mushroom Empire from their comfortable seats.

The Bishop had listened to the story of the anonymous denunciation and to the préfet's wails of woe most suavely and untiringly for close upon an hour. But he was at last showing signs of growing impatience.

"I think, my dear Monsieur Moulin," he said with some acerbity, "you must yourself admit that this affair in no way concerns me. Granville is not even my official residence. I came here for a much-needed rest and, though my support and advice are always at your disposal, I really must leave you and the chief commissary of police to deal with these Chouans as best you can, and with any Bourbon prince who thinks of paying France an unwelcome visit."

He put up his delicate, beringed hand to his mouth, politely smothering a yawn. He appeared absent and thoughtful all of a sudden, bored no doubt by the fussy man's volubility. He was gazing out of the window, seemingly in rapt contemplation of the beautiful picture before him—the setting sun over the Channel, the gorgeous coast scenery, the glowing splendour of the winter twilight.

The préfet considered that he was dismissed. The respect he felt for Monseigneur warred with his latent irritability.

"I won't intrude any longer," he said ruefully, as he prepared to go.

The Bishop, much relieved, became at once more affable.

"I wish I could be of service to you," he said benignly; "but from what I hear you have a very able man at your elbow in the newly accredited agent of His Majesty's Minister. The préfet of Alençon has spoken very highly about him to me, and though he was unsuccessful in the matter of the burglary in my Palace at Alençon last October, I believe he has rendered very able assistance to the chief commissary of police in bringing some of those redoubtable Chouans to justice."

"He may have done that," quoth the préfet dryly, "but I have not much faith in the little grey fellow myself. The problem confronting us here is a deeper one than he can tackle."

A few minutes later the préfet had finally bowed himself out of Monseigneur's presence.

The Bishop remained seated at his desk, absorbed and almost motionless, for some time after his visitor had departed. He appeared to be still wrapped up in the contemplation of the sunset. The hurried footsteps of the préfet resounded on the great flagged hall below; there had been the usual commotion attendant on the departure of a guest: lackeys opening and closing the entrance doors, a call for M. le Préfet's horse, the clatter of hoofs upon the stone-paved court-yard, then nothing more.

The dignified quietude of a well-ordered, richly appointed household again reigned in the sumptuous château. After a while, as the shades of evening drew in, a footman entered with a lighted lamp, which he set upon the table. But still Monseigneur waited, until through the tall window by his side there appeared nothing but an impenetrable veil of blackness. Then he rose, carefully re-adjusted the crimson shade over the lamp, and threw a couple of logs upon the cheerful fire. He went up to the window and opened it, and, stepping out on to the terrace, peered intently into the night.

The north-westerly wind was soughing through the trees of the park, and not half a kilometre away the breakers were roaring against the Dog's Tooth rocks;

but, even through these manifold sounds, Monseigneur's keen ear had detected a soft and furtive footfall upon the terrace steps. The next moment a man emerged out of the gloom. Breathless and panting, he ran rapidly across the intervening fore-court and, almost colliding with the Bishop, staggered and fell forward into the room.

Monseigneur received him in his arms, and with a swiftly murmured, "Thank God!" led him to a chair beside the hearth. Then he closed the window, drew the heavy damask curtains closely together, and finally came up to the new-comer who, shivering with cold and terror, wet to the skin and scant of breath, was stooping to the fire, trying to infuse warmth into his numbed fingers.

"Someone is on my track," were the first words which fell from his quivering lips.

He was a man verging on middle age, short and stout of build, with a white, flabby skin and prominent, weak-looking eyes. His clothes had almost been torn off his back by the frolic of the gale; he was hatless, and his hair, matted and dank, clung to his moist forehead.

The Bishop had remained standing

before him in an attitude of profound respect. "Will your Highness deign to come up to my room?" he said. "Dry clothes and a warm bath have been prepared."

"I'll go in a moment," replied His Highness. He had still some difficulty in recovering his breath, and spoke irritably like a wayward sick child. "But let me tell you at once that our movements have been watched from the moment that we set foot on these shores. The crossing was very rough. The gale is raging furiously. The skipper has put into Avranches. He dropped me at the Goat's Creek and left me there with de Verthamont and du Roy. As soon as we started to come hither we realised that there was someone on our track. We consulted together and decided that it would be best to separate. De Verthamont went one way and du Roy another, and I ran all the way here."

"Was your Highness shadowed after that?" asked the Bishop.

"I think not. I heard no one. But then the wind kept up an incessant din."

"And did Sébastian meet your Highness?"

"Yes! In the Devil's Bowl. He followed

me at a distance as far as your gates. He thought that he, too, had been shadowed all day. Early this morning he reconnoitred as far as Coutances, and there he heard that a couple of regiments of cavalry and a battery of artillery had arrived from St. Lô."

The Bishop made no further comment. His enthusiasm and excitement of a moment ago appeared to have fallen away from him; his finely chiselled face had become serene and pale; only in his deep-set eyes there seemed to smoulder a dull fire, as if with the prescience of impending doom.

A moment or two later he persuaded the Comte d'Artois to come up to his own private apartments. Here a warm bath, dry clothes and a well-cooked supper restored to the unfortunate Prince a certain measure of courage.

"What's to be done?" he asked with a querulous tone in his hoarse voice.

"For the moment," replied the Bishop earnestly, "I would respectfully beg of your Highness to remain in these apartments, which have the infinite advantage of a secret hiding-place which no police agent will ever discover."

"A hiding-place?" muttered the Prince petulantly. "I loathe the very idea of lurking behind dusty panels like a sick fox."

The Bishop did not venture on a reply. He went up to the fine mantelpiece at the opposite end of the room, and his hand wandered over the elaborate carving which adorned the high wainscoting. He pressed with one finger on a portion of the carving, and at once some of the wood-work moved silently upon unseen hinges, and disclosed a cavity large enough for a man to pass through.

"It would only be an hour or so at a time, your Highness," he said with respectful apology; "in case a posse of police makes a descent upon the house."

He explained to his august visitor the mechanism of the secret panel. M. le Comte d'Artois, weary after a long sea journey, fretful and irritable, kept up a constant stream of mutterings *sotto voce*.

"You and the party wished me to come. I never thought that it would be safe, and if I have to remain in hiding in this rat hole, I might just as well be sitting comfortably in England."

Monseigneur, however, never departed

for a moment from his attitude of almost reverential deference. With his own hands he ministered to every bodily comfort of the exalted personage who had found refuge under his roof, and only left him when he saw the Prince comfortably stretched out upon the bed, and was fully assured that he understood the working of the secret panel.

Then after a deep obeisance he finally bowed himself out of the room. Slowly he descended the dimly-lighted stairs which led to his study on the floor below. The pallor of his face appeared more marked than before. A vague feeling of anxiety, not unmixed with disappointment, caused a deep frown to settle between his brows.

The situation, though tense always, had become well-nigh desperate now. With M. le Comte d'Artois under his roof and his movements known to a spy of the Imperial Police, every hour, every minute, had become fraught with deadly danger, not only to him but to every one of his adherents.

Hundreds of men and women around the neighbourhood at this hour were preparing to meet the Prince—the brother of their uncrowned King—for whose sake they were willing to risk their lives. One false move, one act of cowardice or carelessness, and the death of a Bourbon prince would once more sully the honour of France, whilst countless adherents of the Royal cause would again fall victims to their hot-headed loyalty.

But as the Bishop re-entered his study he gave a short bitter sigh, for memory had swiftly conjured up the vision of that un-heroic figure which slept contentedly in the room above, and on whose energy and courage depended the lives of those who still believed in him, and who saw in him only the ideal of a monarchy, the traditions of old France and of the glorious days that were gone.

Monseigneur, on entering the study, saw a man standing there waiting for him.

"Sébastien!" he exclaimed eagerly.

The man had the bearing and ap-pearance of a good-class domestic servant—one of those who enjoy many privileges as well as the confidence of their employer. But to a keen psychologist it would soon become obvious that the sombre, well-cut clothes and stiff, con-ventional demeanour cloaked a more vigorous and more individual personality. The face appeared rugged even beneath the solid mask, and the eyes had a keen, searching, at times furtive, expression in them. They were the eyes of a man accustomed to feel danger dogging his footsteps, to hold his life in his own hands, and to take risks which would make the pusillanimous quake.

"How long have you been here?" asked the Bishop quickly.

"Half an hour, Monseigneur. I did not dare follow His Highness too closely. The town and its neighbourhood are bristling with spies. I have had the greatest difficulty throughout the day in giving at least two prowlers the slip and drawing them off His Highness's tracks."

Monseigneur uttered an exclamation of horror.

"I thought I had one at my heels a moment ago," continued Sébastien; "just inside the gates. Someone, I felt, was dogging my footsteps. I fired a random shot into the night, and as luck would have it, I brought down my man."

"Brought down your man?" exclaimed Monseigneur eagerly. "Then——"

"Unfortunately it was not a police spy

whom I shot," said Sébastien carelessly, "but Grand-Cerf, one of your keepers."

Monseigneur gave a cry of dismay.

"Grand-Cerf! I had posted him just inside the gates to watch for possible prowlers."

"I didn't know that, and I shot him," repeated Sébastien grimly.

"You killed him?"

Sébastien nodded. The matter did not appear to him to have any importance.

"Now if it had been that accursed spy——" he murmured. Then he added more earnestly: "You will have a posse of police over from Granville to-morrow, Monseigneur—they'll search this house. Somehow or other someone has got wind of the affair—I'd stake my life on it."

"Let them come," retorted the Bishop shortly. "Monsieur le Comte d'Artois will be safe behind the secret panel."

Sébastien shrugged his shoulders.

"For half an hour, yes! But if, as I believe, it is that confounded grey chap from Paris who has shadowed us, then no hiding-place or secret panel will screen us from his prying eyes. It is he who tracked down the Spaniard last November, who laid Monsieur de Saint-Tropéze low, who

227

thwarted Mademoiselle Vaillant. Oh!"
added the old Chouan, "if I only had him
here between my hands——"

His powerful fingers twitched convulsively. Monseigneur shrugged his
shoulders.

"That miserable little Man in Grey," he
said dryly, "has had the luck so far, I own,
but it was because his wits were only
opposed to brute force. Monsieur de
Saint-Tropèze was clumsy, the Spaniard
reckless, the girl Vaillant hysterical. Now
we have to defend Monsieur le Comte
d'Artois himself—but not with our lives,
my good Sébastien—'tis our wits which
are going to win the day, right under the
very nose of the Man in Grey."

An hour or two later, in a small dingy
room in one of the most squalid portions
of the town, the accredited agent of His
Imperial Majesty's Minister of Police was
hastily demolishing the remnants of a
meagre cold supper. He appeared foot-
sore and cold. M. Moulin, préfet of St. Lô,
sat opposite to him at the table. He seemed
gravely agitated and anxious.

"We have done all we really could,
Monsieur Fernand," he said fretfully,

"with the material at our command. Monsieur le Duc d'Otrante's spies have been very active, and I don't think that we have any cause to complain of the results."

"Well, let's hear the results," said the Man in Grey curtly.

A sharp retort hovered on the préfet's tongue. He did not like the dictatorial ways of this emissary from Paris, and had it not been for M. le Duc d'Otrante's express orders, the Minister's secret agent would have fared ill at the hands of this hidebound official.

"There has been," he resumed with some bitterness, "great activity among the Chouans that are known to us in this neighbourhood. Our spies have discovered that the Comte d'Artois landed on this coast in the early dawn this morning. Unfortunately, they cannot be everywhere, and up to half an hour ago we had found no trace of him that we can rely on; at the same time we have intercepted a letter——"

"Pshaw!" ejaculated the Man in Grey impatiently. "And did your spies inform you by any chance that three strangers were landed by the brig *Delphine* in the Goat's Creek at dawn this morning?"

"Our informant did not say," remarked the préfet dryly.

"I dare say not," rejoined the Man in Grey. "Nor did he tell you, perhaps, that the three strangers were met at the Devil's Bowl by Sébastien, who is, if I mistake not, confidential valet to the Constitutional Bishop of Alençon."

"That is false!" broke in M. le Préfet emphatically. "The loyalty of Monseigneur is beyond question."

"Perhaps," retorted the other with a grim smile. "At any rate, Sébastien guided the three strangers through intricate passes among the cliffs as far as the Dog's Tooth. Here the party separated: one man went one way, another the other. Sébastien and one of the strangers waited about the cliffs until dusk, then they made their way along as far as the outskirts of Monseigneur's property——"

"I protest!" ejaculated the préfet hotly.

But the Man in Grey put up his slender hand with a commanding gesture.

"One moment, I beg," he said quietly. "The stranger lurked about on the outskirts of the park until it was quite dark, then he slipped in through the gates, with Sébastien close at his heels. The gates were at once drawn to and closed. The stranger disappeared in the night. A few minutes later the report of a musket rang out through the darkness, then the soughing of the gale drowned every other sound."

"Some thief," exclaimed the préfet gruffly, "lurking round the château. No doubt Sébastien suspected him, dogged his footsteps and shot him. It is all as clear as daylight——"

"So clear, indeed," observed the Man in Grey calmly, "that you, Monsieur le Préfet, will at once communicate with the chief commissary of police. I want a squadron of mounted men to surround Monseigneur's château and a vigorous search made both inside and outside the house."

"What! Now?" gasped M. Moulin.

"Yes; now!"

"But it is past ten o'clock!" he protested.

"A better hour could not be found."

"But Monseigneur will look upon this as an insult!" exclaimed the préfet, who was deadly pale with agitation.

"For which we'll apologise if we have wronged him," retorted the secret agent quietly. "Stay!" he added, after a moment's reflection. "I pray you at the same time to tell Monsieur le Commissaire that I shall require a closed barouche, with a strong pair of horses and a mounted guard of half a dozen men, to be ready for me in the stable-yard of Monseigneur's château. Is that understood?"

It was. To have even thought of disobedience would have been madness. The very way in which the Man in Grey uttered his "I pray you" sent a cold shiver down M. Moulin's spine, and he still had in the inner pocket of his coat the letter written in the all-powerful Minister's own hand. In this letter M. le Duc d'Otrante gave orders that his agent was to be obeyed—blindly, implicitly, unquestioningly—whatever he might command, whomsoever he might bid to execute his orders. One look in that pale, colourless face sufficed to show that he knew the power which had been placed in his hands and would use it to punish those who strove to defy his might.

M. Fantin, commissary of police of Granville, was preparing to execute the agent's orders as transmitted by the préfet. The whole matter was unutterably distasteful to him. Monseigneur the Constitutional Bishop of Alençon was a prelate of such high integrity and proven loyalty, that to put such an insult upon him was, in the opinion of the commissary, nothing short of an outrage. He was pacing up and down the uncarpeted floor of his office in a state of great agitation. In a corner of the room, beside the small iron stove, sat the secret agent of His Majesty's Minister. Calm, unperturbed by the mutterings of the commissary, he only exhibited a slight sign of impatience when he glanced at the clock and noted the rapid flight of time. The squadron of mounted police requisitioned by him was making ready to get to horse. It was then close on eleven o'clock.

A moment later one of the police sergeants entered the office with the news that a mounted courier had just arrived from the château, with a message from Monseigneur to the commissary of police.

"I'll see him at once," said the latter, half hoping that this fresh incident would even now prevent the abominable insult to the Bishop.

"What is it, Gustave?" he asked, for he knew the man as one of the grooms in Monseigneur's service.

"An attempt at impudent robbery, Monsieur le Commissaire," replied the man, "which has resulted in a man's death. Monseigneur has sent me over to notify you at once and to ask what he should do in the matter."

M. Fantin threw a look of triumph at the little figure in grey that sat huddled beside the iron stove. The commissary had also advanced the theory of an attempted burglary at the château, and was highly elated to see his deductions justified.

"A robbery?" he exclaimed. "How? When?"

"An hour or two ago, Monsieur le Commissaire," replied Gustave. "Monseigneur will explain. I know nothing of the details except that the rascal overturned a lamp. He was burned to death and nearly set fire to the château. I was sent hither post-haste to see Monsieur le Commissaire——"

"Very good," rejoined the commissary. "Ride straight back to the château and tell Monseigneur that I will be there anon."

As soon as the man had gone, M. Fantin turned complacently to the Man in Grey.

"As you see, my dear Monsieur Fernand," he began, "there is no need to——"

"As your squadron is ready, Monsieur le Commissaire," quoth the agent quietly, "'twere a pity not to give them the exercise. And remember the barouche," he added sharply, "and the mounted guard. Do not on any account leave them behind. My orders are in no way modified."

The commissary swallowed the retort which was hovering on his lips; but he threw a look that was almost vicious at the meagre grey-clad figure.

"Do you accompany us?" he asked with a sneer.

"I will meet you at the château," replied the secret agent simply.

Half an hour later Monseigneur was making the commissary of police welcome at the château. He appeared more upset than he cared to admit by the tragedy enacted inside his house. He was not a young man, and his nerves were severely shaken. When his visitors entered, he was sitting in a large armchair beside the fire in his bedroom; he had a glass in his hand, half filled with some sweet-smelling restorative. One of his male servants was in attendance upon him, bathing his master's forehead with vinegar and water.

Preceded by Sébastien and accompanied by the secret agent and two men of the police, M. Fantin then went to view the scene of the tragedy. The two men remained on guard outside the dining-room, where the drama had taken place. The room still presented a disordered appearance; nothing had been touched, Sébastien declared, in view of M. le Commissaire's visit. But the lamp which hung from the ceiling had been lighted, and by its light the whole extent of what might have been a measureless disaster was revealed to M. Fantin's horrified gaze.

In the centre of the room on the floor, close to the large dining-table, there lay a shapeless mass, obviously a human body, charred beyond identification. Only the lower part, the heavy cloth breeches and high leather boots, though badly scorched, were still recognisable. Beside the body, the rich damask table-cloth lay in a burned and tangled heap, where the wretched man had dragged it down in his fall; and a foot or so away was the heavy lamp which had caused the conflagration. It was lying on its side, with bowl, shade and chimney broken, just as it had rolled out of the man's hand. A narrow streak of oil ran from it to the end of the mantel-kerb. The rich Oriental carpet was burned in several places, and the table itself was severely scorched, while heat and smoke had begun their work of destruction everywhere on the priceless furniture, until water had rendered their work complete.

Sébastien's account of the tragedy was brief and clear. He had had his suspicions aroused during the day by seeing an ill-clad ruffian sneaking around the park gates, and in the evening, feeling anxious, he made a special tour of the château to see that everything was safe. On entering the dining-room he saw a man standing beside the open window, through which he had evidently just made his way. He—Sébastien—at once drew his pistol, and the man turned to fly; but the aim was good and the man appeared to be hit. He gave a snarl like a wild animal, sprang back into the room, apparently with a view to throwing himself upon his assailant, when his strength failed him. With one hand he clutched at the table, but he tottered and fell, dragging with him both the cloth and the table-lamp, which came down with a crash on the top of him, scattering the oil all over his body. His clothing at once caught fire, and Sébastien, realising the danger to the entire house, instantly ran for the buckets of water, which were always kept in the passage for the purpose, and shouted for assistance.

Within a few moments he and another lackey got the fire under control, and no great harm was done, save the shock to Monseigneur's nerves, damage to valuable furniture and the complete obliteration of the felon's identity.

The commissary of police asked Sébastien a few questions for form's sake. He also took some perfunctory notes. He felt irritable and gravely annoyed with the secret agent for having placed him in such an awkward position with regard to Monseigneur.

"A squadron of police to investigate a common attempt at burglary," he growled savagely, as Sébastien was showing him out of the room. "We shall be the laughing-stock of the countryside!"

Sébastien laughed.

"'Tis the Chouans who will be pleased, Monsieur le Commissaire," he said. "They have you safely occupied to-night and can go about their nefarious business un-molested, I am thinking."

The Man in Grey was about to follow, but turned for a moment on his heel.

"By the way, my good Sébastien," he said, "at what time did the tragedy take place which you have so graphically des-cribed to us?"

For a second or two Sébastien appeared to hesitate.

"Oh," he replied, "somewhere about six or seven o'clock, Monsieur. I couldn't say exactly."

"What made you wait so long, then, before you sent to Monsieur le Commissaire?"

"There was a little confusion in the house, Monsieur will understand. Mon-seigneur had given orders at once to send a courier over, but the grooms were at their supper, and it took a little time—we meant to send at once—the delay was unintentional."

"I am sure it was," broke in the com-missary, who was still within earshot. "And now, Monsieur Fernand," he added, "I pray you excuse me. The hour is getting late, and I must make my apologies to Monseigneur."

"One moment, Monsieur le Commissaire," rejoined the Man in Gey. "Will you not at least question the other servants who came to Monsieur Sébastien's assistance?"

"No one came to my assistance," Sébastien assured him. "The whole affair was over in a moment."

"But when the shot was fired——"

"By the time some of the domestics arrived upon the scene I had put out the fire. Then I locked the dining-room door. I knew Monsieur le Commissaire would not wish anything touched."

"Quite right—quite right!" said M. Fantin. "Now, Monsieur Fernand, will you come?"

"One moment, Monsieur le Commissaire," said the secret agent, and suddenly his whole manner changed to one of commanding authority. "There will be plenty of time for excuses presently. For the nonce you will order your captain to make a thorough search of this château and of the grounds around. You will question everyone of the domestics; and remember that I shall be about somewhere—probably unseen—but present, nevertheless, to see that the

240

investigation is minute and thorough. Sébastien will remain in the meanwhile in the custody of these two men here, until I have need of him again."

"By Heaven!" protested the commissary roughly.

"By Heaven!" retorted the Man in Grey loudly, "you'll obey my orders now, Monsieur le Commissaire, or I shall send you straight to Monsieur le Ministre to report upon your own misconduct!"

M. Fantin, at the threat and at the manner in which it was uttered, became as white as a sheet. But he obeyed—at once and without another word. Sébastien's rugged face had shown no sign of emotion as, at a curt word from the secret agent, the two men of the police closed up, one on each side, and marched him into an adjoining room.

The commissary had taken the threat of the Minister's all-powerful agent very much to heart. His men searched the château through and through, just as if it had been the stronghold of some irreconcilable rebel. The secret agent himself appeared and disappeared, while the search was going on, like some grey will-o'-the-wisp—now in one room, now in another, now in a passage, now half-way upstairs, just where least expected. The search took over three hours. During that time Monseigneur himself sat in his room in front of the fire, the very picture of silent and offended dignity. He listened—motionless and dignified—to the commissary's profuse apologies, only now and then accepting the ministrations of the lackey who remained with him throughout, bathing his forehead with vinegar, or mixing a fresh glass of orange-flower water. Of the grey-clad figure which flitted unceremoniously in and out of his private apartments, he took no more notice than if he were a fly.

When presently the police actually invaded his own bedroom, Mon-seigneur's attitude remained one of un-approachable reserve. Even when the agent passed his hands over the wainscoting and presently found the button that worked the secret spring, Monseigneur showed neither interest nor emotion. The hiding-place itself was found to be empty; the Man in Grey walked into it and out again, in a matter-of-fact, impassive manner, as if he were performing a mechanical and useless job.

Neither here nor inside the house, nor in the grounds, nor in any other hiding-place was anyone or anything found to impeach Monseigneur's well-known loyalty.

The unfortunate commissary was covered with confusion. He would gladly have strangled the meddlesome official who had placed him in such an awkward position, or even have relieved his feelings by hurling anathema upon him. But the secret agent appeared indifferent both to the wrath of M. Fantin and to the silent disapprobation of the Bishop. When he was satisfied the search was done, and well done, he took his leave, but not before.

Monseigneur did not vouchsafe him even a look. But he was quite affable with M. le Commissaire, when the latter finally was allowed to depart.

"Have you any further orders, Monsieur Fernand?" queried M. Fantin with bitter sarcasm, when he had bowed his way out of the presence of the outraged prelate.

"Yes," replied the other; "but I will give them to you outside. And stay," he added as the commissary turned on his heel, silent with pent-up rage, "take Sébastien with you and keep him at the commissariat until further orders."

No chronicler could make a faithful record of all that M. Fantin said to himself and to his sergeant even whilst he executed these orders punctually. Fortunately for his feelings on the way home, the Man in Grey did not elect to accompany him. After he had given his final orders he disappeared in the darkness, and M. Fantin was only too thankful to be rid of that unpleasant presence.

In and around the château again reigned that perfect silence and orderliness which pertain to an aristocratic household. The squadron of police had long since departed: even the sound of their horses' hoofs, the clang of metal and rattle of swords and muskets had ceased to echo through the night. For a little while longer soft murmurings and stealthy movements were still heard inside the house as the servants went to bed, and, whilst they undressed, indulged in comments and surmises about the curious happenings of the night. Then, even these sounds were stilled. Monseigneur, however, did not go to bed. He had risen from the armchair, and in it he had installed the man who for several hours had been diligently ministering to him with vinegar and orange-flower water.

"Your Highness is none the worse for the experience, I trust," he said, as he stopped and threw a log or two into the blaze.

"Tired and anxious," replied the Comte d'Artois querulously.

"A night's rest will soon restore your Royal Highness," rejoined the Bishop with deep respect.

"It was a dangerous game to play," continued the prince peevishly. "At any moment one of those men might have suspected."

"It was the only possible game to play, your Royal Highness," rejoined the Bishop earnestly. "The moment those spies were on your track and mine, the search was bound to follow. Think if the police had come whilst you were in hiding in this room or even behind the secret panel! Nay! 'twas a mercy Sébastien shot Grand-Cerf in mistake for a spy. It enabled us to invent that marvellous comedy which so effectually hoodwinked not only the police but even that astute agent of the Minister himself. And now,"

245

added Monseigneur, as a deep sigh of exultation and triumph rose from his breast, "we can work with a free hand. After to-night's work, this house will never again be suspected. We can make it the headquarters of your Highness's staff. It shall be the stepping-stone to your royal brother's reconquered throne."

The words were scarcely out of his mouth when, in an instant, he paused, his whole attitude one of rigid and terror-filled expectancy. Loud and firm foot-steps had resounded upon the flagged terrace, though muffled by the heavy damask curtain which hung before the window. A second or two later the foot-steps halted, the mullion was struck with something that clanked, and a voice called out loudly and peremptorily:

"Open, in the name of the law!"

The Comte d'Artois had smothered a cry of horror. He clung to his chair with hands that trembled as if with ague, his face became deathly white, and he stared with wild, wide-open eyes in the direction of the window, whence that peremptory call had come. He was in a state of acute physical terror bordering on collapse. Monseigneur, however, had not lost his presence of mind: "Quick, the secret panel!" he said, and already the slender hand was manipulating the hidden spring. The Comte d'Artois tottered to his feet; the next moment there was a terrific crash of broken glass, the damask curtain was roughly torn aside, and the agent stepped into the room.

"Resistance were futile, Monseigneur," he said quietly, for with a rapid movement the Bishop had reached the bell-pull. "I have half a squadron of police outside, and six men at my heels."

The Man in Grey came farther into the room, and as he did so he called to two of his men to stand beside Monseigneur. Then he turned to Monsieur le Comte d'Artois:

"I have a barouche and a mounted guard ready to convey your Highness to Avranches, where the brig Delphine with her new skipper is at your disposal for an immediate return trip to England. His Majesty the Emperor deprecates revenge and bloodshed. He might punish, but he prefers to put the culprit out of the way. If Monsieur le Comte d'Artois will offer no resistance, every respect will be shown to his person."

Resistance would, indeed, have been worse than uselsss. Even Monseigneur replied to His Highness's look of appeal with one of resignation. He picked up a mantle which lay upon the bed and silently put it round the Prince's shoulders, then he took the hand which His Highness held out to him and kissed it fervently. Half a dozen men closed in around the Prince, and the latter walked with a firm step over the threshold of the window, his footsteps and those of his escort soon ceasing to echo through the night.

"You have won, Monsieur," said the Bishop coldly, when he found himself alone with the Man in Grey. "I am in your hands."

"Did I not say, Monseigneur, that His Majesty deprecated revenge?" said the secret agent quietly. "You have an estate in the South, a château finer than this one, so I'm told. You are free to go thither for an indefinite period, for the benefit of your health."

"Exile!" said the Bishop bitterly.

"Do you not deserve worse?" retorted the Man in Grey coldly.

"I nearly outwitted you, though," exclaimed the Bishop.

"Very nearly, I admit. Unfortunately for your clever comedy, I happened to know that your valet Sébastien shot a man just outside your gates early in the afternoon. When he told me the elaborate story of the attempted burglary I knew that he lied and, with that knowledge, I was able to destroy the whole fabric of your machinations. As you see, I bided my time. And the moment that you, thinking that you were alone with the Comte d'Artois, threw down your mask I was ready to strike. Let me bid you farewell, Monseigneur," he added in conclusion, and without a touch of irony. "You can have twenty-four hours to prepare for your journey south, and you will remain in your château there awaiting His Majesty's pleasure."

The next moment the Man in Grey was gone, even as the Bishop's parting words struck upon his unheeding :

"Awaiting the return of His Majesty Louis XVIII., by the Grace of God, King of France," Monseigneur called out at the top of his voice.

VI

THE MYSTERY OF A WOMAN'S HEART

THE letter dropped from Mme. de Plélan's thin, white hand. She looked across at her daughter with eyes full of tears.

"And now that Monseigneur has gone," she said mournfully, "I feel as if I had lost the very mainstay of our valient little party."

The girl sighed, somewhat impatiently.

"Monseigneur," she said, "would be the first to bid you smother your regrets for the past, maman, and to concentrate your thoughts on the dangers that still lie ahead."

She was busy at a desk that stood open before her, glancing at a number of papers, classifying some, throwing a great number into the fire which crackled cheerfully in the hearth, whilst others she tied together and put into a small tin box that stood close to her hand.

"It was kind and gracious of Monseigneur," continued Madame la Marquise dolefully, "to think of sending me a courier when he must have been so busy with his preparations for his sudden departure. Oh, that departure!" she added, as once again tears of wrath as well as of sorrow welled up to her eyes, "The shame of it. The humiliation as well as the bitter, bitter disappointment!"

Constance de Plélan made no comment this time on her mother's lamentations. She had apparently completed the work on which she had been engaged, for now she rose, closed the desk, and locking the small tin box with a key which she selected from a bunch at her belt she took it up under her arm. Then she turned to her mother:

"Will you tell me, maman," she said, "just what Monseigneur says in his letter?"

Constance stood there in the grey light of the winter afternoon, with the flicker of the firelight playing on her tall, graceful figure, her arm extended, holding the metal box, her small head carried with the stately dignity of a goddess.

"Those devils will be here directly," continued the girl; and as she spoke the delicate lines of her face were distorted by an expression of intense and passionate hatred. "But we are ready for them. I have only this box to put away in its usual hiding-place—after which, let them come!"

Mme. de Plélan again took up the letter, the perusal of which had caused her so much sorrow. It had arrived by courier a few minutes ago; now, at her daughter's request, she began to read it aloud.

"This is what Monseigneur the Bishop writes," she said. "'My dear friend, immediately on receipt of this missive, set to work at once to destroy any compromising papers you may have in the house. I have no doubt that the posse of police which has just ransacked my place will pay you a visit also. My friendship for you is well known, and your name may appear in one or two of the letters which those brutes have confiscated. Alas! the landing of Monsieur le Comte d'Artois on these shores has ended in disaster. The spies of the Corsican Upstart were on his track from the first. They followed His Royal Highness to my palace, kidnapped him as if he were a bale of goods and shipped him straight back to England. My life and liberty are, it seems, to be spared, but I have been ordered into exile at my château in the Dauphiné, God guard and preserve you all! We must wait

252

for happier times!' "

Constance said nothing for a moment or two. She stood staring into the fire, her lips tightly pressed together.

"And all," she mused after a while, speaking slowly and dreamily, "through the machinations of that extraordinary man, who is said to be a secret agent of Bonaparte's most powerful Minister."

"A man without a name!" added the Marquise, bitter scorn ringing through every word she spoke, "A meagre, insignificant creature, grey and colourless as his coat."

"But clever—and relentless!" said the girl. "That Man in Grey is killing our hopes one by one."

"I loathe the brute!" ejaculated Madame fervently.

"Monsieur de Saint-Tropèze is dead," continued Constance in the same dreary, monotonous voice. "The Spaniard is a prisoner; Marie Vaillant a failure; Monseigneur an exile; and still that Man in Grey is allowed to live. Oh, it is monstrous!" she said, her whole body suddenly quivering with passion. "Monstrous and cowardly! Are there no men amongst us who will rid the King of such a pestilential foe?"

Mme. de Plélan started as if she had been struck. She stared at her daughter, trying to fathom all that was going on behind that smooth young brow and within the depths of those passion-filled eyes.

"You mean——?" she murmured.

The girl nodded. "Why not?" she retorted quite calmly.

"Oh, if we could!" replied Madame. "But he is so cautious, so wary—and lately he has always had two or three spies at his heels."

"There are ways——"

"Oh, as to that, there are a number of our own men who would willingly take every risk in order to rid us of the brute. But in cases of that kind," she added slowly, "failure always means such terrible reprisals—the death of two or three more of our leaders on the guillotine—and we can ill spare them just now."

"I did not mean anything so clumsy," explained Constance quietly. "An attempted murder from behind a hedge is, as you say, foredoomed to failure. From what one knows of the Man in Grey he is not likely to fall a victim to such an artless trap."

"Then what did you mean, Constance?" asked Madame coldly.

"Men have been decoyed before now," replied the girl, as she looked her mother straight between the eyes "and have of their own will walked into traps from which there was no escape. The man in the grey coat may be surrounded by spies, his precious life may be watched over by an army of myrmidons, but he is the most astute as well as the most relentless enemy of our King—and what some women have done before now, surely others can do again."

Mme. la Marquise made no immediate reply. She was gazing almost with awe upon her daughter, who, flushed with ardour, quivering with excitement, appeared the very embodiment of that reckless patriotism which had already sent Charlotte Corday to the scaffold.

"Constance, in God's name," she murmured, "tell me what you mean——"

But before the girl could reply, the words died upon her lips. From the other side of the château there had come the sound of a great commotion, the clatter of horses' hoofs upon the flagged forecourt, the clanging of metal, the champing of bits, and finally loud and peremptory words of command.

"The police!" exclaimed Madame la Marquise in a hoarse whisper.

"Those devils!" ejaculated the girl with savage intensity of hate.

But neither of the women showed the slightest sign of fear, or even of agitation. They were made of that firm nerve which is always ready to meet danger in whatever form, at whatever hour it may present itself. Conspiracy and intrigue were in their blood. They had never become reconciled to the new régime that had sent their King and Queen to the guillotine and kept their present uncrowned King in exile. They had never bowed their necks to the democratic or the military yoke. They still fought tooth and nail for the restoration of a system which they believed was based upon divine right—caring little that that system had been rejected by the entire people of France. And since they could no longer fight in the open—for their party had dwindled to vanishing-point and lacked both men and materials—they plotted in the dark, in secret, but with unswerving

256

loyalty to their King and unbounded belief in ultimate victory.

So now with a posse of police at their gates they did not lose their heads. On the contrary, Madame la Marquise de Plélan's attitude became if anything more dignified and more calm. She arranged her silk dress in prim folds around her, readjusting the set of her lace coif, and took up a piece of knitting wherewith she busied her perfectly steady fingers. Constance, still carrying the metal box, turned to go out of the room.

"I will return," she said, "when I have disposed of this box."

"What have you kept in it?" asked Madame rather anxiously. "From what I hear, secret hiding-places stand but little chance when that grey-coated ferret is about."

Apparently, however, the young girl had not heard her mother's query, for even as the usual ominous "Open, in the name of the law!" rang out through the silence of the château, she ran out of the room and was speeding down the long corridor towards her own apartments.

The Man in Grey, quiet and perfectly

deferential, stood before Mme. la Marquise de Plélan and in a few words explained the duty that lay before him.

"By order of His Majesty's Minister of Police," he added firmly.

Mme. la Marquise de Plélan waved aside his explanations with a quick gesture of her slender, aristocratic hand.

"I know, Monsieur, I know," she said calmly. "French men and women now are little better than slaves. Their very homes, their privacy, have ceased to be sacred in the eyes of the State which should be their protector, rather than their tyrant."

A search in a private house in those days was no small matter. Ordered by the Minister of Police or his accredited representative, it consisted in a thorough and rigid examination of every nook and cranny, of every corner wherein compromising papers might be hidden. The high-born gentlemen and ladies, suspected of furthering the Cause of the exiled Bourbon princes by aiding and abetting the Chouans in their nefarious practices, were known to be past masters in the art of concealing every proof of their own guilt or that of their friends; the women especially, who reckoned on a certain amount of chivalry on the part of police officers, were the chief custodians of the papers and records belonging to those organised bands of marauding freebooters.

Madame la Marquise had only thrown one glance at the hated enemy when first he entered the room, but already she had appraised him in her mind: "Relentless in the exercise of duty," she thought. "Cold and dispassionate; no mercy or consideration could be expected from him. If only Constance has burned everything that was compromising—there was the tin box and papers which related to the agency at Jersey—and many more records which might mean the guillotine for some of us if they were found——"

Madame noticed that the moment the agent entered the room he cast one rapid look in the direction of the hearth, where the fire was half-smothered beneath a heap of burned paper. On this, however, he made no comment; only his glance appeared to harden and the orders to his men became more peremptory and more sharp. He asked Madame for her keys. She took a bunch from her basket and gave them up to him without remark beyond the curt statement:

"My daughter has the others."

The Man in Grey opened the desk and the drawers of other pieces of furniture in the room, then he left his men to do their work. Madame sat beside the fire, quietly knitting. When she was respectfully asked to move she did so with lips tightly pressed, as if determined not to give vent to her indignation. Cushions and stuffings of chairs and sofas were searched through and through; three men were busy in this room, others were dispersed throughout the house. They tested the wainscotings and the window recesses; they climbed up the chimneys and tapped on the ceilings and the walls. The calm, colourless eyes of the Man in Grey appeared to be everywhere. Even Mme. la Marquise felt a hot flush rising to her pale cheeks when she encountered that searching gaze, which seemed to probe her very thoughts.

"If only Constance would return!" she sighed to herself impatiently.

The shades of evening were beginning to draw in. The police were now busy in other parts of the house; only the secret agent was still in the room. His fingers were wandering over the elaborate carving of

260

the wainscoting. Madame was silent, her ear strained to catch the sound of Constance's footfall on the corridor outside.

Suddenly she heard the familiar light footstep, and, strangly enough, the young girl's voice, clear as a bird's and exquisitely trained, singing an old French *chanson*. The next moment the door was opened and Constance stood under the lintel. She had changed her plain morning dress for a clinging gown of soft silk, embroidered in tiny, coloured rose-buds; her neck and arms were bare, and round her shoulders she had wound a diaphanous scarf of old lace. Her golden hair was dressed high in the prevailing fashion of the day; her cheeks and lips were slightly rouged, her eyes shone with intense excitement. It was obvious that she had been at pains to enhance her great personal attraction. Even the perfume of sweet peas which emanated from her was intended to intoxicate, and of a truth she presented an altogether adorable picture of youth and beauty, as well as of gay and childlike spirits.

Madame smothered the exclamation of astonishment which at sight of her daughter had risen to her lips, whilst the Man in Grey turned from his engrossing occupation and was gazing at the exquisite apparition in the doorway, offering it that tribute of silent admiration which no man—however hidebound—will ever grudge to a beautiful woman.

"Ah, Monsieur!" said Constance gaily, as with perfect unconcern she stepped into the room and turned a pair of appealing blue eyes to the impassive secret agent, "I entreat you, come to the rescue! Your sergeant insists that he must turn out all the things in my bedroom. Oh, he is a very worthy man!,' she added, and a light of saucy mischief began to dance in her eyes; "but he—he tells me that he is not a married man, and–and he is too young—Monsieur, I pray you—must he look over my things?—my—my—you understand? Why, it is not *convenable*! Is it maman?"

"Constance!" came involuntarily from Madame, together with a look of horror and reproach.

Even the Man in Grey appeared slightly embarrassed.

The young girl ran up to him and suddenly linking her hands around his

262

arm tried to drag him towards the door.

"Monsieur," she entreated, and, under the charm of her gaiety and her girlishness, the icy reserve of the police agent already seemed to thaw. "I can trust you—I don't know if you are married, but—but I feel that you are more respectable than your sergeant—I entreat you, come! If my—my—you understand—are to be turned over by rough masculine hands, I feel that I could endure it if those hands were yours."

"Mademoiselle," protested the Man in Grey, who was making somewhat feeble efforts to disengage his arm, "I——"

"Oh, you won't refuse!" she pleaded with tender reproach.

Her lovely face was very close to his; the subtle scent of sweet peas rose to his nostrils and somewhat clouded his usually cool and discerning mind. Moreover, no male creature living could have withstood for long the appeal of those shimmering blue eyes. After all, she was not asking very much. Only that he should himself perform a duty which the clumsy sergeant might perhaps not have performed quite tactfully.

She was still clinging to his arm, still

pleading with her eyes. After a brief hesitation, more assumed than real, he assented coldly.

"I am at Mademoiselle's service."

She gave a cry of pleasure, and he followed her out of the room.

Madame la Marquise was left bewildered, half-thinking that she must have been asleep and dreaming when she saw that dainty and puzzling apparition just now—Constance, her daughter, putting forth her powers of fascination to please that odious and vulgar creature! It was unbelievable!

Charles, the footman, entered with the lamp. Madame did not speak; she was wrapt in moody contemplation. Gradually a strange expression of disquietude and then of weird misgiving spread over her pale face, and once or twice she put a handkerchief to her lips as if to crush a cry.

Gradually the commotion in the house became stilled. A while ago Madame had heard the tramp of those hateful police creatures going down the stairs in the direction of the offices and the servants' quarters; then for a time all was still in that part of the château. But presently, as

264

Madame sat pondering and listening, she heard a sound which—though familiar and reassuring enough—caused her to jump to her feet in an access of abject horror. Her knees shook under her—she could hardly stand.

"My God!" she murmured. "Not that—Don't let her do that——".

All that the Marquise had heard was the soft strain of a spinet and a young girl's pure, fresh voice singing an old French ditty.

Mme. de Plelan stood rigid, as if turned to stone. The dim light of the lamp shone upon her face, which was the colour of pure snow. Then she slowly went to the door and out of the room. She walked along the corridor and up the stairs. Her daughter's rooms gave on the landing immediately above. Madame had to cling to the banisters as she went up, or she would have fallen. An icy horror gripped her heart; she was only conscious of a wild desire to interfere, to place herself at once and by any means athwart those schemes taking shape in Constance's turbulent brain.

The door of Mademoiselle de Plélan's boudoir was wide open. Opposite the door was the spinet at which the young girl sat, playing and singing. The light from the lamp gleamed through the soft tendrils of her golden hair, and the pure lines of her delicate profile were silhouetted against the glow. Not far from her stood the agent of His Imperial Majesty's Minister of Police, the most bitter enemy her friends and kindred had ever known. Constance was looking at him as she sang, and his deep-set eyes, usually so colourless, were fixed with a gaze of ardent admiration on the beautiful singer. On a table at his elbow was the tin box, with its lid thrown open. Only a few papers remained at the bottom of the box; the others he had in his hand.

Mme. de Plélan tottered as if ready to fall. An extraordinary emotion, born of a nameless terror, was paralysing her limbs. In trying to cross the landing she felt faint and all but measured her length on the ground. A weak cry escaped her lips. In an instant Constance ceased playing and, seeing her mother, ran to her side. The next moment her arms were round Madame's shoulders, and she almost carried her back into the room.

The Man in Grey had also made a

266

movement as if to run to Madame's assistance; then he stood by, looking confused and awkward, as men are apt to do when women are ill. However, he helped Constance presently to lead Madame to a chair, and the girl immediately threw him a grateful look.

"Maman is over-fatigued," she said softly. "She has gone through a great deal this afternoon."

Her tone of tender reproach and the glance which she cast him from the depths of her blue eyes completed the confusion of the Man in Grey. He stammered an apology, feeling that he was an unmitigated brute. At once Constance stretched out her hand to him.

"I did not mean to complain," she said gently, "You have been so kind—so considerate—I——"

Her voice broke in a sob. The secret agent, deeply moved, took her hand and pressed it to his lips. Then, hurriedly, he gathered up the remaining papers out of the tin box, slipped them into his pocket and left the room.

By and by his firm voice was heard giving orders to his men to mount.

But as soon as his slim, grey-clad figure

had disappeared across the landing, Constance ran to the door and closed it with a bang. For a moment she stood quite still, gazing in the direction whence came the sound of the enemy's retreating footsteps. An unmistakable look of triumph and satisfaction filled her eyes. The next instant, however, she was down on her knees beside her mother, half-sobbing, half-laughing, her cheeks flushed even beneath the rouge.

"There was nothing in the tin box, maman," she cried somewhat wildly. "Only a few worthless letters, with nothing in them to compromise any of us seriously. Oh, but I have got him, maman! I have got him as surely as he got Monsieur de Saint-Tropèze. In a month from now I shall be able to twist him round my little finger—and then—and then——"

But Mme. de Plélan did not hear the girl's strange, half-hysterical ravings. She was lying unconscious, her pale face looking ghostlike against the silk cushion of her chair.

Less than a month later, on a clear, cold afternoon early in February, a woman, wrapped from head to foot in a dark mantle, was making her way along the main road which cuts straight through the Cache-Renard woods between Alençon and Plélan. She came from the direction of the château and walked briskly, holding her mantle closely round her shoulders.

When she arrived at the clearing where cross-roads met and intersected the main one, she paused for a moment, listened intently for a second or two, then struck into the wood along a side track on her left. She followed this track for two hundred metres or so, then suddenly plunged into the thicket.

The undergrowth here was very dense. Overhead the grey light of the late winter's afternoon filtered through the branches of the trees, guiding the woman on her way. Suddenly, out of the thicket, a gruff voice called out "Who goes there?" and the woman without hesitation replied, "One who has courage and courts success."

Immediately a dark form detached itself from out the undergrowth.

"Is it you, Blue-Heart?" asked the woman sharply.

"At your service, Mademoiselle," said the rough voice which first had challenged her.

"It is all right," said Mademoiselle, "Are you prepared?"

"Oh, I am prepared right enough!" retorted the man whom she had called Blue-Heart. "My musket has been ready for that vermin this past fortnight. I've been here every afternoon," he continued, "since first I had my orders."

"It couldn't be managed sooner, my friend," answered Mademoiselle, "The fox was wary; he would not walk into the trap."

"It was baited often enough for him."

"Oh, yes! He met me in town. He walked with me through the streets or along the river bank. He even came to church with me once or twice." she added with a strained laugh. "But, unlike a beast of prey, he would not come out of nights."

"Did he suspect you, Mademoiselle?" asked Blue-Heart; "or Madame?"

"Oh, no!" replied the girl. "Instinctive caution has saved him so far; nothing more."

"Think you he will come?"

"I am sure," she replied decisively. "You'll hear our voices—mine you will recognise. You'll not miss him?" she added with a strange quiver in her voice.

"Miss him?" retorted the man with a savage oath. "Ever since he killed Hare-Lip and Mole-Skin last November not a hundred metres from this very spot, I have prayed that a bullet from my musket might lay him low."

The girl said nothing more. The man grasped his musket more firmly and cowered into the thicket, and she turned and went back towards the cross roads.

At this very moment a man was walking rapidly towards the same cross roads, but from the opposite direction. He, too, held his cloak wrapped closely up to his chin, for the air was cold. But soon he paused, threw back his mantle and unfolded a scrap of paper he had been holding tightly squeezed in his hand. Once again he read the lines which were so familiar to him, and when he had finished reading he pressed the precious scrap of paper once or twice to his lips. Then he continued on his way.

Some time before he reached the cross roads, he saw Constance de Plélan coming towards him. A moment or two later he was by her side, confused and shy, hardly able to speak owing to the overwhelming

271

sense of happiness.

He tried to take her in his arms, but she evaded him, slipping away from him like a mischievous elf of the woods.

"Let us walk a little," she said.

He was ready to do anything she wished. His calm, reserved demeanour appeared in strange contrast to her exuberant vitality. He hardly could believe in the reality of this supreme moment, and he moved along beside her like a sleepwalker in a dream. He tried to lead the way towards the cross roads.

"There is a side-track there," he said, "sheltered against the wind and carpeted with moss. We should be more lonely there."

But she demurred and, with a laugh, clung to his arm and made him turn back towards the city. She talked at random, almost wildly, about irrelevant things, whilst he wished to speak of nothing but of his love for her—born on that afternoon when she had sung to him and with her own white hands had given him the tin box. The papers it contained were worthless perhaps; but he had been deeply moved by her trust in him and his admiration had quickened into love. Since

272

then he had dreamed of the happy times when she would trust him more fully and allow him to walk by her side and to sit with her, untrammelled by the presence of strangers. Hitherto she had been very shy and reticent, though at times she met him in the town when she was up for a day's shopping or to see her friends. Once or twice she had sent him a treasured little note, telling him that she would be going to church alone.

These had been happy times, and his love had grown in intensity with every meeting. But still he longed to have her all to himself. Timidly he ventured to suggest a walk in the woods or in the park of the château. And this morning the measure of his happiness appeared complete. She sent him word that she would walk in the woods as far as the cross roads close to the château, and would meet him there in the late afternoon. He was too unsophisticated and unversed in the usages of Society to marvel at Mademoiselle de Plélan's agreeing to a clandestine meeting with a man far beneath her in station and at an hour when only flirts were wont to walk abroad. He was far too infatuated by this time to see in this unconventional act aught but graciousness on her part.

But now, somehow, he felt disappointed. she insisted on keeping to the main road, where, at this hour, there were many passers-by. The Caën—Alençon coach had only just rattled past with much blowing of horn and clanging of metal chains.And there was such a beautiful side-track he knew of, if only he could induce her to follow him thither!

The time went by all too quickly. Constance de Plélan appeared anxious to go home.

"I have arranged to meet Annette," she said, "my mother's maid. Her mother lives in the cottage on the road to Plélan. Annette has been spending the afternoon with her, and we have agreed to walk back to the château together. I would not wish her to see you."

And the police agent, smothering a sigh of regret, escorted her back as far as the edge of the wood. He would have liked to walk on with her to the château, but this she resolutely forbade him to do.

"We must not be seen together by Annette," she reiterated somewhat tartly.

Fernand had not yet earned the right to insist. The parting was more disappointing than even the meeting had been. Constance de Plélan now appeared desperately anxious to be rid of him. He tried to take her had, but even this privilege was denied him.

"The cottage is just round the bend of the road," she said with forced gaiety. "Annette may appear before us at any moment."

Whereupon she turned and left him standing alone and disconsolate, his longing eyes watching her graceful figure as she moved swiftly along and soon disappeared round a sharp bend in the road.

Then, with another bitter sigh, he, too, turned on his heel and started to walk back through the wood.

Constance de Plélan had walked on very rapidly, only looking back now and again to see whether the police agent had followed her. The road was now quite lonely; not even a belated passer-by was in sight. After a few minutes, the girl halted where a side-track, inches deep in mud, struck at right angles, and, cutting across an intervening meadow, plunged into a dense part of the wood at some distance from the road. For a few seconds Constance appeared to hesitate; she pressed her trembling hands against her heart, which was beating so furiously that she felt sick and faint. Next moment, however, she started to run down the side-track as fast as the muddy ooze would allow her. A few minutes later she had reached the margin of the wood and, no longer hesitating, boldly entered the thicket.

The road along which the police agent was striding with his habitual quick and firm step wound in and out of thick masses of coppice; the footpath which Constance de Plélan followed so unerringly led by a direct short cut straight to the thicket where Blue-Heart lay in wait.

The shades of evening were falling fast; the wintry sunset had long since ceased to glimmer among the trees. Blue-Heart was cowering in his hiding-place, grasping his musket and marvelling why Mademoiselle had not yet led her quarry into the trap which had been so carefully prepared. The hated police agent had not yet come. But Blue-Heart was patient and content to bide his time. He knew that the hatred he felt for the Man in Grey had its counterpart in the heart of Constance de Plélan. The secret agent had only been in the province four months, and already the Chouans had felt the weight of his relentless courage, his astuteness and his power. M. le Comte d'Artois, brother and messenger of the uncrowned King, had been sent back to England with ignominy, through the instrumentality of this one man, and when Mademoiselle de Plélan had asked for a volunteer to lay this powerful enemy low, Blue-Heart had offered himself, heart and soul, ready to strike and take every risk. If only the quarry would come, Blue-Heart's musket was not likely to err.

Suddenly the Chouan drew in his breath. His whole attitude grew at once more rigid and more tense. Cowering in the thicket, he shouldered his musket. The road stretched out before him, through a veil of coppice, for a length of some thirty feet or so and at a distance of less than twenty paces from the spot where he crouched, on the alert, holding his breath now that his keen ear had detected the sound of approaching footsteps.

Soon these footsteps drew nearer and Blue-Heart muttered an imprecation: "Malédiction!" came between his clenched teeth. "Mademoiselle said that the devil would come along!"

But his rough, nervy hands grasped the musket with undiminished vigour. If the hated police agent came escorted with a whole posse of his own men, Blue-Heart was not going to be done out of his vengeance.

Then suddenly the footsteps stopped and the melancholy call of a screech-owl pierced the silence of the night.

"White-Beak!" muttered the crouching Chouan as he lowered his musket. "What is he doing here at this hour?"

He, too, raised his fingers to his mouth, and the cry of a screech-owl rang shrilly through the wood. Next moment three or four men pushed their way cautiously through the thicket.

"Well, is it done?" queried the foremost amongst them, as soon as he had become conscious of Blue-Heart's presence close by.

"Done? No" growled the latter. "What have you come for?"

"To lend you a hand," replied White-

Beak, "with the body of the vermin."

"Too soon! I haven't got him yet."

"No hitch, I hope," broke in one of the others.

"None."

"Then we can give you a hand now as well as later. The fox may be armed."

"He may," rejoined Blue-Heart. "Go to the other side of the road," he added, "so as to intercept him in the rear. You have your musket?"

"No."

"Then you can hold him while I use mine. It will make assurance doubly sure."

They spoke in whispers scarcely audible above the manifold murmurs of the wood. Now, like creeping furtive beasts of prey, White-Beak and his companions crawled on hands and knees through the thicket and across the road, and thence under cover once more. The trap was indeed well set for the quarry, which could not fail to walk into it very soon. Indeed, less than five minutes later there came from some little way down the road the sound of a measured and firm footfall.

With rapid steps the hated police agent was drawing nearer. A grim chuckle escaped the lips of the old Chouan as he once more shouldered his musket. The evening gloom was gradually enfolding the wood in its embrace. On either side of the road the miscreants in their hiding-place were peeping through the undergrowth, watching for the approach of their prey. Presently they could discern the vague outline of his slender figure walking unhesitatingly towards them. Within a few seconds he would be passing right in front of them, at a distance of less than twenty paces. Blue-Heart thought that he would wait and take no risks and only pull the trigger when the victim was quite near, the aim sure, and the fast gathering darkness not likely to play him any illusive trick. Not a sound, not the flutter of a dead leaf nor the crackling of a twig would have revealed to an untrained ear the presence of a band of assassins, and for another minute or so the police agent walked along, wary and alert as was his wont but, as yet unsuspicious. His footstep sounded unhesitating and firm.

Then suddenly he paused and threw a quick, searching look around him.

"Who goes there?" he called in a loud and firm voice.

His ear, attuned to the faintest breath which might be drawn around him, had warned him, all at once, of the danger which awaited him if he continued on his path; it had betrayed to his keen consciousness the presence of human beings, living breathing, close by—somewhere in the thicket—hiding and crouching in the darkness; obviously with evil intent.

Next moment something definite stirred in the thicket not twenty paces from where he stood; there was a faint click which to a trained ear was unmistakable. In a twinkling Fernand had drawn a pistol from his pocket and, with a swift and sudden spring, he threw himself against a tall beech which bordered the road; and here he stood, with his back against the massive trunk, pistol in hand and his keen eyes searching the darkness around him.

There was a moment of tense suspense and of absolute silence, and in an instant the Man in Grey felt his arm seized from behind, the pistol was knocked out of his hand, a rough fist was thrust into his face, and he found himself pinioned against the tree, whilst a hoarse voice shouted lustily;

"You can shoot friend Blue-Heart. No

chance of missing the vermin in the dark. We've got him tight."

Then it all happened in a second. A musket-shot rang through the evening air; its sharp report came simultaneously with a loud and piercing cry which rang right through and above it. The cry proceeded from a woman's lips; it was immediately followed by a violent imprecation from one of the Chouans. The Man in Grey, dazed, bewildered, not understanding, had only heard that cry, straight in front of him, right from out the thicket whence had come the report and flash of the assassin's musket. The rough hands that held him relaxed, and there was wild confusion of cries and oaths and a scrambling and scrimmage in the undergrowth behind him.

What had happened within the depths of the shadows in front of him he did not know, but at a bound he cleared the intervening width of the road, and Constance de Plélan fell staggering in his arms.

"Constance!" he exclaimed, still mystified by the turn of events, "you are hurt!"

"No, no!" she said in a strange, hoarse

282

whisper. "I am not hurt. Only save yourself—— Go, in God's name, ere I forget that I am a woman and again think of you only as the enemy of my King."

"You have saved my life!" he said, as the horror of the situation rose with staggering vividness before his mind "and at risk of your own."

But already she had disengaged herself from his arms. She struggled to her feet and, as he tried to assist her, pushed him with amazing strength away from her.

"Go, I tell you!" she said, and she tried to steady her voice, which came feeble and panting from her throat. "The hand that fired the first shot might fire another ere I could prevent it—and the others might come back."

"I'll not go," he rejoined firmly, "until I am sure that you are not hurt."

"Hush!" she retorted hurriedly. "I am not hurt, I say. And even if I were, you must go now—at once. Have I not said that I might repent? Behind that thicket lurks the man whom I employed to kill you—I came back here to gloat over his work. Yet, somehow, when the time came, and I saw you in the grip of those assassins, I could not bear to see you

283

die—not like that—five against one—it was too horrible, too cowardly. But you must go. And you and I must never meet again, unless indeed you set your spies on us to-morrow and send us all to the guillotine."

"How you hate me, Constance!" he protested with passionate reproach.

"Perhaps I do," she rejoined softly. "I do not know. But believe me that the guillotine would have no terror for me. I have betrayed a great trust, for you are the enemy of my kindred and my King, and I ought not to have failed when the choice lay betwixt your life and theirs."

She tottered, and he thought she would fall.

"You *are* hurt!" he cried hoarsely.

"Even if I were dying," she parried feebly, "I would not have you help me now. If we did not part at this hour, perhaps—who knows?—I might become even a blacker traitor than I am. You and I, Fernand, can have nothing in common. Our ways must for ever lie as far apart as are our ideals. The man who at my bidding would have been your murderer will carry me home and minister to my needs. He and I have everything in common—faith, friendship, community of ideals and disappointments of hopes and of sorrows. He is rough, uncultured, a potential assassin; but he and I strive for the same Cause and weep over the same failures. In thought he is my friend—you can never be aught but an enemy."

And suddenly, without giving him another look, she plunged into the thicket. For a few seconds only it seemed to the Man in Grey that he could see her slender form moving among the undergrowth and that he heard the crackling of dead twigs beneath her feet. She had gone for comfort and protection to the assassin who was still in hiding. She went to him because, as she had said, with those savage Chouans she, the irreconcilable Royalist, had everything in common.

Whereas with him, the stranger, the plebeian police agent, the obscure adherent of the newlyfounded Empire, she could have nothing to do. Nay, she had actually persuaded an assassin to shoot him—vilely—in the back, when, at the fateful minute of crisis, a thought of womanly compassion had prompted her to save him from his doom. And, on his part, what was there for him to do but mourn the only illusion of his life? It served him right for being a visionary and a fool!

And with a bitter sigh of enduring regret, the police agent turned on his heel and went back the way he came.

VII

THE LEAGUE OF KNAVES

ONE of the letters written to the Man in Grey by Fouche, Duc d'Otrante, is preserved in the Archives of the Ministry of Police. It is dated February 17th, 1811, and contains the following passage:

"Do not let those official asses meddle with the affair, my good Fernand, for they are sure to mismanage it completely. That man de Livardot is an astute brigand and a regular dare-devil. To apprehend or to deport him would not be of the slightest use to us; he has escaped out of three different prisons already, and has come back once—none the worse—from Cayenne. To murder him from behind a thicket would be more useful; but for the fact that he has many secrets of that damnable Chouan organisation in his keeping, which would be of incalculable value to us, if we could get hold of them. At any rate, see what you can do, my dear Fernand. I rely on your skill and discretion. De Livardot has left England for Jersey; he is at St. Hellier now. I'd stake my life that he is on his way to France. The Emperor will be at Caën within the next month. Remember Cadoudal and his infernal machine, and for the love of Heaven keep an eye on de Livardot!"

For obvious reasons the Man in Grey did not communicate the actual contents of the letter to the prefet of Caën, M. Laurens, a typical official of not too assured loyalty, or to M. Carteret, chief commissary of the district. But both these worthies had had news, through police spies, of the arrival of de Livardot in Jersey, and were alive to the fact that the wily Chouan leader was probably meditating a secret landing on the shores of France.

Everyone was on tenter-hooks, with nerves on edge at the prospect of the visit of the Emperor, who in less than a month would be spending half a day and a whole night at the house of Marshal Cormier, lately created Duc de Gisors in recognition of magnificent services rendered during the last Austrian campaign.

The Man in Grey, as was his wont, listened unmoved and in silence to the many expressions of loyal fears, anxieties and unswerving resolutions which flowed so freely from the lips of the various official personages who visited M. le Préfet that morning. But when the last caller had departed, and only he and the commissary were left to take their leave, he said quietly but significantly:

"I shall leave you a free hand for a few days, Monsieur le Préfet. You have the list of persons on whom I have enjoined you and Monsieur le Commissaire to keep a watchful eye. I pray you do not slacken your vigilance during my absence."

"You are going away, Monsieur Fernand?" queried the préfet, who tried to show some concern, even though in his heart he could not but rejoice at the prospect of being so soon rid of this interfering and dictatorial nincompoop from Paris.

"I am going to meet de Livardot when he lands," replied the Man in Grey simply.

"But you don't know where to find

him!" exclaimed the commissary with a complacent laugh.

"I dare say I shall contrive to find that out," rejoined the secret agent with a smile. "In any case," he added with deliberate solemnity, "remember while I am gone to double the number of your spies and not to slacken your vigilance either day or night. The most precious life in the whole world will be in your keeping for close on twenty-four hours, and France will hold you answerable for its safety."

There was something curiously impressive about the small colourless, grey-clad figure while this solemn warning crossed his usually silent lips. Both the préfet and the commissary, despite their covert antagonism to this obscure personage who had so authoritatively been placed above their heads, were conscious of a sense of respect and awe.

"But you will be back here in time for the Emperor's visit, Monsieur Fernand?" rejoined the commissary, trying to speak lightly.

"Such is my intention," replied the secret agent. "But we are all going to be at grips with a man who is both resourceful and utterly unscrupulous—and one never knows. If I do not return, you must take it that de Livardot has proved the stronger of us two."

"But you are not going alone?" interjected the préfet, throwing a quick glance at the slender form and delicate hands of this mysterious creature who, of a truth, appeared more of a dreamer than a man of action.

The Man in Grey laughed.

"The last time" he said carelessly, "that de Livardot landed in France, our friend Carteret here had a whole squadron of police ready to arrest him—we all know with what results. Murder, pillage, robbery, endless intrigues went on for three whole months, after which our crafty brigand disappeared as cunningly as he had come. Well, we are not going to repeat that blunder, are we, Monsieur le Préfet?" He added more seriously, "This time I go to meet de Livardot—and I go alone."

The next moment he was gone, leaving the two worthies puzzled, wrathful and contemptuous.

"And de Livardot will do for you," growled the commissary after him with an oath. "And serve you right, too, you interfering, impudent shrimp, you!"

In the narrow, sparsely furnished room, dimly lighted by tallow candles fixed in pewter sconces, the men sat waiting.

It was a cold but brilliant night; a small fire smouldered in the little iron stove in one corner of the room. The window beyond was open, as was the communicating door; and from time to time violent gusts of wind would blow the flame of the candles about and cause the grease to trickle and splutter upon the unpolished table-top. Every now and again one of the men would get up, go through to the other room, and, leaning out of the window, peer up and down the dark and narrow street. Then he would rejoin his comrades, who sat listlessly round the table, sipping wine out of pewter mugs.

"I think we had best make up our minds," said one of them after a while.

"I've feared it all along." said another.

"The moment White-Beak returned with the news that that accursed grey-coated ferret was lurking in the neighbourhood of the Goat's Creek," continued he who had first spoken, "I for one——" He shrugged his shoulders, leaving the sentence unfinished. But the others understood. There was no need to put into words the fear that was uppermost in their minds.

One of the men took up the metal snuffers, and with studied care cut the wick of the smoking candle.

"Why White-Beak did not put a bullet through the grey fox, I cannot imagine," he said slowly.

"I would have done so if I could," retorted he who was called White-Beak because his lips appeared absolutely bloodless; "but he never came within range of my gun. And when I tried to creep closer he disappeared."

"That cursed spy bears a charmed life," growled the other.

"Methought de Livardot should have broken the spell," here interposed a third.

"De Livardot may have been detained in Jersey," suggested another. "And the weather in the Channel has been very dirty of late."

"Bah! From what I hear, Livardot is not like to be detained by bad weather. By all accounts he is a regular dare-devil," assented White-Beak with a laugh.

"Blue-Heart here says that, even as a lad, he had the pluck of Satan."

"Tell us some more about him, Blue-Heart," added White-Beak. "The chiefs say we've got to do as he tells us, and we've all got a mighty lot at stake now. We ought to know something of the man who is going to lord it over us. What is he like?"

"Well," replied Blue-Heart after a moment's thought, "I used to see him when he was a lad and Monsieur le Chevalier his father lived in the house yonder, which now belongs to Marshal Cormier. It's because de Livardot comes from these parts, and knows the house so well, that the chiefs are sending him over from England to help us in our work."

"But if he hasn't seen the place since he was a lad——"

"Even so! There are plans of the house and——"

"Hush!" broke in White-Beak peremptorily.

A sudden silence fell upon them. From away down the narrow street had come the weird and mysterious hooting of a screech-owl calling through the night.

Blue-Heart jumped to his feet and in a trice was over the threshold in the other room. He strode across to the window and, leaning out, peered up and down the street.

Before him, about a kilometre outside the city, the pointed roofs and tall chimneys of Les Acacias peeped above the low houses opposite. It was the residence of Marshal Cormier, Duc de Gisors, and here the Emperor and his suite would sleep on the following night. The wintry moon picked out the metal ornaments of the roofs and the crests of the tall, encircling trees with shimmering lines of silver.

Blue-Heart uttered a comprehensive curse.

"Without de Livardot," he muttered between his teeth, "we shall fail!"

He was about to close the window, thinking that once again his comrades' ears and his own had been deceived, when a solitary pedestrian at the far end of the street arrested his attention—a man walking very slowly, as if he were infinitely weary. He wore an old-fashioned three-cornered hat, and a voluminous mantle was wrapped closely round his shoulders. Blue-Heart waited, while the pedestrian came leisurely down the street. Presently he paused and, with nose in the air, studied the outside aspect of the houses. Then he put the fingers of both hands to his lips and once more the melancholy call of the screech-owl rang out through the night.

Blue-Heart was holding his breath. His companions behind him had jumped to their feet and stood in a compact knot in and around the communicating doorway. Blue-Heart with his hand motioned them to be still; then he leaned still farther out of the window, and, in a voice scarcely above a whisper said, as he looked straight down on the passer-by:

"The fearful wild-fowl is abroad."

And the other, raising his head, gave reply:

"And the wild duck comes with a feather in her mouth."

"De Livardot!" exclaimed the men excitedly.

Helter-skelter some of them ran down the stairs to greet the leader whom their chiefs were sending to command them, whilst the others placed a fresh jar of wine, some meat and a hunk of bread upon the table. A moment or two later the stranger entered.

To those who had so eagerly expected

him, de Livardot appeared as a short spare man, prematurely grey, with face drawn, eyes sunk and cheeks wan with obvious fatigue verging on exhaustion. He sank into a chair beside the iron stove and eagerly drank the wine offered him.

"I have been three weeks on the road," he murmured hoarsely; "and haven't tasted food for two days."

He dragged his chair to the table and they allowed him to eat and drink in peace, after which he felt better and answered the inquiring glances of the men with an encouraging nod.

"That cursed police-spy nearly did for me," he said.

"We thought something of the sort had happened," muttered Blue-Heart with a savage oath.

"The Captain of the *Foam* put me off at the Goat's Creek," continued de Livardot in a steadier voice. "Then he left me there to make my way inland, as I intended to do. I knew my way well enough, and my intention was to walk by night and to lie hidden by day where and how I could. I had no misgivings, but nevertheless my eyes and ears were on the watch for spies. I had climbed to the top of the Dog's Tooth;

the coast seemed deserted—not a soul was in sight and the night had set in dark and stormy. I was standing on the edge of the cliff and at my feet the breakers were dashing themselves against the rocks two hundred feet below. All at once something sprang on me from behind a boulder. The attack was so violent and so sudden that, even as I veered round and closed with my assailant, I felt I was doomed. He was small and spare like myself, but he had unusual strength. We fought desperately—both of us—for our lives. Fortunately," continued de Livardot lightly, "I have spent my best years in England, where the art of self-defence is at its best. With a dexterous movement which I had learnt from a champion wrestler, I slipped out of his grip; the next moment he lost his footing. For a second or two his hands clawed the air, and then with a piercing shriek he fell, two hundred feet on to the rocks below.

"Et voilà!" concluded the Chouan leader as he threw a look of triumph on his breathless hearers. "But that accursed spy, whom Satan now hath in his keeping, managed to dislocate my knee ere he went to join his colleagues in hell, with the result

that I have been very slow in coming. Ofttimes in the last three weeks, as I dragged my weary limbs along those interminable roads, I feared I would be just too late to be in at the death of the Corsican."

"Thank God you are here now!" ejaculated one of the men fervently.

"All our work is ready," added Blue-Heart, "But if you hadn't come we shouldn't have known what to do—afterwards."

De Livardot rose and, holding his mug of wine aloft, said firmly:

"Afterwards we'll proclaim his gracious Majesty Louis XVIII, King of France. We'll assemble here and march in triumph to the Hôtel de Ville at the break of dawn, with banners flying, singing a Te Deum. Then by the time the city is astir the fleur-de-lis will be waving above every public building, and the worthy bourgeois of Caën will realise that France has awakened from her nightmare and that her lawful King sits upon his throne again."

He sat down amidst loud applause from the group of ill-kempt, unwashed, surly-looking brigands around him. Mugs were re-filled and deep draughts of wine drunk to do honour to the toast.

"And now to work, my friends!" continued de Livardot briskly.

"To work!" exclaimed White-Beak, "I thought you were dog-tired."

"So I was," he replied gaily, "till we drank that toast."

He took out a bundle of papers from the pocket of his coat and glanced rapidly through them.

"I shan't want all these in future," he said. "And the less of this sort of thing one has about one the safer for the rest of us."

He turned to the iron stove which was close to his hand and, selecting some of the papers, dropped them into the fire one by one, keeping up a running comment on their contents the while.

"Here goes the list of your names, you fellows," he said. "Blue-Heart, whom I haven't seen since I was five; White-Beak, I knew you at once; Great-Fang, Green-Eye—I recognised you all. The chiefs spoke to me about you. And here goes our pass-phrase. I had such trouble to commit it to memory. But now I feel that I shall never forget it again! Would you fellows have admitted me if I had made a mistake?" he added with a light-hearted laugh.

"No," replied Blue-Heart curtly. Then he said more quietly, as if to atone for the bluntness of his negative: "Think of all that we have at stake——"

"I know, of course," rejoined de Livardot earnestly. "I only wished to test the measure of your caution. And now," he continued, "here is the plan of Les Acacias, just as it was in my father's time."

He drew his chair in closer to the table and spread the map out before him. He bent over it, shielding his face with his hand. The flickering light of the candles threw into bold relief the grim and sinister faces of the Chouans as they pressed eagerly round their new leader.

"Now tell me what you've all done!" said de Livardot.

"We followed closely the instructions you sent us from Jersey," Blue-Heart explained, as his grimy forefinger wandered along the surface of the map. "Great-Fang obtained work in the garden of Les Acacias and soon located the disused shaft you spoke of, quite close to the house. It had, just as you said, been used at one time for lowering wine barrels into the cellar. It was no trouble to Great-Fang, in the course of his work, when no one was about, to loosen the stone which closed the mouth of the shaft, and after that matters were quite easy."

"I used to leave the postern gate on the latch," interpolated Great-Fang; "and the others took it in turns, two by two, to steal into the grounds by night. We very soon found the trap-door at the bottom of the shaft which gave directly on the cellars underneath the house, and when we had removed that our work was practically done."

"Now we've got two kilogrammes of gunpowder stored down there," added the man who was called Green-Eye.

"We carried it over, keg by keg, of nights," interposed BlueHeart.

"Our time-fuse is set," quoth White-Beak.

"Even if you hadn't come, we should have fired it," concluded another. "We were not going to have our work for nothing."

They all spoke at once, eager to have their say, anxious that the leader lately come from England should know the share everyone had had in the work which was to rid France of her Emperor.

"Thank Heaven I am in time, then," concluded de Livardot fervently. "When does the Corsican arrive?"

"To-morrow afternoon," replied Blue-Heart.

"And he sleeps at Les Acacias?"

"For one night."

"There is to be a big fête in the evening. Marshal Cormier issued hundreds of invitations," added White-Beak.

"Nothing could be better!" exclaimed de Livardot.

"And of course we wait till the guests have departed, and everyone in Les Acacias, including the Upstart, has gone to bed. Yours, Blue-Heart," he continued, "will be the honour of firing the time-fuse, which will send Napoléon Bonaparte to a tea-party among the stars. In the meanwhile all of your men must spend the best part of to-morrow in seeking out the friends you know of, who are at one with us in this great undertaking, and convene them in my name to a meeting in this house directly after the event. In fact, the explosion itself shall be the signal by which we'll all rally together for that glorious proclamation of our lawful King and our triumphal march to the Hôtel de Ville. Is that understood?"

"Perfectly!" they cried with one accord.

The next half-hour was devoted to the discussion and copying out of the names of various personages, whom the Chouans suggested as having been chiefly concerned in the present affair—men and women in and around the city who were ardent Royalists and would not shrink from a direct attack on the man whom they deemed a usurper; men and women for the most part who had countenanced, if they had not directly participated in many of those hideous crimes which had already sullied the Cause they professed to uphold, and who would see in the base murder of the Emperor whom they hated nothing but an act of lofty patriotism.

Wary and cunning, they had hitherto escaped apprehension; though many of them were suspected, few had ever been confronted with proofs of actual conspiracy. They were wise enough to employ men like Blue-Heart or White-Beak to do their dirtiest work for them, men who had neither scruples nor conscience, and who hid their deeds of darkness behind weird masks of anonymity.

It was long past midnight ere the party round that table was broken up. De Livardot was the first to go; he had given his orders and he knew he would be obeyed.

"You will see nothing of me all day," he said when he finally took leave of his comrades. "I am too well known in these parts to dare show my face in the open. At dusk we shall meet here for a final word. Until then let our password be as before: 'The fearful wild-fowl is abroad,' and the counter-pass: 'And the wild duck comes with a feather in her mouth.' I have not forgotten it this time!" he concluded with a hearty laugh, which found its echo in the grim chuckle of his men.

The visit of the Emperor had sent Caën wild with enthusiasm. All day the streets leading towards Les Acacias were thronged with people eager to keep in sight the roofs and chimneys of the house which sheltered the Emperor. The town itself was magnificently beflagged, and all day the cheering was both constant and deafening. In the evening there was a popular fête with display of fireworks in the grounds of the Old Château on the north side of the town, whilst the rout given at Les Acacias by the Duc de Gisors to the notabilities of the neighbourhood, at which His Majesty himself was graciously pleased to be present, was the most brilliant affair the province had ever known. People had journeyed from far and wide to attend the rout; many who came from a distance had taken lodgings in the town for the occasion. Never had Caën been so full of strangers of quality.

On the great night the stream of equipages which set down the guests at Les Acacias extended for close on a kilometre from the park gates to the confines of the city, and those who were not watching the fireworks at the Old Château stood about on the road, in spite of the cold, to see the gorgeous liveries, the painted coaches and caparisoned horses which were a regular feast for the eyes. For hours the streets were thronged. Only the narrow little Rue aux Juifs in the outskirts of the city appeared dark, solitary and unfestive. It consisted for the most part of tumbledown, half-derelict houses, the owners of which had been out of France for many years. And to-night, when the rest of Caën was out to make merry, only one of the low, grim-faced houses showed any sign of life. Here a feeble light shone dimly through the cracks of an ill-fitting shutter on one of the floors above, and anyone who had taken the trouble to be on the watch would have seen dark forms, wrapped to the chin, gliding furtively in and out of the door.

But the military, the police and the municipal servants were alike engaged in keeping watch over Les Acacias, the stately residence which sheltered the most precious life in Europe.

The rout was kept up till the small hours of the morning. It was two o'clock before the last equipage drove through the monumental gates of Les Acacias, and these were finally closed upon the departing guests. But for an hour after that the roads around the house were still thronged with people too excited to go to bed. They swarmed around the encircling wall, above which they could only see the glimmer of lights behind the shuttered windows, tried to peer through the wrought-iron gates, happy to see how completely their Emperor trusted them, and that he disdained the usual paraphernalia of military guards and sentinels—the relics of bygone times. The house was lighted up; no doubt a number of lackeys would be astir keeping watch over the illustrious guest, but there was no glimmer of fixed bayonets within the gates, no tramp of martial feet up and down the circular drive.

Only at three o'clock did the citizens of Caën finally decide to go to bed. By half-past three the approaches to Les Acacias, as well as the streets, were at last deserted; the houses in the city had closed down their lights; only in the distance the house in which the Emperor slept was illuminated from within; but it, too, now appeared absolutely still.

Then suddenly the slumbering city was awakened by an awful sound—a terrific crash which broke the window panes of hundreds of houses, and which reverberated for many kilometres around. Fragments of wood and stone and tiles appeared to rain down from the skies like deathdealing projectiles, crashing through the roofs of some houses in the confines of the city and causing much damage, fortunately without any loss of life.

There was hardly a citizen inside the

town who did not immediately jump out of bed, with beating heart and blanched cheeks and lips that quivered with horror, as he murmured the ominous words;

"Les Acacias! The Emperor! My God!"

Within a few minutes the garrison was astir. The whole sky was now suffused with a weird and lurid glow. In the direction of St. Martin, where stood Les Acacias, vivid tongues of flame were seen to leap intermittently into the night. The streets leading thither soon became crowded with people, clad in promiscuous garments, all running in the one direction, and headed by a company of infantry and a squadron of cavalry, rushing along with buckets, pumps and ladders, in the wake of the hastily summoned official fire-brigade. The confusion threatened to grow serious. The city police were quite unable to cope with it, and the military alone were in a measure able to enforce some semblance of order.

Only the Rue aux Juifs, with its crazy houses, remained as before, silent and comparatively deserted. The distant conflagration lit up with a weird glow the ramshackle facades which lined the narrow thoroughfare. Neither the police, nor the military, nor yet the few sightseers who drifted down the street in search of a short cut to the scene of excitement, had a mind to notice the sombrely clad passersby who halted outside the door of one of these grim-faced abodes, about half-way down the street.

Two men, dressed in rough blouses, and with widebrimmed hats pulled over their eyes, appeared to be on guard at the door, and as each person passed from the street into the house, one of these men uttered a whispered challenge: "The fearful wildfowl is abroad." And instantly was heard the equally whispered reply. "And the wild duck comes with a feather in her mouth."

After which the gloom beyond appeared to swallow up the new-comer. But a number of these, as they went by, added a quick and eager query:

"Has he come?"

And one of the men invariably replied:

"Yes! Last night. Just escaped being murdered by one of those accursed spies."

Outside were noise, bustle, wild excitement, made up partly of horror, partly and mainly of eager curiosity. Folk rushed aimlessly hither and thither; the military charged the populace with loud commands to make way; the police shouted and used their swords to cut a passage through the crowd for the firemen; everybody yelled or screamed; some women fainted; on everyone's lips was the one agonised query: "The Emperor! Is he dead?"

But inside the derelict house in the Rue aux Juifs a dignified hush reigned. The narrow double room on the floor above was filled with a throng as passionately excited as was the one which shouted itself hoarse in the streets; but the men and women assembled here only spoke in whispers, even though the query which was on everyone's lips was not a whit less eager: "De Livardot! Is he here?"

"He and Blue-Heart fired the fuse," said White-Beak in reply. "No doubt they are held up by the crowd. They will be here soon."

A score or so of men and women wandered about aimlessly from room to room, or sat on the gimcrack chairs and the steps of the rickety stairs. They talked in whispers, communicating their excitement to one another. Only now and then a young voice would be raised in sudden, half-hysterical laughter.

The shutters were hermetically closed so that no sound should filter through. The usurper was dead, but his sycophants were still abroad and his paid minions still in power, and the populace was still intoxicated with the glamour which Austerlitz and Wagram, Jena and Rivoli had cast over the hated Corsican's name. Therefore the conspirators, though certain of victory, still went about with bated breath, whilst an air of mystery still clung to the shabby, tumbledown house in the Rue aux Juifs.

White-Beak and his mates, who had prepared the foul crime which had just achieved its grim culmination, stood apart from the rest of the company, in the narrow hall below—at respectful distance from the noble ladies and gentlemen who had paid them to do their cowardly task.

But, noble and peasant alike, all these Chouans to-night—a veritable league of knaves—were here assembled in order to proclaim their triumphant exultation at the cold-blooded murder of the Emperor, and to hail the return of their rightful King.

Despite the cold outside, the rooms and staircase felt overpoweringly hot. The tallow candles flickered and guttered in their sconces; weariness warring with excitement was depicted on every face.

Then, suddenly a woman's voice rang out buoyantly:

"Why should we wait for de Livardot ere we drink the health of His Majesty the King?"

"Why, indeed?" came in lusty response from every side.

The effect of the suggestion was electrical. In a moment mugs and flagons were produced. The gentlemen poured out the wine, whilst everyone crowded round the table in the centre of the room. It seemed as if a load of anxiety had been lifted from every shoulder; the younger people began to laugh aloud, weariness fled as if by magic. The shutters were flung wide open. Of a truth, what need was there now for fear or mystery? Perish the last misgivings, that unshakable sense of impending doom! The usurper is dead! Long live the King! And let every passer-by, an he would, pause to hear the rousing, loyal toast:

"The usurper is dead. Long live His Majesty Louis XVIII., by the Grace of God, King of France!'

And the echo of the enthusiastic cry reverberated from attic to cellar of the old house. White-Beak and his mates in the hall below joined in the acclamation with a rollicking shout. The veil and gloom of doubt had lifted; spirits ran high, laughter rang from end to end of the narrow, fusty rooms.

It was when these transports of delight were at their highest that the street door was suddenly thrown open, and Blue-Heart, panting, half-exhausted, with shaking knees and trembling hands, staggered into the narrow hall and fell headlong in the arms of his comrades.

"We are betrayed!" he gasped. "They are on us! *Sauve qui peut*!"

"We are betrayed!" The awful, ever-recurring cry of the conspirator, of the man who concocts deeds of evil under cover of darkness, and who mistrusts every hand he grasps! All these men, accustomed as they were to this ever-present danger—a danger which hung over them, even when they felt most secure—paused neither to question nor to reflect; they scarcely paused to warn the noble ladies and gentlemen above, who were still engaged in toasting the triumph

313

of their Cause.

"We are betrayed! *Sauve qui peut*!" they shouted and, not waiting to hear whether the warning were heeded, scrambled for the door.

"Too late!" gasped Blue-Heart, as with trembling hands he strove to detain his struggling mates. "They were on my heels!"

"They? Who?" queried the others hoarsely.

"The police!"

"Bah! The police!" exclaimed White-Beak, a feeble attempt at swagger. "The Corsican is dead. We have no cause to fear the police."

But already a nameless terror, like a pale, mysterious ghost, had floated upwards through the house. It had reached a small group of young men and women gaily chattering at the head of the stairs.

"We are betrayed!"

"Did you hear that?" asked someone, and suddenly excitement died away as if stricken down by a poisonous breath, and within a second or two the whisper was on every lip. "We are betrayed!"

"Who said it?"

"The men below!"

There was a swift rush for the stairs, while one man hastily re-closed the shutters. Another was leaning over the banisters, trying to learn the truth.

"White-Beak!" he called. "Is that you? What does it mean?"

"That the police are on us!" was the gruff reply.

"The police!" shouted those above. "Why, the Corsican is dead and——"

"Hark!" came peremptorily from the men.

And all the conspirators held their breath, listening. The sound was unmistakable; a number of men were outside the door. Quick words of command could be heard; the clanging of steel and the snorting and pawing of horses.

"But the usurper is dead!" glided as a reassuring cry from a woman's lips.

"He is not dead!" retorted Blue-Heart firmly.

"Not dead? But the explosion—the fire——"

As if to confirm these words, a gigantic sheet of flame in the direction of Les Acacias suddenly lit up the whole sky again, with such brilliancy that, despite the closed shutters, a lurid glow penetrated the house, throwing for an instant into bold relief the pale, haggard faces, and illumining them with a light which was the colour of blood.

At the same moment, in the distance was heard the sound of prolonged cheering. Louder and louder it grew as it seemed to spread to every corner of the town, till it became absolutely deafening. A wild medley of sounds filled the air with clamorous din; people rushed excitedly to and fro, shouting "*Vive l'Empereur!*" and singing the "Marseillaise." Horses galloped by at breakneck speed; the roll of coach-wheels went thundering along the cobble stones; from the château close by came the echo of bugle calls.

And in the derelict house of the Rue aux Juifs there reigned silence as if of the dead, though wellnigh two score men and women were there, huddled together in one common and agonising fear. What had happened no one could as yet even conjecture; all they knew was that Napoléon had escaped by a miracle and that the police were at the door.

"And de Livardot? Where is he?" was

one of the many questions on trembling lips.

But to this query even Blue-Heart could give no conclusive reply. He had been with de Livardot until after they had fired the time-fuse together, then de Livardot ordered him to go back to the Rue aux Juifs and there to wait for him till he arrived, and in the meanwhile to tell all the friends to drink and make merry. He—Blue-Heart—had walked rapidly for a time, then curiosity had mastered him and he waited until the terrifying explosion rent the air and gave him assurance that his task was indeed accomplished. Then he turned back towards the city.

When he reached the Rue aux Juifs he saw that it swarmed with police-spies. He heard words and whispered commands which left no doubt in his mind that somehow or other the conspiracy had been betrayed, and that a descent on the Chouan meeting-place was in contemplation. At first he made light of the affair. Was not the Corsican dead? And he—Blue-Heart—and his friends, were they not triumphant? What cause had they to fear the minions of an Empire

317

that was now defunct? Nevertheless, he hung about the street under the shadows of doorways, on the *qui vive*. Then suddenly the rumour spread throughout the town that the Emperor was safe. He had left Marshal Cormier's house along with his host and the latter's family and entire staff of servants and retainers, directly after the last guest had departed.

Not a soul was left at Les Acacias when the explosion occurred. Blue-Heart, realising that the plot must have been discovered and that the deadliest danger now threatened all his friends, contrived to reach the door of the meeting-place undetected, and to sound the note of warning which, alas! had already come too late.

The house was surrounded. The police were swarming everywhere. The Chouans—save for a few of the gentlemen who wore their swords and one or two who carried pistols—were practically unarmed. They put up a certain measure of resistance, however; some of the men fired pistol shots through the windows, and there was a mêlée on the stairs, in the course of which several of the police were wounded; but these were armed with swords and muskets, and from the first the Chouans knew that they were doomed. After a struggle which lasted less than a quarter of an hour, they were forced to surrender; they were doing neither themselves, nor their Cause, nor the women who were with them, any good by senseless resistance.

When the last of them was disarmed and men and women alike were marched as prisoners down the stairs, a whisper went round among them which was not destined for the ears of their captors:

"Thank God," they said, "that at any rate de Livardot has escaped!"

Blue-Heart and his comrades, who were in the forefront, walking under strong escort—as they had offered by far the most determined and most savage hostility—caught the whisper and, pointing down in the hall where a man in a grey mantle and wearing a three-cornered hat stood in the midst of a group of police officers, one of them said with a grim oath:

"Escaped? Not he! There he is, like the rest of us, already half-way to Bicêtre."

"Livardot? Where?" came in an eager query from his fellow-prisoners.

"Why, there!" said Blue-Heart, once

more pointing to the man below.

"That's not Livardot!" retorted one of the prisoners emphatically, whilst the police laughed grimly, as at an excellent joke.

"Of course, it's not de Livardot," added one of the women. "You are dreaming, Blue-Heart. That's that beastly spy, whom we all know to our cost as the Man in Grey."

"But," stammered Blue-Heart, who, bewildered and utterly uncomprehending, was staring down before him like a man suddenly brought up against a measureless abyss; "the police-spy was killed by de Livardot on the Dog's Tooth rocks——"

At this moment the Man in Grey looked up and caught Blue-Heart's glowering eyes and those of his mates fixed almost crazedly upon him.

"Nay! friend Blue-Heart," he said quietly—in the weird silence which had fallen upon the throng—"the police-spy, as you call him, arrived safely in the Rue aux Juifs, just in time to learn the details of the plot which you and these gentlemen and ladies were so confidently hatching. Your friend de Livardot, whom I certainly met face to face on the Dog's Tooth rocks, is quietly awaiting his friends in Bicêtre."

Then, while a string of muttered imprecations fell from the lips of the miscreants whom he had so cunningly outwitted, he gave the final word of command.

"Forward! March! The carriages for the ladies are in the front; those for the men in the rear. Guard your prisoners well, my men!" he added. "They are as crafty as a tribe of foxes. Forward, now, and may God always protect the Emperor!"

Napoléon thanked the Man in Grey personally for the superb way in which he had not only saved his Emperor's life, but had also succeeded in gathering so many Chouans into his net.

"How was it done, my good Monsieur Fernand?" His Majesty asked graciously.

"Quite easily, sire," replied the Man in Grey. "Your Majesty's spies in Jersey gave us warning some time ago that de Livardot was making preparations to embark for France. My business then was to find out where he would land. This I did by watching the best-known Chouans in the district. One of them led me to the Goat's

Creek, which I then kept in observation. A week later de Livardot did land there. I had him waylaid and arrested, and took possession of his papers. One of these gave me a pass-phrase and the address in the Rue aux Juifs, another was a map of the house and grounds of Les Acacias.

"It was not difficult to imagine a connection between that map and your Majesty's visit; nor would it, I hoped, be difficult to assume the personality of a man whom, presumably, they had not seen for years (I mean de Livardot), and to learn the whole of the plot against your Majesty's life. At any rate I chose to take the risk. From one or two of the papers I had gathered that he was being recommended by certain Chouan chiefs to a number of their followers who did not know him by sight. I went to the address in the Rue aux Juifs and there obtained full details of the infamous plot. My hope, of course, was not only to frustrate that plot, but also to bring the conspirators to justice. This I was able to do through your Majesty's gracious co-operation in leaving Les Acacias secretly at my suggestion, together with your host and retinue; and also through Monsieur le Duc de Gisors' lofty patriotism in allowing his magnificent mansion to be sacrificed. The explosion I knew was to be the signal for the rallying of the *infâmes* who schemed in secret, while they left their humbler followers to do the poisonous work for them. Now the trap has closed on them all and your Majesty's clemency alone can save them from the gallows."

VIII

THE ARROW POISON

WHEN the secret agent of His Majesty's Minister of Police selected Hippolyte Darnier to be his messenger for the occasion, he knew he had a man whom he could trust.

Darnier was married: he was a man of middle age, who had served the Republic first, then the Consulate, and finally the Emperor with unswerving loyalty, in circumstances which more often than not entailed grave personal risks. He had always extricated himself from difficult and dangerous positions with marvellous coolness and acumen, and it was but natural that when the autograph letter signed by M. de Trévargen—which implicated the noble Marquis and his family in the late abortive conspiracy against the life of the Emperor—had to be sent to M. le Duc d'Otrante, the latter's secret agent should choose a man of proven courage and address for the purpose.

The Man in Grey took leave of his messenger at his lodgings in the Rue de Bras, and at the very last moment of the leave-taking gave him the precious letter, which Darnier immediately secreted in the inside breast pocket of his coat. Then he was ready for the journey

In those days the Paris diligence started from the Hôtel du Portugal in Caën every morning at eight o'clock, reaching Lisieux—the first stage—at five in the afternoon. Darnier had secured his seat on the banquette by the side of the driver, for although the day was cold he felt that he would be safer there than huddled up between other passengers inside the coach, some of whom might be unpleasantly light-fingered. There was a fair number of travellers that morning. An elderly pair of bourgeois on their way to Evreux and a well-to-do shopkeeper's wife going to

Paris to visit her son, who was employed in the new aerial telegraphs, had secured the *coupé* in front. Two or three commercial travellers, a couple of young officers on leave from the war, a portly fish-wife from Caën, and a round-cheeked country wench occupied the interior. At the small posting inn of the "Mouton Noir," just outside the city, another woman got in. She had no luggage and apparently she had not booked her place, for she had to be content with one on the narrow back seats of the inside, wedged in between the round-faced country wench and the fish-wife from Caën. However, the newcomer seemed quite satisfied with her surroundings; she sat down placidly and, pulling her hood well over her face, took up a book and thereafter remained absorbed in reading, looking neither to right nor left, and taking no part in the vapid conversation, engendered by boredom, which was carried on around her. Her fellow-travellers put her down as belonging to some sort of religious community, for she wore a voluminous black cloak with a hood which only allowed the point of her chin to peep out below it.

At Mézidon, where halt was made for dinner, everyone trooped into the coffee-room of the "Cheval Blanc." Hippolyte Darnier asked to have his meal served in a private room, and as he was provided with special credentials bearing the seal of the Ministry of Police, his wishes were at once acceded to, and he was served both promptly and obsequiously, in a small room adjoining the one where the other passengers were dining together.

The woman in the black cloak had been the last to leave the diligence. She had remained in her seat, immersed in her book till everyone had scrambled out of the coach. Then she, too, got out, and walked very slowly in the wake of the jovial party ahead. But she did not appear to be in any hurry to join her fellow travellers, for while they settled down with noise and bustle at the well-spread table, she strolled away in the direction of the river.

The dinner was over and coffee had been handed round when she entered the coffee-room. The wine had been good, and everyone was hilarious. As she closed the door behind her, she was greeted with jovial calls.

326

"Here, reverend sister, come and sit down."

"You must be famished!"

"The roasted gigot is positively excellent!"

But the woman paid no heed to these well-meant civilities, beyond a few whispered "Thank you's." Her hood still covered her face, all but the point of her chin, after the manner adopted by professed nuns of cloistered orders when men are about. She crossed the coffee-room rapidly to the door of the private room beyond, where Hippolyte Darnier was having his solitary dinner.

The serving-maid tried to stop her.

"There's a gentleman in there," she said, "who wishes to be alone."

"Oh!" said the woman quietly, "that is quite all right. I am travelling in his company."

With that she opened the door and went into the inner room.

There was so much noise going on in the coffee-room at the time that no one was able to state positively afterwards how Darnier greeted the intruder, and whether or no her statement was true that she was travelling in his company. Certain it is that, after a quarter of an hour or so, she came out again, as quietly, as silently as she had come, re-crossed the coffee-room, and went out, leaving this time a curious, almost uncanny air of mystery behind her.

"I have never been fond of these female *callotins* myself" said one of the young officers after a while.

"I cannot stand people who make no noise when they walk," asserted the worthy bourgeois of Evreux.

The well-to-do farmer's wife, conscious of undisputed respectability, added with some acidity;

"Strange that a professed nun should be travelling alone in a man's company."

After that comments on the occurrence became freer and more ribald, and very soon the absentee had not a shred of reputation left in the minds of the worthy but intensely bored people congregated around the festive board of the "Cheval Blanc."

At two o'clock the ostler in charge announced that the diligence was ready to start. Jean Baptiste, the jocund host of the "Cheval Blanc," was going round the table, collecting payment for the good *déjeuner* which had been served to his more than satisfied clients.

"What shall I do about the gentleman in there?" asked the serving-maid, pointing to the door of the private room. "He was asleep the last time I went in."

"Wake him up," replied Jean Baptiste.

"I have done all I could to wake him," answered the wench. "He doesn't seem inclined to move."

"He'll have to move," rejoined Jean Baptiste with a laugh; "or the diligence will go without him."

With that he strode across to the door of the private room, kicked it open with his foot, and called out in his lusty voice, which, as someone remarked, was loud enough to wake the dead:

"Now then, Monsieur, 'tis time to wake up! The diligence is about to start. You'll never get to Paris at this rate."

The door had remained wide open. The travellers in the coffee-room could see the figure of M. Darnier sitting huddled in a chair, and half-leaning against the table, like one who is in a drunken sleep.

"Give him a good shake, papa Baptiste!" called one of the young officers waggishly. "Your good wine has been too much for him."

Jean Baptiste stopped and gave the huddled figure a good shake. Then suddenly he uttered a horrified "Oh, mon Dieu!"

"What is it?" queried the travellers anxiously.

"The man is dead!"

Never had the Paris diligence been so late in starting from Mézidon; and when finally, with much cracking of whips and rattling of chains, it thundered along the cobble stones of the Grande Rue, it was without its full complement of passengers.

M. le Commissaire de Police had ordered the detention of most of them as witnesses of the occurrence which culminated in the death of Hippolyte Darnier, who was known to the commissaire as an employé on the police staff at Caën.

It was no use grumbling. No one who had seen or spoken to the woman in the black cloak could be allowed to leave the city until M. le Procureur Impérial in Caën had granted them leave to do so.

In the meanwhile M. le Sous-Préfet, who was quite hopelessly out of his depth, interrogated the witnesses without eliciting more than a noisy and confused account of the events of the past few hours wherein the weather, the bad state of the roads, and the good wines of the "Cheval Blanc" vied in importance with the doings of a so-called mysterious nun, of whom nothing had been seen by anybody, save the point of a chin and a voluminous black cloak and hood. By the time that the sous-préfet had jotted down these miscellaneous depositions, it was discovered that the mysterious personage in question had disappeared. Whereupon search parties were sent abroad in every direction, with strict orders to bring any woman who was seen wearing any kind of a black cloak forthwith before M. le Commissaire, whilst the sous-préfet, freely perspiring under the effort, wrote out a detailed and wholly unintelligible report of the incidents, which he dispatched by mounted courier to his chief at Caën.

The search parties, after two or three hours' diligent scouring of the neighbourhood, brought back an inoffensive farm servant, who was trudging home from her milking, wrapped in a black shawl; the kitchen wench from the Hôtel de Madrid, who had gone out to meet her sweetheart and had borrowed her mistress's black cloak for the occasion; and old Madame Durand, the caretaker at the church of St. Pierre, who always wore a black gown as an outward symbol of her official position and responsible calling.

One lad, more intelligent than the rest, while wandering along the tow-path of the river, had espied a black cloak and hood floating down-stream until its progress was arrested by a clump of rushes. The lad fished for the cloak with a barge-pole and succeeded in landing it. He brought it in triumph to Mézidon, where he became the hero of the hour.

Late in the evening, M. Laurens, préfet of Caën, received his subordinate's report. At once he communicated with M. Carteret, the chief commissary of police. The two, fearing that the officious secret agent would keep them out of their beds for the next two hours, with God knows what orders to proceed to Mézidon in the middle of the night, decided to say nothing to him until the morning. After all, the matter was not of such paramount importance. Darnier, they argued, had had too much to drink and had a fit of apoplexy in an overheated room.

But next morning, when the chief commissary did present himself before the Minister's agent with the Mézidon report, he for one felt that he would far sooner have sacrificed a night's rest than endure the icy reprimand and the cooly worded threats wherewith the insufferable little man had greeted his news.

"By your culpable negligence," the Minister's agent had said in his quiet monotone which made every official conscious of some unavowed peccadillo shiver, "you have given the murderer an added chance to escape."

"The murderer!" protested M. Carteret, with a feeble attempt at swagger. "What in the world makes you think that Darnier has been murdered? Why, the leech——"

"Because an ignorant country apothecary finds no sign of violence upon a dead body" retorted the Man in Grey coldly, "unanswerable logic must not be deemed at fault."

"But what motive would anyone have for murdering poor Darnier?" argued the commissary with a shrug of his wide shoulders.

"You forget that he was the bearer of an

important report from me to the Minister," replied the Man in Grey.

The commissary gave a long, low whistle. He certainly had forgotten that all-important fact for the moment.

"And you think," he said, "that the woman in the black cloak was an emissary of those cursed Chouans, and that she murdered Darnier in order to steel that report——"

"Together with the autograph letter of Monsieur le Marquis de Trévargan, which implicates him and his family in the plot against the Emperor," broke in the secret agent. "I should have thought it was self-evident."

He wasted no further argument on the commissary, who, bewildered and helpless, scratched his head, as if to extract therefrom a solution of the weird mystery.

An hour or so later Madame Darnier, the widow of the murdered man, called at the préfecture in answer to a hurried summons. As someone must break the terrible news to her, the Man in Grey undertook the task, speaking as sympathetically and as gently as he could. She was a delicate-looking woman, still in the prime of life, and with justified pretensions to good looks. She took the news badly, for, as she explained later when she was calmer, she had been devoted to her husband and he to her, and they had only been married five years. She had no children, she said, in answer to the secret agent's kindly inquiries, and her dear husband's death left her practically without means of support. The assurance that His Majesty's Minister of Police would provide generously for the widow of a man who had died in the service of the State gave her some small measure of comfort, and when she finally took her leave, she appeared, if not more consoled, at any rate more tranquil.

Madame Darnier had been unable to furnish the police with any clue which might guide them in their investigations. She was quite sure that her husband had no enemies, and whilst she had been aware that his work often entailed grave personal risks, she knew nothing about the work itself, nor, in this case, had he told her anything beyond the fact that he was going to Paris and would be absent about ten days. She repudiated with indignation the suggestion that he had been travelling in the company of some woman unknown to herself, and of her own accord threw out the suggestion that some of those *méchant* Chouans—knowing her husband's connection with the police—had not scrupled to slay him.

The Château de Trévargan, situated upon a lonely piece of coast midway between the mouths of the Orne and the Dives and about ten or a dozen miles from Caën, had remained one of the beauty spots of the neighbourhood. Though its owners had emigrated at the outbreak of the Revolution and their domain had become the property of the State, it had been brought nominally by a man named Leclerc, who had been the Marquis's agent, and who held it thenceforward and administered it with unswerving loyalty, in the name of his former master. Leclerc with his wife and family had settled down in the château, and together they looked after the house, the park and the estate during the Marquis's prolonged absence abroad. They always appeared plentifully supplied with money, which no doubt came to them through one of the many agencies in Jersey, and when M. le

Marquis returned to France some five years ago he found his house in perfect order; and it is supposed that he rewarded his faithful steward generously, for the latter retired with his family to a little estate close by, where they continued to live in undiminished affluence.

M. le Marquis de Trévargan had obviously not brought a fortune back from exile; nevertheless, he and Madame la Marquise kept up a good deal of style at the chateau. They also went to Paris and made their obeisance to the Emperor at Versailles, and hitherto not the slightest suspicion of disloyalty to the new regime had attached to them.

The discovery of the outrageous plot against the life of the Emperor during the latter's visit to Caën in February had left the Trévargans unscathed, even though close upon a score of their personal friends were implicated in the affair. It was only three weeks later that M. le Marquis learned that the one foolish letter he had written in the whole course of his cautious career had fallen into the hands of the police. He had written to his friend the Comte de Romorantin, urging him to keep aloof from the conspirators until he was sure that the Corsican had really been sent to Hades.

"Madame la Marquise and myself do not intend to appear at Caën until we know for certain that the *coup* has been successful. We have done our share in the matter of providing funds, but we prefer to let Blue-Heart, White-Beak and the other ruffians do the work for us. We shall be ready to proclaim His Majesty King Louis XVIII. in the Hôtel de Ville as soon as we know that all fear of failure or discovery is at an end. I entreat you to do likewise and to destroy this letter as soon as read."

Unfortunately, M. de Romorantin had not destroyed the letter. He had it in his pocket at the very moment when the police made the raid on the house in the Rue aux Juifs and arrested the Chouan conspirators redhanded. The letter was seized, together with every other paper which happened to be in the possession of the prisoners, and it was that same highly compromising letter which Hippolyte Darnier was taking to Paris when he died so mysteriously in the private room of the "Cheval Blanc" at Mezidon.

Investigation at the chateau on the day following the discovery of the plot had led to no result. M. le Marquis watched with lofty indifference and disdain the turning over of his private papers and belongings by the heedless hands of the police. Except for that one letter, he had never committed an indiscretion or written an unguarded word in his life. But there was the letter! And it was this very search which, coming as a bolt from the blue, had assured him that he was no longer immune from suspicion.

The day following the death of Hippolyte Darnier, M. le Marquis de Trévargan received another visit from the police, this time in the person of M. Carteret, the commissary, whom he knew personally, and who came accompanied by a small, insignificant-looking personage dressed in grey. Once more, secure in the knowledge that nothing that could in any way compromise him would be found inside his château, the Marquis received his visitors with condescending hauteur.

"Ah, *ça*, my good Carteret," he said to the commissary somewhat tartly, "when am I and Madame la Marquise to be free from this insolent interference? Since when are the loyal subjects of His Majesty to be treated as if they were criminals?"

The worthy M. Carteret felt hot and cold all over. He had an enormous regard for M. le Marquis de Trévargan and a wholesome terror of the Minister's secret agent, and between the two he did not know to which saint he should pray for protection.

"Loyalty is a matter of degree," here interposed the Man in Grey in his usual monotone; "as Monsieur le Marquis well knows."

"I only know, Monsieur," retorted the Marquis haughtily, "that certain aspersions have been cast upon my good name, chiefly on the strength of a forged letter——"

"A forged letter, Monsieur le Marquis?" interposed the Man in Grey with a smile. "Monsieur de Romorantin has owned to its authenticity."

"Monsieur de Romorantin was scared out of his wits." rejoined the Marquis, "or he never would have been taken in by such a clumsy forgery. And," he added haughtily, "I might have a chance of proving the truth of what I say."

"It is just because the letter has been stolen," stammered M. Carteret, "and the messenger murdered that we are here to-day, Monsieur le Marquis."

While he spoke a door at the farther end of the room opened, and a tall, handsome woman appeared upon the threshold. When the commissary finished speaking, she broke into a ringing laugh.

"A pretty story indeed!" she said harshly. "A monstrous accusation hurled at Monsieur le Marquis de Trévargan! And when he demands to be confronted with proofs of his guilt, these proofs are said to be destroyed, whilst a vague hint of murder goes to swell the iniquitous charge. A pretty pass, indeed!" she continued, as with stately steps she advanced into the room. "Fortunately His Majesty has some friendship for Monsieur le Marquis and myself, and we can appeal to him to punish those who have put this affront upon us."

"Your pardon, Madame la Marquise," answered the Man in Grey, as soon as she had finished her impassionate tirade. "Monsieur le Commissaire said that the letter had been stolen; he did not say that it had been destroyed."

An almost imperceptible shadow seemed to pass as in a flash over the

Marquise's handsome face; but the very next second she shrugged her handsome shoulders and said flippantly:

"The same thing, my good man."

"I trust not, Madame la Marquise," rejoined the Man in Grey.

"Oh, we all know," here interrupted M. le Marquis with a sneer, "that in your unmentionable profession, Monsieur, you are bound to send a certain number of unfortunates to what you call justice, whether they are guilty or not, or you would lose your highly lucrative employment. Isn't that so?"

"Our employment, Monsieur le Marquis," replied the Man in Grey imperturbably, "is not likely to find favour in your sight."

"Well!" rejoined Madame with a harsh laugh, "so long as you don't trump up a charge of murder against some poor innocent this time——"

"Murder, Madame la Marquise!" queried the secret agent with a look of mild astonishment in his colourless eyes. "Who spoke of murder?"

"I thought," parried the Marquise airly, "that some spy or other of yours was murdered and robbed of the forged letter, which was supposed to convict Monsieur le Marquis de Trévargan and myself of disloyalty."

"One of our men was certainly robbed of a letter written by Monsieur le Marquis de Trévargan to Monsieur de Romorantin on the eve of the conspiracy against the Emperor" said the Man in Grey, "but I am happy to say that he is alive at the present moment——"

A terrific crash of broken china drowned the rest of his speech. The table against which Madame la Marquise had been leaning fell over, scattering precious *bibelots* in every direction.

"How clumsy of me!" exclaimed Madame in some confusion, whilst the commissary of police, agitated and obsequious, crawled about on his hands and knees, trying to collect the fragments of priceless china which littered the carpet. "Do not trouble, I pray you, Monsieur le Commissaire," said the Marquise with affable condescension. "The servant will clear away the rubbish."

She sank into a chair, as if tired out with the interminable interview, and put her aristocratic hand up to her mouth, smothering a yawn.

"As you were saying, Monsieur—er—" she drawled wearily.

"I was not saying anything, Madame la Marquise," rejoined the Man in Grey, smiling.

"Your spy or messenger, whatever he was——" interposed the Marquis impatiently. "You were saying something about him."

"Oh! nothing that would interest Monsieur le Marquis," replied the secret agent. "He was stabbed in the hand with a pin steeped in a deadly arrow poison, which in ordinary circumstances would have killed him in less than five minutes. Fortunately for him the assassin was either inexperienced or clumsy, or perhaps the poison had become stale by keeping. At any rate, poor Hippolyte Darnier was nearly killed—but not quite. He is still very ill—half paralysed; but the leech assures me that he will recover."

This time there was no mistaking the shadow which once more passed across the Marquise's handsome face, whilst for the space of a second or two the somewhat high colour of her cheeks changed to a leaden hue. The Marquis instinctively came forward a few steps, obtruding his

344

stately figure between the police agent and his wife. Next moment, however, Madame had regained her composure. She rose from her chair, tall, dignified, unspeakably haughty.

"So much the better for your friend, Monsieur—er—I forget your name," she said coldly, "And now," she added as she walked majestically towards the door, "if you or Monsieur le Commissaire have any more senseless questions to ask, you must be content with the information Monsieur le Marquis condescends to give you, I confess to being weary of this folly."

She pushed open the door and sailed out of the room, as arrogant as any queen of the old régime dismissing an importunate courtier. Then the door fell to behind her and her firm step soon died away along the marble corridor.

The commissary of police was pining to take his leave, and much to his relief the Man in Grey put no further questions to M. le Marquis, and after a few seconds declared himself ready to go. M. de Trévargan was quite pleasant to poor M. Carteret, who obviously greatly disapproved of this intrusion on the privacy of the stately château.

"The man is a veritable pest!" he contrived to whisper in the Marquis's ear, behind the back of the secret agent. "I would wish to assure Monsieur le Marquis——"

"Do not trouble to do that, my good Monsieur Carteret," interrupted M. de Trévargan impatiently. "Your assurances are unnecessary. You were obeying orders: and the man, I suppose, was fulfilling what he believed to be his duty."

Somewhat comforted, the commissary went downstairs in the wake of the Man in Grey, who was waiting for him in the vast entrance hall below, and was gazing in rapt admiration at the pictures and statuary which would not have shamed a royal residence.

"It is a rare treat," he was saying to the pompous major-domo who was waiting to usher the visitors out, "for art-lovers to have the opportunity of seeing these priceless treasures. Are they not sometimes shown to the public?"

"Oh, no, Monsieur," replied the major-domo sententiously. "As Monsieur and Madame de Trévargan are in residence, it would not be seemly to allow strangers to wander about the château."

"Ah!" said the Man in Grey, "then my sister was lucky indeed. She saw all these beautiful pictures and statues yesterday!"

"Yesterday, Monsieur?" queried the man, as haughtily as his master and mistress would have done. "I do not understand."

"It's quite simple," rejoined the secret agent. "My sister is the intimate friend of one of the maids here, and yesterday, as Madame la Marquise was away all day, this friend smuggled my sister into this part of the château and showed her all these marvellous art treasures——"

"This would be a pretty story, Monsieur," here broke in the major-domo impatiently, "if it were based on some semblance of truth. Madame la Marquise did not happen to be away at any time during yesterday."

"But surely——" protested the Man in Grey.

"Madame la Marquise was indeed very much at home," continued the other with becoming sternness, "seeing that she entertained the children of the Convent School here to *déjeuner* at midday and games all the afternoon."

347

The secret agent now appeared overwhelmed with confusion at his stupid blunder.

"I am very sorry," he murmured haltingly. "There's some mistake on my part—I understood my sister to say that she was here yesterday—it must have been some other day——"

"Very likely!" retorted the major-domo with a sneer; and giving the plebeian police agent the supercilious stare which so much impertinence deserved, he finally closed the imposing doors of the chateau upon the unwelcome visitors.

"Another snub!" remarked the commissary of police as he descended the steps beside his silent colleague. "And why you trumped up that story about your sister and a maid, I cannot imagine!" he added with withering contempt.

But the Man in Grey apparently did not hear him. He was murmuring under his breath: "Clever enough to have secured an alibi! I might have guessed it! And such an actress! But, then, how in Heaven's name was it done? How? And by whom?"

The Man in Grey had allowed the commissary of police to return to Caën, but he seemed to find it impossible to tear himself away from the neighbourhood of Trévargan. He felt that the lordly château held a grim secret within its walls, and he could not rest until he had wrung it from them.

All day he hung about the approaches of the park and, as soon as night fell, managed to creep into the depths of the shrubberies before the gates were closed. Here he remained on the watch, peering through the thicket at the stately pile, the windows of which soon became lighted from within, one by one. What he expected to see he could not have told you, but Night is the great guardian of dark mysteries and unavowable deeds, and the secret agent hoped that the gloom would mayhap give him the key to that riddle which had baffled him in broad light of day.

From where he was crouching he commanded a view both of the front of the house and of the path which led to the back. He had been lying in wait for nearly two hours, and a neighbouring church clock had just struck ten, when through the darkness he perceived the figure of a woman, wrapped in a cloak, walking quickly towards the château. At first he thought it might be one of the maids returning from a walk, but as the figure passed close to him, something vaguely familiar in the poise of the head and the shape of the cloak caused him suddenly to crawl out of his hiding-place as noiselessly as he could, and to follow the woman until a bend in the avenue afforded him the opportunity which he sought. In one second he had taken off his mantle and, springing on her from behind, he caught her in his arms and threw the mantle over her head, smothering the cry which had risen to her lips. Though he was short and slight, he had uncommon strength, and the woman was small and slender. He lifted her off the ground and carried her along the avenue and down a side-path, until he had reached a secluded portion of the park.

Here he laid his burden down and unwound the mantle which was stifling her. Then he turned the light of his dark lantern upon her.

"Madame Darnier!" he murmured. "Just as I thought!"

Then, as the woman was still lying there almost unconscious, he threw back her cloak and looked at her hands. There was nothing in them. He felt for the pockets in her cloak and in her dress; his hands wandered over the folds of her gown; his ears, attuned to the slightest sound, listened for the crackling that would reveal the presence of papers concealed about her person. But there was nothing, and he frowned in deep puzzlement as he encountered her large, melancholy eyes, which were following his every movement with the look of a trapped animal watching its captor.

"What are you doing here in Trevargan?" he asked sternly.

"Help me to get up," she replied almost fiercely, "and I may tell you."

More puzzled than before, he raised her to her feet.

"You remember me?" he asked.

"Of course," she replied. "How could I forget the man who first held the cup of such bitter sorrow to my lips?"

"Someone had to tell you," he rejoined more gently, "and your husband was in my employ."

"And died in your employ," she answered roughly.

"Will you believe me," he retorted,

"that, had I known of the terrible risk which he was running, I would have undertaken the errand myself?"

"Yes," she said dully, "I know that you are not a coward."

"Will you tell me why you are here?" he reiterated firmly.

She looked round her, right into the gloom in the direction where the lights of the château glimmered feebly through the trees. Then, turning to the Man in Grey, she said calmly:

"There was a suspicion gnawing at my heart. I came to see if I could confirm it, or lull it for ever to rest."

"You suspect the Trévargans of having had a hand in the outrage against your husband?"

"Don't you?" she retorted.

He made no reply, and even through the darkness she could see that he appeared deeply buried in thought. He had turned off the light of his lantern, and by the dim light of the moon, partly hidden behind a veil of clouds, they could only distinguish one another's outline against the dense background of the shrubberies.

"Will you allow me to escort you home?" he asked abruptly.

She nodded in assent, and he, knowing the way, guided her along the less frequented paths of the park till he came to a locked postern gate. Asking her to wait a moment, and, drawing a small tool from his pocket, he coolly picked the lock, and a moment or two later he and Mme. Darnier were walking rapidly down the main road in the direction of the city.

Next morning, when the Man in Grey arrived at the commissariat of police, he was greeted with sneers and acid reproaches by M. Carteret and M. le Préfet.

"I must say," said the latter with becoming pomposity, "that your attitude with regard to Monsieur and Madame de Trévargan is exceedingly reprehensible. You have placed my colleague and myself in a very awkward position. Monsieur le Marquis is one of the most influential, as he has always been one of the most loyal, personages in the province, and I have no doubt that he will visit his displeasure upon us both, though, Heaven knows! we have done nothing but follow your foolish lead in the matter."

"I pray you have patience, my good

Monsieur Laurens," said the Man in Grey with unruffled calm. "The matter to which you refer is on the point of reaching its culmination."

"I was alluding to the affair of Hippolyte Darnier," said the préfet.

"So was I," retorted the Man in Grey.

"Are you about to discover who murdered him?" queried M. Carteret, with a touch of taunt.

"Yes," replied the secret agent. "With the help of Madame Darnier, whom I have summoned hither."

The préfet shrugged his shoulders with marked impatience.

"And I must ask you," added the Man in Grey in his blandest tones which admitted of no argument, "not to interfere in anything I may say to Madame Darnier in the course of our interview; to express no surprise and, above all, not to attempt to contradict. And you know, Monsieur Laurens, and you, too, Monsieur le Commissaire," he added sternly, "that when I give an order I intend it to be obeyed."

Hardly had this peremptory command fallen from his lips than Madame Darnier was announced.

She came in, looking even more fragile and more delicate in her deep mourning than she had done before. Her large, melancholy eyes sought, as if appealingly, those of the three men who had half-risen to greet her. The Man in Grey offered her a chair, into which she sank.

"You sent for me, Monsieur?" she asked, as she pressed a black-bordered handkerchief to her quivering lips.

"Only to give you the best of news, Madame," the secret agent said cheerily.

"The best of news?" she murmured. "I do not understand."

"My friend Hippolyte Darnier," he exclaimed, "your husband, Madame, is out of danger——"

She rose suddenly, as if some hidden spring had projected her to her feet, and stood rigid and tense, her cheeks the colour of yellow wax, her eyes so dilated that they seemed as black as coal. The préfet and the commissary had, indeed, the greatest difficulty to maintain the attitude of impassivity which the Minister's agent had so rigidly prescribed.

"Out of danger," murmured Mme. Darnier after a while. "What do you mean?"

"No wonder you are overcome with emotion, Madame," rejoined the secret agent. "I myself did not dare breathe a word to you of my hopes at Trévargan last night, for I had not had the leech's final pronouncement. But I have had hopes all along. We transported your dear husband's inanimate body to my lodgings after his—er—accident the other day. He was totally unconscious; it almost seemed as if *rigor mortis* had already set in. But I suppose the deadly arrow poison, which a murderous hand had injected with the aid of a pin, was either stale or ineffectual. Certain it is that my dear friend Darnier rallied, that he is alive at this moment, and that I shall have the pleasure of conducting you to his bedside immediately."

While he spoke the Man in Grey had kept his eyes fixed steadily upon the woman. She was still standing as rigid as before and clinging with one hand to the back of the chair, whilst with the other she continued to press her handkerchief to her lips. Nor could the other men detach their eyes from her face, which appeared like a petrified presentation of abject and nameless horror.

"Darnier," continued the Man in Grey relentlessly, "is slowly regaining consciousness now. The leech desires that the first sight which greets his eyes should be that of his beloved wife. Come, Madame, it is a short walk to my lodgings. Let me conduct you——Ah!" he suddenly exclaimed, as with his usual agility he literally threw himself upon the staggering woman. "Stop that, now! Stop it, I say!"

But he was too late. Madame Darnier had fallen back into her chair. From a deep scratch across her hand drops of blood were oozing freely. The commissaire and the préfet were gazing, horror-stricken and helpless, upon her face, which was slowly becoming distorted. A curious, jerky quiver shook her limbs from time to time.

"She has killed herself with the same poison wherewith she sent her unfortunate husband to his death," said the secret agent quietly.

"To his death?" gasped the préfet. "Then the story of Hippolyte Darnier's recovery——"

"Was false," broke in the Man in Grey. "It was a trap set to wring an avowal from the murderer. And we must own," he

357

added earnestly, "that the avowal has been both full and conclusive."

He threw his mantle over the wretched woman, who was already past help. But he dispatched one of the servants of the préfecture for the nearest leech.

"But what made you guess——?" queried the commissary, who was gasping with astonishment.

"The fact that Madame Darnier was the daughter of the man Leclerc, who for years devoted himself to the fortunes of the Trévargans. He and his family are attached heart and soul to the Marquis and his cause. The daughter has proved herself a fanatic, a madwoman, I should say. She killed her husband to save the family she loved."

"But those accursed Trévargans——" said the prefet.

"Their punishment will not long be delayed. I sent a copy of the compromising letter to the Minister—the original is still in my keeping."

IX

THE LAST ADVENTURE

THE riders put their horses to a walk. It was getting late in the afternoon, and the sun, crimson and cheerless, was setting in a sea of slate-coloured mist. A blustering wind from the south-west blew intermittent rain showers into the faces of the two solitary wayfarers. They had ridden hard all day—a matter of over thirty miles from Evreux—and one of them, at any rate, a middle-aged, stoutish, official-looking personage, showed signs both of fatigue and of growing ill-temper. The other, younger, more slender, dressed in colourless grey from head to foot, his mantle slung lightly from his shoulders, his keen eyes fixed straight before him, appeared moved by impatience rather than by the wind or the lateness of the hour.

The rain and the rapidly falling dusk covered the distant hills and the valley beyond with a mantle of gloom. To right and left of the road the coppice, still dressed in winter garb, already was wrapped in the mysteries of the night.

"I shall not be sorry to see the lights of Mantes," said M. Gault, the commissary of police of Evreux, to his companion. "I am getting saddle-sore, and this abominable damp has got into my bones."

The other sighed with obvious impatience.

"I would like to push on to Paris to-night," he said. "The moon will be up directly, and I believe the rain-clouds will clear. In any case the night will not be very dark, and I know every inch of the way."

"Another six hours or more in the saddle!" growled the commissary. "No, thank you!"

"I thought you were anxious about those escaped prisoners of yours," observed the Man in Grey.

"So I am," retorted M. Gault.

"And that you desired Monsieur le Ministre to hear of the escape through your lips, before rumour hath played havoc with the event," continued the other tartly.

"So I do—so I do!" grunted the commissary. "But those damned Chouans only got away last night from Evreux, where they should never have been brought. They were apprehended at Caën;

the outrage, which you were able to avert, had been planned and was discovered at Caën; the knaves should have been tried and hanged at Caën. Instead of which," continued M. Gault wrathfully, "they were marched to Evreux, on their way to Paris. At Evreux we had neither the facilities nor the personnel to guard such a *rusé* gang adequately—they gave us the slip——"

"And," interrupted the Man in Grey, in his iciest manner, "the men who planned to murder the Emperor are now at large, free to concoct a further outrage, which, this time, may prove successful!"

"Through no fault of mine!" protested the commissary.

"That will be for the Minister to decide," concluded the Man in Grey.

But even this thinly-veiled threat failed to instil new vigour into M. Gault. Alarmed at the possible effects upon his future career of what might be deemed official negligence, he had wished to place his excuses personally before His Majesty's Minister of Police, ere the latter could hear through outside sources that the desperate gang of malefactors who had planned the affair of the infernal machine against the Emperor's life had escaped from Evreux, and that such astute and reckless criminals as Blue-Heart and White-Beak were again at large. In spite of M. Gault's anxiety, however, to be the first to gain the Minister's ear, his whole middle-aged, over-indulged person protested against any prolongation of what had become torturing fatigue.

"You are young, Monsieur Fernand," he added dolefully. "You do not realise—— Malédiction! What was that?" he ejaculated, as his horse gave a sudden jump to one side and nearly unseated him. The animal had shied at something not at present visible to its rider. It was still retreating, with ears set back, nostrils quivering, its body trembling with fright, so that M. Gault had the greatest difficulty alike to keep his seat and soothe the poor beast.

"I wonder what the brute shied at," he said.

But already the Man in Grey had dismounted. He led his horse across the road, and then to a spot where, on the farther side of the intervening ditch, a large, dark mass lay huddled, only vaguely discernible in the gloom. He peered with anxious eyes into the darkness; then he called to the commissary.

"I pray you hold my horse, Monsieur Gault," he said peremptorily.

"What is it?" queried the latter as—still with some difficulty—he brought his horse alongside the other and gathered up the reins which Fernand had thrown to him.

"That is just what I wish to ascertain," replied the Minister's agent simply.

He jumped lightly over the ditch and approached the huddled mass. This proved to be the body of a young man with fair hair and beard, dressed in rough peasant's clothes. The linen blouse he wore was smeared round about his shoulders with stains of a dull crimson colour, whilst the dead leaves beneath him were soiled in the same way. In a moment, Fernand had passed his slim, experienced hand over the face of the man, over his body and his feet, which were bare. These were cold and rigid, but the stains upon the blouse and upon the bed of dead leaves were yet dank to the touch.

"What is it?" queried the commissary again, more impatiently.

"Murder!" replied the Man in Grey

laconically.

"The high roads are not safe," remarked M. Gault sententiously. "And even in this district, where those *satané* Chouans do not ply their nefarious trade, the police seem unable to ensure the safety of peaceable travellers."

He gave an involuntary shiver and gazed anxiously behind him.

"I pray you, Monsieur Fernand," he said, "do not let us linger here. This is an affair for the local police, and we must get to Mantes before dark."

"You need not linger, Monsieur le Commissaire," rejoined the Man in Grey. "I pray you, tie my horse to the nearest tree and continue your journey, if you have a mind."

He had risen to his feet and appeared to be examining the ground closely all round the spot where lay the body of the murdered man. M. Gault uttered one of his favourite oaths. Indeed, he had no mind to continue his journey alone, with those murdering footpads lurking in the woods and the road to Mantes lonely and unsafe.

"What are you looking for now, Monsieur Fernand?" he queried sharply.

"Surely, the police of Mantes can deal with the affairs. Are you looking for traces of the miscreants?"

"No," replied the other, "I am looking for the murdered man's boots."

"The murdered man's boots!" exclaimed the commissary crossly. "Why the fellow is just a rough peasant, and no doubt he walked barefoot."

"No doubt," agreed the Man in Grey.

Nevertheless, he continued his search and even plunged into the thicket, only to emerge therefrom in a minute or two, as the darkness made it impossible to distinguish anything that might be hidden in the undergrowth.

"I don't know why you should be so obstinate about those boots!" growled the commissary.

But to this remark the Man in Grey vouchsafed no reply. He had resumed his mount and was already in the saddle.

"I am going on to Paris," he said briefly.

Poor M. Gault heaved a doleful sigh.

"To Paris!" he ejaculated pitiably. "But I——"

"You'll stay at Mantes," enjoined the Minister's agent emphatically, "and there await my orders or those of Monsieur le

Ministre. You are on no account to leave your post," he added sternly, "on pain of instant dismissal and degradation."

With that he put his horse to a sharp trot, heedless whether the unfortunate commissary followed him or not.

The Man in Grey was sitting, travel-stained and weary, in the dressing-room of M. le Duc d'Otrante, Minister of Police to His Imperial Majesty. He had ridden all night, only halting now and again to give his horse a rest, as he could not get a change of mount during the whole distance between Mantes—where he had obtained a fresh horse, and where he left M. Gault comfortably installed in the best hotel of the place—and Paris, where he arrived an hour after daybreak, stiff, aching in every limb, scarcely able to tumble out of the saddle.

But he would not wait even to change his clothes or get a little rest. Within a quarter of an hour of his arrival in the capital he was knocking at the monumental gateway of M. le Duc's magnificent palace. Obviously he was a privileged person as far as access to the all-powerful Minister was concerned, for no sooner had his name been metioned to M. le Duc's confidential valet than he was ushered into the great man's presence.

The police agent had the power of concise and rapid diction. Within a very few minutes the Minister was in possession of all the facts connected with the mysterious murder of the unknown person on the highway to Mantes.

"The man's clothes were rougher and more shabby than his physical condition suggested," Fernand remarked in conclusion. "His hands were not those of a peasant; his feet were quite clean though the roads were muddy. Clearly, then, his boots had been taken off by the murderers, presumably in the hope that some valuables might have been concealed inside them. At once my mind jumped to thoughts of a written message—sent by you, Monsieur le Ministre, perhaps. At any rate, I left old Gault at Mantes and rode another sixty kilometres to ascertain as quickly as possible what my conjectures were worth."

"Describe the man to me," said the Minister.

"Age under thirty," replied Fernand; "short, square beard, fair hair slightly

367

curled——"

"Hector Duroy," broke in the Minister.

"Then he was your messenger?"

"Yes! He started for Evreux early yesterday morning. I wished him to meet you there."

"To tell me what, Monsieur le Ministre?"

"That the Emperor left Versailles incognito yesterday in response to the usual request from the ex-Empress. You know how he literally flies to do her behests."

"Alas!" said the Man in Grey with something of a sigh. "But I don't understand," he added inquiringly, "if the Emperor has gone to Malmaison——"

"Not to Malmaison this time," interposed M. le Duc. "The ex-Empress is at Chartres, staying at the Hôtel National, and she desired the Emperor to go to her there. This time she seems to have pleaded family imbroglios. She is always ready with a pretext whenever she desires to see him; and with him, as you know, her slightest whim is law. Enough that he set out for Chartres this morning, in the strictest incognito, accompanied only by one of his valets—Gerbier, I think.

Fortunately he apprised me yesterday of his project. I begged him to let me send an escort to guard him, but—well! you know what he is. The future Empress is already on her way to France; the Emperor, naturally, guards very jealously the secret of his continued visits to Joséphine. Curtly enough he forbade me to interfere. But, knowing you to be at Evreux, I sent a courier to you, telling you what had occurred and suggesting that perhaps you could send a posse across to Chartres to keep watch quietly and discreetly while the Emperor was there. He will be there to-night, of course," concluded the Minister with a weary sigh, "and no doubt he will return to-morrow. But these incognito visits of his are always a terror to me, and this time——"

"This time," concluded Fernand as the Minister paused, hardly daring to put into words all the anxiety which he felt, "the courier whom you dispatched to me was waylaid and murdered, and your message, which, I imagine, gave some details of the Emperor's movements, is in the hands of a band of Chouans."

"Chouans?" exclaimed the Minister. "What makes you think——"

"Some of the rascals whom we arrested at Caën in connection with the affair of the infernal machine, and who were being conveyed to Paris in accordance with your instructions, escaped from Evreux prison the night before last. The commissary of police and I were on our way to report the matter to you when we came across the body of the murdered man in the woods outside Mantes."

"Malédiction!" ejaculated the Duc d'Otrante; and though during his arduous service he had been faced with many and varied dangers which threatened at different times the life of his Imperial master, his cheeks became almost livid now, when the vista of horrible possibilities was thus suddenly conjured up before his mind. Then he continued more calmly; "Which of the villains have escaped, did you say?"

"The Marquis de Trévargan, for one," replied the Man in Grey.

"And the Marquise?"

"No. We had not arrested her yet. She was not directly named in the affair, and we can always lay our hands on her, if occasion demands."

"Anyone else?"

"Those two villains they call Blue-Heart and White-Beak, the most daring and most infamous scoundrels in the whole crowd."

"One of them was paid by Mademoiselle de Plélan to murder you," remarked the Minister dryly.

To this, however, the Man in Grey made no reply; only his cheeks—always colourless—became a shade more ashen in hue. M. le Duc d'Otrante, who knew something and guessed a great deal of this single romantic episode in the life of his faithful agent, smiled somewhat maliciously.

"The last we heard of the Plélans, mother and daughter," he said, "was that Madame had joined some relatives in the south, but that the beautiful Constance had remained at Evreux. She is a niece, remember, of Monsieur de Trévargan, and France does not hold another conspirator quite so astute and so daring as either of these two. De Trévargan is a model of caution and Constance de Plélan is recklessness personified; but both will stake their all for the Cause of those degenerate Bourbons——"

"And both are at large," added the Man

in Grey somewhat impatiently; "while the Emperor is travelling without escort upon the high roads."

"Do you suppose that Constance de Plélan had anything to do with the escape of the Chouan prisoners at Evreux?"

"I imagine that she was the prime mover," replied Fernand calmly; and even the Minister's sharp, probing eyes failed to detect the slightest sign of emotion in the grave face of the police agent at this significant mention of Constance de Plélan's name in connection with the recent Chouan affair. "No doubt she gave Monsieur de Trévargan and his gang all the help they required from outside, and shelter afterwards. But time is getting on, Monsieur le Ministre," he continued eagerly, "and the Emperor, you say, is on his way——"

"He left Versailles at six o'clock this morning," rejoined the Minister. "He will be at Chartres by nightfall."

"He will never reach Chartres," announced the Man in Grey, "if—as I believe—Blue-Heart and his gang waylay him on the road."

"That is just what is in my mind," assented the Minister with a shudder. "It is close on seven o'clock now, and I can have a posse of police on the way within half an hour; but whether they can reach the Emperor in time to be of service is very doubtful. According to arrangement, he will have left Versailles an hour ago. He is travelling in his private *berline*, harnessed with his four bays, which, as you know, fly over the ground with almost unbelievable swiftness. He will get relays on the way and proceed with undiminished speed. Our men have not the horses wherewith to cover the ground at such a rate."

"Let me have a horse out of your stables, Monsieur le Ministre," rejoined the Man in Grey. "I'll cover the ground fast enough."

"You, Fernand!" exclaimed M. le Duc. "What can you do—by yourself?"

"I don't know. I can always take short cuts and gain ground that way. I can overtake the Emperor's *berline* and warn him that assassins are on his track. He has a postilion, I presume, and Gerbier is with him, you say. Well! with the coachman, we should be four of us to divert a musket-shot from the most precious life in France."

"But, my good Fernand," argued the

373

Minister, "I cannot even tell you which road the Emperor has taken. As you know, he can either go by the main Paris—Chartres road—which, of course, is the more direct, but also the more public—or he can go by way of Houdan and——"

"Both roads converge at Maintenon, and I can intercept him there by cutting across fields and meadows, if you will give me your swiftest horse, Monsieur le Ministre. If you don't know which road the Emperor is taking," he continued with unanswerable logic, "the Chouans do not know it either. They also would have to waylay him somewhere past Maintenon."

"Unless they are in full force and patrol both roads——" suggested the Minister.

"They would hardly have had time to make such elaborate arrangements. Moreover, both roads are very open and moderately frequented. It is only after Maintenon that the single road strikes through the woods and becomes very lonely, especially at nightfall. A horse, Monsieur le Ministre!" entreated the Man in Grey, his keen, deep-set eyes glowing with ardour and enthusiasm. "A horse! Ten years of my life for the swiftest horse

z
374

in your stables!"

The Minister said nothing more. He, too, was a man of energy and of action; he, too, at this hour, was filled with passionate fervour for the Cause which he was desined so soon to betray, and he knew how to appreciate the ardent spirit which irradiated the entire personality of this insignificant little Man in Grey. At once he rang the bell and gave the necessary orders. Within twenty minutes Fernand was again in the saddle. Fatigue and weariness both had fallen from him like a discarded mantle. He had no time to feel tired now. Ahead, the *berline* harnessed with the four swift bays was thundering down the Chartres road, and the most valuable life in France was threatened by a band of assassins, shrewd enough to have planned a desperate *coup*. Somewhere on the broad highway the murderers were lurking, and the Emperor—unguarded, unsuspecting—might even at this hour be falling into their hands.

On! On, Fernand! The four splendid bays from the Imperial stables have two hours' start of you! In the streets of Paris, the life of the great city is running its usual course. Men are hurrying to business, women to their marketing, soldiers or officials to their duties. One and all pause for an instant as the hoofs of a powerful grey strike showers of glowing sparks from out the stones of the pavements, and a horse and rider thunder past at break-neck speed on the way to Versailles.

Just before the main Paris—Chartres road plunges into the woods, about a kilometre from Maintenon, where two narrow roads, which lead, the one to Houdan and the other to Dreux, branch off from the diligence route, there stood in this year of grace 1811 an isolated inn by the wayside. The house itself was ugly enough; square and devoid of any engaging architectural features, it was built of mottled brick, but it nestled at the cross roads on the margin of the wood and was flanked by oak and chestnut coppice, interspersed here and there with a stately beech or sycamore, and its dilapidated sign bore the alluring legend, "The Farmer's Paradise."

The Paris—Chartres road with its intermittent traffic provided the "Paradise" with a few customers, with some, at least, who were not to be scared by the uninviting appearance of the house and its not too enviable reputation. Wayfarers, coming from Houdan or from Dreux on their way to Chartres, were forced to halt here in order to pick up the diligence, and would sometimes turn into the squalid inn for a cup of that tepid, acid fluid which Alain Gorot, the landlord, so grandiloquently termed "steaming nectar." But during the greater part of the day the place appeared deserted. The light-fingered gentry—footpads and vagabonds—who were its chief customers, were wont to use it as a meeting-place at night, but during the day they preferred the shelter of the woods, for the police were mostly always at their heels.

On this cold winter's afternoon, however, quite a goodly company was gathered in the coffee-room. A log fire blazed on the open hearth and lent a semblance of cheeriness and comfort to the bare, ugly room, in which the fumes of rank tobacco and wet, steaming clothes vied with the odour of stale food and wine to create an almost insufferable atmosphere.

The Paris—Chartres diligence had gone by an hour ago, and had picked up one solitary passenger at the cross roads. Soon after that a hired chaise, coming from Dreux, had driven up to "The Farmer's Paradise." A lady and a gentleman had alighted from it and gone into the house, while the driver sought shelter for his horse in the tumbledown barn at the back of the inn and a warm corner for himself in the kitchen.

It was then three o'clock in the afternoon, and the roads and the country around appeared desolate and still. M. le Marquis de Trévargan sat with his niece, Constance de Plélan, at a trestle-table in a corner of the coffee-room. It was they who had driven over from Dreux in the hired chaise. The landlord had served them with soup, which, though unpalatable in other ways, was, at any rate, hot and therefore very welcome after the long, cold journey in the narrow, rickety chaise.

Three or four men—ill-clad, travel-stained and unwashed—were assembled in the opposite corner of the room, talking in whispers, and near the door a couple of farm labourers were settling accounts with mine host, while a third, seemingly overcome by Papa Gorot's "nectar," was sprawling across the table with arms outstretched and face buried between them—fast asleep.

Gorot, having settled with the two labourers, shook this lout vigorously by the shoulder.

"Now, then," he shouted roughly. "Up you get! You cannot stay here all night, you know!"

The sleeper raised a puckered, imbecile face to the disturber of his peace.

"Can't I?" he said slowly with the deliberateness of the drunkard. And his head fell down again with a thud upon his arm.

Gorot swore lustily.

"Out you get!" he shouted into the man's ear. "You drunken oaf—I'll put you out if you don't go!"

Once more the sleeper raised his head and stared with dim, bleary eyes at his host.

"I am not drunk," he said thickly and with comical solemnity. "I am not nearly so drunk as you think I am."

"We'll soon see about that," retorted Gorot. "Here!" he added, turning at once to the ruffians at the farther end of the room. "One of you give me a hand. We'll put this lout on the other side of the door."

There was more than one volunteer for the diverting job. One of the men without more ado seized the sleeper under the armpits. Gorot took hold of his legs, and together they carried him out of the room and deposited him in the passage, where he rolled over contentedly and settled down to sleep in the angle of the door even whilst he continued to mutter thickly: "I am not nearly so drunk as you think I am."

When the landlord returned to the coffee-room he was summarily ordered out again by M. de Trévargan, and he, nothing loth, accustomed as he was to his house being used for every kind of secret machinations and nameless plottings, shuffled out complacently—unastonished and incurious—and retired to the purlieus of the kitchen, leaving his customers to settle their own affairs without interference from himself.

As soon as the door had closed on Alain Gorot, M. de Trevargan promptly addressed the ill-clad loafers in the corner.

"Now that we are rid of that fellow at last," he said with marked impatience, "tell me just what you have done."

"We carried out your orders," replied

one of the men, a grim-looking giant, bearded and shaggy like a frowsy cat. "We strewed more than a kilo of nails, bits of broken glass and pieces of flint across both the roads, at a distance of about a kilometre from here, and then we covered up the lot with a thin layer of earth."

The others chuckled contentedly.

"When the *sacré* Corsican comes along in his fine chaise," said one of them with a coarse laugh, "he'll have two or three spanking bays dead lame as soon as they have pranced across our beautiful carpet."

M. de Trévargan turned to his niece.

"We couldn't think of a better plan," he said, "as we could only muster one musket among us, and that one we owe to your kindness and foresight."

Constance de Plélan did not reply at once. She took up an old and dilapidated musket from the nook behind her and examined it with deft fingers and a critical eye.

"It will serve," she said coldly after a while.

"Serve? Of course it will serve," rejoined M. de Trévargan lightly. "What say you, Blue-Heart?"

"That I wish you would let me have it,

Monsieur le Marquis," answered the old Chouan. "I'd guarantee that I would not miss the accursed Corsican."

"And I'll not miss him either," said M. de Trévargan, as he rose from the table and stood before his ruffianly followers the very embodiment of power and determination. "And I myself desire to have the honour of ridding France of that pestilential vermin.

"And now 'tis time we went," he added authoritatively. "Two of you go up the Paris road—and two up the Dreux road. take cover in the thicket, and as soon as one of you perceives the rumble of wheels in the distance, give the signal. We'll all be on the watch for it and hurry to the spot ere the first of the bays goes lame."

M. de Trévargan then once more turned to his niece.

"If we succeed, Constance," he said, and with sudden impulse he took her hand and kissed it almost reverently, "the glory of it will be yours."

"I only did my duty," she replied coldly. "I am thankful that I happened to be at Evreux, just when you wanted me most."

"Nay, dear child," he rejoined earnestly. "You must not belittle the services you have rendered to me and to the King. If you had not known how to bribe our warders at Evreux, and how to send us word and succour, we could not have effected our escape. If you had not given us shelter we must certainly have been recaptured. If you had not conveyed me hither, I—in my indifferent state of health—could never have followed the others across country; and if you had not found that old musket for us, we could not have done for the Corsican at this hour, when God Himself is delivering him into our hands. That is so, is it not, my men?" he concluded, turning to his followers.

"Aye! Aye!" they replied unanimously.

"God grant you may succeed!" said Constance de Plélan, as she gently disengaged her hand from his.

"We cannot fail," he declared firmly. "One or more of the Corsican's horses must go dead lame over the carpet of nails and broken glass and flint. The carriage must then halt, and the coachman and postilion will get down to see to the injured beasts. That will be our opportunity. Blue-Heart and the others will fall on the men and I shall hold Napoléon at the end of my musket, and though it may be old, I know how to shoot straight and my aim is not likely to err. And now let us get on," he added peremptorily. "The Corsican's carriage cannot be far off."

Constance, without another word, handed him his hat and mantle. The latter he fastened securely round his shoulders, leaving his arms free for action. Then he turned to pick up the musket. Blue-Heart and White-Beak were ready to follow. They and the two others strode towards the door, with backs bent and an eager, furtive look on their bearded faces, like feline creatures on the hunt. Constance de Plélan was standing in the middle of the room and her eyes were on the door, when it was suddenly thrown open. The figure of the drunken labourer appeared, clear-cut against the dark passage beyond. In an instant he had stepped into the room, closed the door to behind him, and was now standing with his back to it and holding a loaded pistol in his right hand.

It all happened so quickly that neither M. de Trévargan nor any of the others had time to realise what had occurred; and for an instant they stood as if rooted to the spot, staring at the unexpected apparition. Only Constance de Plélan understood what the presence of this man, here and at this hour, portended. She was gazing at him with fixed, dilated pupils, and her cheeks had become livid.

"You!" came in a hoarse murmur through her bloodless lips.

Next moment, however, M. de Trévargan had recovered his presence of mind.

"Out of the way, you lout!" he cried roughly.

And he stretched out his hand to grasp the musket, still believing that this was merely a drunken boor who was feeling quarrelsome and who could easily be scared away.

"If you touch that musket, Monsieur le Marquis," said the man at the door quietly, "I fire."

Then only did de Trévargan, in his turn, look steadily at him. As in a flash, remembrance came to him. He recognised that pale, colourless face, those deep-set grey eyes which once before—at the Château de Trévargan—had probed his very soul when investigating the secret of Darnier's assassination.

"That accursed police agent!" he muttered between his teeth. "*A moi*, Blue-

385

Heart. Let him fire and be damned to him!"

But even Blue-Heart and White-Beak, those desperate and reckless Chouans, who were always prepared to take any and every risk, and who counted life more cheaply than they did the toss of a coin, paused, awestruck, ere they obeyed; for the Man in Grey, with one of those swift and sudden movements which were peculiar to him, had taken one step forward, seized Constance de Plélan by the wrist, dragged her to him against the door, and was even now holding the pistol to her side.

"One movement from any of you," he said with the same icy calm; "one word, one step, one gesture, and by the living God, I swear that I will kill her before your eyes!"

Absolute, death-like silence ensued. M. de Trévargan and the four Chouans stood there, paralysed and rigid. To say that they did not stir, that they did not breathe one word or utter as much as a sigh, would but ill express the complete stillness which fell upon them, as if some hidden and awful petrifying hand had suddenly turned them into stone. Constance de Plélan had not stirred either. She also stood, motionless as a statue, her hand held firmly in a steel-like grasp, the muzzle of the pistol against her breast. Fearlessly, almost defiantly, she gazed straight into the eyes of this man who had so reverently worshipped her and whom she had so nearly learned to love.

"From my soul," he whispered, so low that even she could scarcely hear, "I crave your pardon. From my soul I worship you still. But I would not love you half so dearly, Constance, did I not love my Emperor and France more dearly still."

"You coward!" came after a moment or two of tense suspense, from the parched lips of M. de Trévargan. "Would you seize upon a woman——?"

"The Emperor's life or hers," broke in the Man in Grey coldly. "You give me no other choice. What I do, I do, and am answerable for my actions to God alone. So down on your knees every one of you!" he added firmly. "Now! At once! Another movement, another word, and I fire!"

"Fire then, in the name of Satan, your friend!" cried Constance de Plélan loudly. "Oncle Armand, do not hesitate. Blue-Heart, seize this miscreant! Let him kill me first; but after that you will be five against one, and you can at last rid us of this deadly foe!"

"Down on your knees!" came in a tone of frigid calm from the police agent. "If, ere I count three, I do not see you kneel—I fire!"

And even before the words were out of his mouth, the five Chouans dropped on their knees, helpless before this relentless threat which deprived them of every vestige of will-power.

"Oh, that I had not stayed Blue-Heart's hand that day in the woods!" cried Constance de Plélan with a sigh of fierce regret. "He had you then, as you have us now——"

"As he and the others would have the Emperor," rejoined the Man in Grey, "if I allowed my heart to stay my hand."

And that relentless hand of his tightened its grip on Constance de Plélan's wrist, till she felt sick and faint and fell back against the door. She felt the muzzle of the pistol against her side; the hand which held it neither swerved nor quaked. The keen, grey eyes which had once radiated the light of his ineffable love for her held no pity or remorse in them now: they were watching for the slightest movement on the part of the five Chouans.

Slowly the afternoon light faded into dusk. The figures of the Chouans now appeared like dark and rigid ghosts in the twilight. The ticking of the old clock in the ingle-nook alone broke the deathlike silence of the room. Minute sped after minute while the conspirators remained as if under the ban of some evil fairy, who was keeping them in an enchanted castle in a dreamless trance from which perhaps they would never wake again. Minute sped after minute, and they lost count of time, of place, of very existence. They only appeared alive through the one sense of hearing, which had for them become preternaturally acute. In the house, too, every sound was hushed. The landlord and his servants had received their orders from the accredited agent of His Majesty's Minister of Police, and they were not likely to risk life and liberty by disobedience.

Outside, the air was damp and still, so still that through the open casement there could be heard—very far away—the rumble of carriage wheels and the patter of horses' hoofs on the muddy road.

It seemed as if an electrical wave went

right through the room at the sound, and the police agent's grip tightened on Constance's wrist. A slight tremor appeared to animate those five marble-like statues who were kneeling on the floor.

The carriage was drawing nearer: it was less than a hundred metres away. The clang of hoofs upon the road, the rattle of metal chains, the shouts of the postilion, could already be distinctly heard. Then suddenly the carriage had come to a stop.

A bitter groan went right through the room, like the wail of condemned spirits in torment. But not one of the Chouans moved. How could they when a woman's life was the price that would have to be paid now for the success of their scheme?

Only a heartrending cry rose from Constance de Plélan's lips:

"In Heaven's name, Oncle Armand," she entreated, "let the man fire! Think you I should not be glad to die? Blue-Heart, has your courage forsaken you? What is one life when there is so much at stake? O God!" she added in a fervent prayer, "give them the strength to forget everything save their duty to our King!"

But not a sound—not a movement came

in response to her passionate appeal. Through the open casement a confused murmur of voices could be distinctly heard some distance away, up the side-road which ran from Dreux. The Emperor's carriage was obviously being held up. One, if not more, of the spanking bays had gone dead lame while trotting across Blue-Heart's well-laid carpet. The rough, stained hands of the Chouans opened and closed till their thick knuckles cracked in an agony of impotence.

How long the torture of this wellnigh intolerable suspense lasted not one of those present could have told. The twi-light gradually faded into gloom; dark-ness like a huge mantle slowly enveloped those motionless, kneeling figures in the coffee-room of "The Farmer's Paradise."

But if some semblance of hope had crept into the hearts of the Chouans at sight of the beneficent darkness, it was soon dis-pelled by the trenchant warning which came like a blow from a steel-hammer from the police agent's lips:

"If I hear the slightest movement through the darkness—one flutter, one creak, even a sigh—I shall fire," he had said, as soon as the gloom of the night had begun to creep into the more remote corners of the room. And even through the darkness the over-strained ears of the kneeling Chouans caught the sound of a metallic click—the cocking of the pistol which threatened Constance de Plélan's life. And so they remained still—held more securely on their knees by that one threat than by the pressure of giant hands.

An hour went by. Through the open window the sound of the murmur of voices had given place to renewed clanking of metal chains, to pawing of the ground by high-mettled horses, to champing of bits, to snorting, groaning and creaking, as the heavy travelling chaise once more started on its way.

After that it seemed like eternity.

When once again the silent roads gave forth signs of life and movement; when, from the direction of Paris, there came the sound of a cavalcade, of a number of horses galloping along at breakneck speed; when after a while it dawned upon these enchanted statues here that a posse of police had arrived at "The Farmer's Paradise," and the men were even now dismounting, almost a sigh of relief rose from five oppressed breasts.

They knew the game was up; they knew that all that they had staked had been swept aside by the ruthless, unerring hand of the man who had terrorised and cowed and bent them to his will.

Constance de Plélan was resting against the door in a state of semi-consciousness. Two or three minutes later the landlord, who, acting under the orders given him by the secret agent, had gone to meet the posse of police on the road and guided them to his house, now led them to the back entrance of the coffee-room. The arrest of M. de Trévargan and the Chouans was an easy matter. They were, in fact, too numb and dazed to resist.

All five were tried for the murder of Hector Duroy, the police messenger, and for an attempted outrage against the person of the Emperor, and all five were condemned to penal servitude for life. At the Restoration, however, M. de Trévargan was publicly absolved of participation in the murder, and honoured by the King for having made such a bold, if unsuccessful, attempt to "remove" the Corsican usurper.

But Constance de Plélan was never

brought to trial. Powerful influences were said to have saved her.